Lake Laps

Staci Andrea

Lake Laps

Vanguard Press

VANGUARD PAPERBACK

© Copyright 2024
Staci Andrea

A CIP catalogue record for this title is available from the British
Library.

ISBN 978 1 80016 933 3

*Vanguard Press is an imprint of
Pegasus Elliot Mackenzie Publishers
Ltd.*www.pegasuspublishers.com

First Published in 2024

**Vanguard Press
Sheraton House Castle Park
Cambridge England**

Printed & Bound in Great Britain

For my husband of twenty-five years, Dustin, the best wingman out there, and for my daughters, Paige and Skylar, and son-in-law, Zach, thanks for all of the story ideas that come from your life's adventures, I live through your eyes. For my family, who have tread water next to me in the murky undercurrent for so long, thanks for pulling me to shore. And to my Aunt Peg, who blessed me with her love of writing, thanks for listening and letting me sort it all out, I know you are hearing me. Look Mom and Dad, I did it!

Acknowledgements

I would love to humbly acknowledge Killer Nashville for seeing the beauty and potential in this dark tale, naming *Lake Laps* as a finalist in the prestigious 2022 Killer Nashville Claymore Awards for best suspense. I was honored to take my place among the greats.

Preface

They sat out there in the fading evening sun; her three-year-old body sprawled out lazily over his belly. The warm August lake water was gently lapping at the side of the boat, as the scent of sunblock hung thick in the air. Her life jacket was snuggly riding up under her chin as she laid there giggling with one hand holding her blanket and the other fishing around in a half-eaten bag of cheesy poofs, searching for damp survivors. Her ocean-blue eyes were squinting as they watched her sister and grandpa out on the jet-ski.

He took it all in. Her curly blonde hair blowing in the soft warm air, the belly laugh she would let out as her sister rode by on the jet-ski with Grandpa splashing them. The little face with a smile full of teeth who grinned at him.

"Hey Magoo," he called out her nickname, watching her struggle with the sippy cup as the boat gently rocked side to side, water lapping at the sides of the boat.

"Huh, Dad?" she answered as she spun around to face him, blanket still under one arm and a damp cheesy poof bag in the other.

"Stay three Ms. Magoo. Just stay three," he pleaded as she giggled and threw her baby soft face into his neck, dropping the cheesy poofs, but managing to keep the beloved blanket tucked under her armpit.

These are the memories that you cling to when you realize that eighteen years went by when you blinked, and it just wasn't enough. The memories that you lay with in the middle of the night when you are cold and alone and the ones that haunt you in your sleep like a long-lost puppy with pleading eyes, begging you to be the savior.

You question if you would do it all again if given the chance, knowing how it would all play out, and the answer comes swiftly and hard on your heart, you would choose those eighteen years every damn time, no matter how it would end...

Introduction

"Tell me she's still alive!" I pleaded into the phone. I could feel my throat closing as the words fought to escape my lips. My heart was pummeling my chest with such a force that I could barely hear. I took a deep breath in to fill my lungs that no longer cared if they were to sustain my life or not. Panic began to slowly lick at my soul, but only briefly. My scattered thoughts went from questioning the enormity of what I had just done, to then soothing myself and reassuring my heart that if she made it out alive, what I had done would have been worth it.

She's my daughter after all, I would give my life for hers and dance with the devil himself if that's what it took, and dance we did.

It was at this moment that I began to lose my grip on reality. Not in any of the nightmarish months that had built up to this catastrophic night, not any of the times I sat hunched over in the shower silently crying so no one would hear my heart breaking. Not when I took off after arguing with her, or with my husband, not sure where I would go or what I would do, but talking myself back into sanity as I drove tirelessly around the lake, pleading for answers from a God that I doubted existed any more. I stayed sane while I hid all the guns in the house and suffered through sleepless nights fearing that he would kill her, or himself or all of us. I didn't crack when I had to write the note that to this day sits in my top desk drawer at the office to alert anyone that if I should die, this Joker was who they should be looking for.

It was none of these events that led me to dance on the edge of reality, slowly letting the warm sensation of a false reality begin to engulf my soul. It was in this moment right here that I walked the line, hanging on to my every breath, waiting for my estranged husband to speak the words that I needed to hear to stay sane.

"Damn it Max, are you listening?" I faintly heard him on the line, screaming with frustration into the phone. "Did you hear what I said?" I was busy letting my mind lapse from this hellish reality that had become our home, to see his face in my mind, the boy that I met at the age of sixteen, the man that I married at nineteen. We had our first daughter when I was twenty-two and second when I was twenty-five. We had owned six homes together through the years and amassed a treasure trove of picture-perfect snapshot memories. We had worked hard and built our road to greatness, forged on hard work and sacrifice. We were inching ever so slowly towards a retirement that would eventually allow us to spend all our time with the grandchildren that we would be blessed with and to travel. It's why we owned such a tiny house. It's why we have made sacrifices time and time again. We bought the girls their first cars, helped pay for college, paid for their cell phones, insurance and paid for a wedding. We had scrimped and saved our way to this point in our lives, setting our daughters up for a good future and allowing us to enjoy the second half of our lives. And it was wonderful. We were the fairytale... Until we weren't.

"What? What? No... no Gage, I... I..." There were just no words to answer with at this point. The small cell that I was being held in suddenly became smaller and although it was cold and uncomfortable, I still felt as though I had risen out of the situation and was watching this whole thing unfold as a spectator and not as a player in the game. This wasn't us. This couldn't be us.

Not my family from the small town in Iowa with two daughters, a dog, a cat and a house near the lake. Not my daughter, who up until about a year ago was part of a picture-perfect slide show of life. And damn sure not me, a woman who loves her family fiercely and who only a short time ago was consumed with graduation planning for the girls and a wedding to get off the ground in the fall for my oldest daughter. I looked down at this sad soul, broken and sobbing on her hands and knees in her cell, unable to recognize the empty shell that I had become.

I was utterly unrecognizable. I had aged ten years in twelve months. My hair had dulled and thinned, my muscles had grown weak, and my fingernails had cracked and peeled. My skin had paled, and I had lost any glow that had ever sparked my soul. My green eyes that once danced with ideas had dimmed in a wretched sadness as my soul had been consumed with hate and my heart had been paralyzed in fear. My body was tired of hanging on and my mind had begun to let go. My joints ached, my skin hurt and I just wanted off of the ride.

"I said she's breathing on her own! She's still out of it, but she's a fighter! Max... Maxine! Do you hear what I am telling you? God damn it, will you say something!" I could hear the desperation in his voice, but that wasn't what reached my soul. I knew that the events of the last few months had driven my husband and I too far apart to make it back to each other again. It wasn't that we fell out of love, it was just that all the anger and pain had seeped in and splintered our relationship, festering away until there was a great divide. We had fought to hang on as long as we could, but I couldn't save us all. Somewhere in my soul, I had already made peace with that. It's amazing the things that you are willing to sacrifice to save your child.

My estranged husband had said to me once that she had broken him, that he didn't know how to care any more and that terrified him. This tiny human that we had put our whole hearts and souls into had turned on us in a matter of months, ripping off the protective barrier and exposing who we all were underneath... just broken souls trying to survive. What did bring me back from the depths of insanity, from the dark space that was threatening to anchor me to my own hell, was the sliver of hope that she will make it. Her survival was worth giving up all my dreams, all of my heart and all of my sanity for.

I gasped at the air that was thick and burned with a fury in my lungs with each gulp. Pain and fear, anxiety and depression and a million other ailments had weighed my heart down for so long that it was hard to want to breathe, to will myself to keep going on. I choked on the oxygen, and as tears escaped my stinging eyes and slid down my burning cheeks, I blurted out the only thing that was left to ask…

"What about Him? Gage, tell me that fucker is dead."

Chapter 1

What we didn't warn her about…

It's never the things in life that you spend your time warning your kids about that will lure them into the darkness. We spend years lecturing about strangers and no-no spots. Say no to drugs and no drinking and driving. Go pee in groups of three and leave no one behind. Leave the party with the people you went with and check the backseat of your car before you get in. Be leery of white vans with no windows. Carry your keys like a weapon, and for God's sake girls, don't dress to get raped.

In today's world, my girls had a healthy dose of fear instilled in them, along with the multiple lectures of 'There is nothing worth dying for', that basically was my way of saying suicide was no way out no matter what the 'problem' may be… Think teen pregnancy, drugs and just the disappointment lectures in general. My girls knew that I would pick them up in the middle of the night, no questions asked to get them home safe. Hell, I thought they always knew that I would crawl army style through an inferno to the ends of the earth for them. But maybe that's where the line starts to blur, because maybe one of them never truly understood just how far her mother's love would push her to go.

I remember in my first conceal and carry class, one of the first things that we were told was that if we shoot someone, anyone, in any situation, we would most definitely be arrested. At the conclusion of the first class, we were handed a card with the name of an attorney who specialized in this very type of litigation. At the time I took that class, my mindset was very different. I wanted to be more comfortable around our handguns. I wanted to know that when my husband was away on business, that I could protect and defend our family.

There were basic rules. When defending your home, the intruder couldn't just be in the garage, they should be in your home in order to shoot them. Preferably, they should be facing you because if you shoot them in the back, it means they were leaving your home and you would have been using deadly force that wasn't warranted. Always be aware of what is behind your target before you shoot. And never, never shoot unless it is your last line of defense. The problem with that last one is how do you know what is considered your last line of defense? How many times previously do you need to defend yourself before it's acceptable to forcibly remove the problem? I suppose I should have studied that designation a little bit more thoroughly...

As I write this for the lawyer, for the judge, for the jury and for my family, I just want it to be known that this was never about hate, although it was there. It was never about revenge. It was always about saving her from herself, ensuring her survival and the survival of our family. In order to do that, I also had to decide what was worth saving, who was expendable and what I was willing to trade.

Hang on, I need to grab the sheet from my cot. It's not much, but I find that since I have tumbled into this lonely abyss, I'm cold a lot. Like, cold to my bones. I remember this feeling from when I was a kid. I think it was right around when I was fourteen or fifteen and going through some basic 'depression' type of tendencies, as we all do when we are young and stupid. I can remember sitting out on the back deck of my parent's house in our suburban middle-class neighborhood alone, looking into the woods and thinking of how lonely I felt.

I didn't really like school and had a couple of friends, but never really felt like I was 'enough'. That loneliness that stung your bones, the shiver that runs up your back when there is no breeze. The darkness that shrouds you and makes you want to curl up in a ball. That familiar old friend of a feeling has come back to me now. But I am a long way from fifteen, and this time, the depression has made its home within my guts and rightly so.

I like to think that I was a pretty good kid. I was only a shit for about a year or so, hanging out with the wrong crowd and being mouthy. I was never into drugs and too terrified of disappointing my family to try drinking or partying too hard. I wasn't even good at lying. I tried a cigarette at my best friend's house one night, puked after inhaling once and came home and told my mom about it.

What I was pretty good at was becoming pretty invisible. We moved a lot as a kid. By the time I hit eighth grade, it was my fourteenth school. My parents weren't gypsies or hippies or anything, they just worked hard at different jobs that led to different opportunities. I started out in Iowa, headed to Florida, where they both worked at the Kennedy Space Center, then back to Iowa, on to Minnesota and headed back to Iowa to raise my kids as an adult later on in life.

All of that moving did two things for me in those formative years. First, it taught me how to blend in. One thing you never wanted to do as the new kid was stand out. I just learned how to pay attention, test the waters and survive. In high school, I was great at walking into a classroom and deciding which of the local gangs would be the best bet to sit by that day. Even as kids, survival is ingrained in us. This has served me well over the years, and a skill that I gripped when I was tossed into this hell of a jail cell.

The second thing that all of the moving around had done for me growing up was to instill the value of family. We were a pretty small family, just my mom, dad, sister and myself. We had no brothers, so if anything needed to be moved, hauled, picked up or cleaned out, we were one of the boys. When my dad worked a lot, or was on a different shift than my mom, I watched her become the man of the house too. She was such a tiny person, but her strength was insane, which led us to dubbing her Mighty Mouse. We thought nothing of her hanging pictures by herself, chasing snakes out of the house and changing toilet seats, which somehow was always my job in my married life as well. We were just always close. Not touchy-feely close, but close. We weren't the family that openly professed our love towards each other and hugged all of the time, but we just knew it. There is a loyalty in some families that I truly believe is just ingrained through history and respect. This was us. And this is what I brought into my family.

If I was the one that brought the loyalty and closeness to our family, it was my husband's upbringing that brought the touchy-feely side. Again, he was raised with only one sister. They didn't move around, and he went to school with the same group of kids his whole life. Of course, he was popular, he played hockey and was cute as hell. His dad liked to learn and was in school for most of the time the kids were growing up. So, he also watched his mom have to be the strong woman that she needed to be, although he and his friends were fiercely protective of her. They were huggers though. They freely expressed their adoration for each other, and it was a concept that was so foreign to me at first. I really didn't know how to hug like that, like they meant it. I caught on quick though and easily became the mama later in life that just adored her kids and slobbered all over them.

My husband and I both did actually. We always praised the girls for their minds, their hearts, their souls.

We cheered for all their accomplishments and cried along with them at their heartbreaks. We always wanted them to know their worth in this world, and to know that although they were beautiful, brains and heart needed to back that up. We hugged them all the time. We were just completely in love with these little beings and spent our adult lives making sure that they had everything that they needed and tried to make their childhood the type that someday they would look back on fondly and tell their grandkids how great it all was.

By all accounts and recollections, it all looked good on paper. Anyone would think that these girls would have a great self-esteem and know their self-worth. They should demand better for themselves. They should set high goals and not be afraid to make a run for them. But life has a funny way of working out.

They couldn't be more different if they had tried. Shiloh is the oldest, she's the one that I had been so preoccupied with wedding planning for this past year, and what an event it was!

Growing up, she was a bit of a tomboy, helping her dad work on cars, playing on four wheelers and snowmobiles, fishing, boating, just being her dad's mini me. Her sixth birthday party was a construction truck theme and to this day, her favorite cartoon is Bob the Builder. She was never built to lie, she was shyer in the classroom and had to struggle through learning comprehension difficulties to chase every good grade she ever got. She recently graduated with her elementary teaching degree with endorsements in special education, and she's going to make one hell of a teacher. Fairness matters to her. Integrity matters to her. She's strong when she needs to be but has a gentle soul. She fiercely values her family and isn't too comfortable with all of the touchy-feely-ness that I have become accustomed to.

Shiloh had a boyfriend through school, but they were young and on two different paths in life. While in college, she met her actual soulmate. I am a firm believer that when someone enters your life and they are supposed to be there, you just know. I like to think that people fall into three categories, first there are the people that you meet and get the feeling that they are nice enough, but you know that they won't be in your orbit for long. Then there are the people who you meet, and you instantly know they need to get their toxicity out of your orbit, you can feel it. Like they were never meant to be part of your story. Then there are the third kind, the best kind. These people are the people that you meet and feel instantly connected too, like seeing your best friend after they have been gone for a while. These people feel familiar from the first time that you meet. These are what I like to call, your forevers. Shiloh's now husband, Brody, entered our lives in this manner.

Shiloh met Brody not too long after she had broken up with what she thought was the love of her life. (I knew he wasn't; you could feel it. He just wasn't the forever type of soul.) They met over a dating app. As a mom, this terrified me to know that she met a possible serial killer

25

over the internet and invited him to her home. Oddly enough, it's not the obvious people that you have to look out for in life after all. The day that Shiloh brought Brody home, it happened to be Harvestfest in our little cozy town. What's Harvestfest you ask? Let me enlighten you…

Picture a very Norman Rockwell looking sleepy little town in the fall, leaves falling, pumpkin rolling contests, salsa tasting, grape stomping, all of the shops open and open-air vendors in the street, the view of our little lake in the background. There is even a trolley giving leaf tours. (I told you; it has a very small-town vibe!)

Now here is the catch, wine. Iowa has a pretty large population of local wineries, so during Harvestfest, the town closes down main street, the wineries set up shop, and all of the local ladies get hammered and shop. This is how I met my future son-in-law.

To be precise, I was on what is called the Lady of The Lake, an old paddle boat that docks at shore for the event. In truth, I believe as he was walking up to me to say hello, I was in the middle of convincing my mother-in-law that she didn't need to try to stand on the bar to reach a bag of chips at that exact moment. There I stood, half lit, or fully lit, alongside my mom, mom-in-law, sister, sister-in-law and grandmother trying to pull my shit together and shake this boy's hand.

The second my eyes locked on that boy; I knew I didn't have to worry about this one. He was one of the good ones. It was as though he had been the little kid who grew up down the street from us. I felt like I had known him his whole life and instantly wanted to Mama Bear the situation and love him and protect him forever. That was it.

He became one of us just like that and after about five months of dating, he asked her to marry him in front of the whole family while we were vacationing in Florida. The wedding planning began!

They spend their time hunting deer, ducks and turkey and raising chickens and sheep on their little farm. Life was good. My heart was full. I couldn't wait to be a grandma. (But not 'Grandma', I had already decided that I like the Italian name for Grandmother instead, which is Nonna, and we would call my husband [estranged now] Grumps instead of Gramps because it just fit him.)

For all of the ways that our dear Shiloh was quiet, shy, even tempered and liked to test the water first, her sister Maisey was at the other end of the pool, diving right in. From the minute that sweet baby face could make a sound she was laughing and talking. Big blue eyes and a head full of curls, that kid's heart never met an animal she didn't like or couldn't try to save.

She was always all girl all of the time. She had Barbies and carried babydolls on her hips. She had such a free spirit and a bit of a wild side, never really stopping to test the waters for anything. She welcomed everyone and made sure no one was ever left out. If her mouth was big, her heart was even bigger.

As she got older, school came pretty easy for her. She really didn't have to study much and cracked good grades.

She was pretty patient and respectful, and treasured the time she spent with her family, which included everyone from her young cousins to her great grandparents. She was always just such a good kid, such a beacon of light.

She really didn't get too serious with anyone in high school, but she dated boys and definitely had a 'type'. Looks wise, we teased her because she seemed to always fall for the tall string beans with blonde hair. Her boyfriends were literally carbon copies of each other. The one thing that they had all had in common was that they were broken in one way or another. If they weren't running from a broken home, they were struggling with a mental illness or low self-esteem. Not once did she bring home a soul that wasn't broken, except of course for her best buddy Moby. Moby moved to town right before their freshman year of high school. Actually, they met when they were both working at the local daycare. Legend has it that when they first met, she thought he was cocky and wouldn't give him her phone number. But the universe has a way of sorting itself out, and I have no doubt that because Moby was one of her 'forevers', she couldn't resist that boy if she tried.

The crazy thing about Moby and Maisey was that they have always held dangerous crushes for each other, but it was always at the wrong time. When she thought about dating him, he had a girlfriend and when he looked at her that way, she would be involved with someone. So their friendship just kept rolling on with a hint of flirtatious undertones.

They were so magically good together, they just made sense. Maisey would tell Moby when she thought he was acting like an ass and Moby would mend Maisey's heart when a boy would crush it. No girl was ever good enough for Moby in her eyes and he couldn't ever stomach any of the guys she brought home either. Moby only tried to kiss her once when they were in school, and it was just at the wrong time and terrified Maisey so badly because she couldn't imagine a life without her Moby and was scared to go there and possibly lose him like all of the other boyfriends that she let herself get too close to. Those two had one other fatal flaw… They were both fixers.

One night at dinner when Moby was over and we were touching very lightly on the subject of Maisey's current potentially disastrous relationship, something had occurred to me. Moby had never broken up with a girl. Ever. And this kid is insanely adorable with such charisma and old school charm. Maisey also had never broken up with a guy. She was beautiful, smart and fun. Together, these two were the ultimate Ken and Barbie, yet they both carried the same dangerous quality. Their hearts were so good, so pure that they never wanted to cause harm. They walk gently in the lives of people around them, even though they enter your life in a ball of fire and excitement and make you want to get out there and start living life again. They both had the innate need to leave people better than when they found them. This is why I never doubted Maisey's desire to be a nurse. Her heart has always been set on mending the broken souls and healing the wounded.

When we were talking at dinner that night, I pointed this out to them both. I pointed out to them that they never valued themselves enough to walk away from someone when they knew that they deserved more. Moby even had a girl head off to college and cheat on him but still let her do the ending of the relationship. What they said haunted me when I questioned them about it all, and I still think about it even now while sitting alone in this cell.

Maisey looked me dead in the eye that night and said, "Well mom, I never want to be responsible for someone's downfall. I couldn't live with myself if they went off and tried to kill themselves or something stupid like that over me. I'm not worth dying for."

As my heart froze at that statement and I sat wide eyed, Moby jumped in, "See! This is exactly why we are best friends! We think alike. I can't hurt anyone either. It's just easier for me if I wait long enough, they will find new happiness and move on. I never want to be the bad guy. We just don't want to go through the pain of what happened with Steele again."

Aghhhhhh. There it was. The elephant in the room that no one likes to speak of, but he is always one halted breath, one stalled heartbeat away. Steele was the kids' classmate. He was a likable kid, soft spoken with a good heart. He liked to boat and hang out with his buddies near the water. He partied a little, as most high schoolers do, and had a few girlfriends. Tall and thin with blonde hair and bright blue eyes. His family was pretty well off and he was best friends with his older sister. From the outside looking in, he looked like the vision of happiness, even the type of character that a person would cast as a lead role in a high school dramedy or love story. As we all know too well, anyone can hold up appearances if they just try hard enough. Anyone can make people believe their charade if they put the effort in.

Steele was found in a small patch of woods, known to be one of his favorite hunting spots. Earlier that night, he went to the local football game and was last seen high fiving his buddy in the parking lot and wishing luck to one of the members of the marching band who was heading to a solo competition the next day. He smiled that toothy smile to a girl walking by and waved out his truck window at one of his buddies crossing the street. There was nothing remarkable about his last night on earth. No arguments, no crying, no acting odd. It was as if he had just walked out of their lives, ready to move on to better things.

He drove out to the woods behind Cutty's Creek and parked his old Ford pickup. I imagine he must have sat there for a little while, just thinking about the way his life had played out. Thinking about whatever made him feel so alone, and I could imagine that coldness hitting him to the bones as the air got thin around him. Whatever demons that were in Steele's mind died with him that night, by his own hand and his dad's 9mm. He had left no note.

I think that was the most gut-wrenching part and the thing that all of the kids really struggled with. There were no easy answers and because of this, there were accusations thrown around towards everyone, fingers pointing everywhere. It got ugly, from accusations of his ex-girlfriend breaking his heart to questioning his sexuality. Had he been abused in the past? Was there a drug problem? What had he done that he felt couldn't be forgiven? The student body was small, only ninety kids per grade, and this was the second student lost within two years, not to mention the loss of their dearly loved principal to cancer just months ago.

A loss such as this, with no real answers, left the kids staggering to grip a sense of normalcy again. The school tried to move on rather quickly, and I believe they may have feared that too much focus on Steele's suicide would spark others to do the same thing.

Maisey's locker was next to Steele's. One day he was standing there grinning at her and trying to get her to give him answers to homework, and the next day he was gone. Permanently gone. For the rest of the year, she would glance over at his locker daily only to see dying flowers or notes taped to the space that his grinning soul had once been. This shook her. This shook them all. They realized then that you never really know what a person is going through and how easy it is to affect each other's lives. Maybe this is why they began to move silently, trying to fix people, trying to save them.

Maybe Steele's death started the downward spiral of Maisey's loss of self-worth, her loss of value on her own soul that she, and Moby, would so easily sacrifice to rescue someone else.

What we couldn't have known that night at the dinner table was just how much pain these two hearts would have to endure in just a few months' time. Because my daughter devoted her life to fixing the wounded and healing stray dogs, not only would she sacrifice her own happiness, but she would end leaving dear Moby clinging to a lifeline as well. These sweet souls who have clung to each other in the worst of times, built each other up when they were knocked down and laughed away a thousand tears while doing a lake lap, would soon lose their footing and it would take losing it all to find their way back to each other again.

Chapter 2

Intro to Joker

Maisey had broken up with her last boyfriend about six months before He entered our lives. (One thing you should know is that I will never refer to that wretched human by name. To me, He is the guttural puke you feel right before something is about to go horribly wrong. He is, and always has been, a ghost to me, someone not worth the air that He breathes. In fact, it was only a couple of months into their relationship that I looked my sweet girl in the face and told her that He was dead to me.) As the town reads this, family reads this, His mother reads this, they will all know to whom the 'He' is that I am referring to. But I digress… (Losing my train of thought here. It's hard because they have me so medicated! I was a real ball of fire when they hauled me in last night…)

I have absolutely no problem writing a confession, I own what I have done. My biggest complaint is that if I want this written for the world to read, I want to be sure that the full story is represented. The world needs to know what we have endured at His calculating hands. It needs to be known how hard we fought to stay together, to stay alive.

He is so good at disguising the truth and twisting the perception of reality, that I feel the last line of defense I have as her mother is to be sure that all truths are told, no matter how callused and hard and ugly those truths may be. (It's hard to stay in the right frame of mind when my keepers here in this hell keep telling me to calm down and medicating me. Honestly though, when you have become as broken as I have, and have witnessed one of the great loves of your life get lost within herself, struggling to keep her head above the murky cesspool that He had created in our world, a little medication is a blissful burn to my veins.)

I am going to try and fight off sleeping for a while if I can, as there is so much that my frantic mind wants to be sure to say. I haven't fought for her for a year to let the story end here, like this. Wait... oh... there it is. Damn, when those drugs kick in, it's such a warm feeling. It starts in my arms and then warms my cold heart. Suddenly, the brain gets a little fuzzy and it's hard to keep my head up. It's a little like a good jello shot filled with the welcoming burn of Everclear, or maybe the first big drag of a joint. Calmness... Just serenity and warmth like I have been chasing for a year now... But I am just so damn tired of fighting, of running, of holding on...

I see her in my mind as a three-year-old, and somewhere in this mama's heart, that is how I keep her. Big blue eyes, innocent of all the things that will fall onto her shoulders and eventually break her soul. Crazy blonde curls, and when she was a little sweaty, they would form ringlets that framed her sweet face. Her smile... Oh, I can see it now! All teeth! From when she was just a peanut, she would light up the room and you could see her heart in her smile. That was my Magoo. My hip rider. One of my best buddies. She and her sister Shiloh were the best girls. Best friends. Gorgeous and bold and fiercely smart. They clung to each other. Those big blue eyes never knew what lay ahead, never knew of the danger that was coming her way.

I see her as a scared eighteen-year-old, pale and broken. When she looks at me now in confusion, in anger and in pain, her eyes no longer dance with love, but flicker with flames of hate and deception. She no longer knows her reality or owns her own history any more. She has lost the horizon and can't remember where *He* ends, and she begins. The lies, the deception, the manipulation had led her to this point, and here she stood and wept with her whole-body trembling... Because when you are tiptoeing between reality and a nightmare, what else can you do? It's only a matter of time until you are so weighted down, so broken, that you begin to feel that there is no turning back. Someone has to go, and at that point of desperation, if she couldn't save Him, she felt like she couldn't save herself either. And then she cried. And then she screamed. And then she hurled all the anger at me.

It's always this part of the dream that would haunt me and yet it always played out the same. In an instant, I watched one of the lights of my life flicker and fade away. I saw this radiant creature that I brought into the world slowly wither away and all I am left with is an ache to save her, to run to her, to lay down my life for her. That's what Mama Bears do. I could feel her, smell her, sense that she needed me and every bone in my body was aching to break free and rescue her.

Again and again, I will rescue her.

Even now in my cell, in the darkness of night, I am comforted by my senses. Like a Mama Bear, I cling to her scent in my heart when the loneliness becomes suffocating. I can sense her, smell her, feel those delicate curls slip through my fingers as I reach for her, and barely brush by her oddly sand papered feeling hands, left scarred from years of eczema as a small child, as they are reaching for me now. Against all darkness, her beaming face still illuminates the night as a three-year-old with that beaming smile full of teeth and those pleading eyes. This is where my mind goes when my heart begins to suffocate. I fight off the sting of loneliness here by recalling our lives before *Him*, the nightmare with a joker smile. When she still laughed and smiled.

When her family was everything to her and mama was a superhero. When she knew that life was worth living.

"Max. Max! Your attorney is here. Hey! Get up!" I must have been drifting off because it took the guard a couple good shouts to wake me. Bud was just sadly shaking his head as I tried to get up in my drugged state. Side note: when your husband has worked for the local police force for as many years as mine has, you know them all like family, including Bud, the jailer. A couple of nights

37

ago, at least I think it was a couple of nights ago, or maybe just last night, when I was brought in, Bud was the first one to see me. I feel for this poor man who has held my babies in his arms, watched them grow, and lived through the past year with us. I know his heart is hurting. I know it's hard for him to put the cuffs back on me. I know that he knows what I have done and exactly why I had done it. In fact, all of Gage's police force family had known for months of our situation. He had even discussed with them all that if he called any of them, they needed to come get him at that moment because it meant that he was about to do something that he wouldn't be able to come back from. That is where we had been pushed to. That is the reality we had been living in.

I remember late night discussions just a few months ago with Gage detailing all of the 'what ifs' as they applied to the life we were trapped in. We always made sure the doors were locked, security cameras were on and guns were hidden. I would hold my breath many nights questioning who was in my house when she came home at night. I would have nightmares of what he would do to us. I feared for her, I feared for my pets, I was terrified for us all. My 9mm was always ready to go in the nightstand and Gage's was in his bedside table as well. We concealed knives beneath the mattress.

After Gage and I separated and he moved out, my anxiety was even worse, and I was up all hours of the night. I slept with the bedroom door locked, a hammer at my fingertips and the gun in the nightstand. To be paralyzed in so much fear is exhausting. To try and fight something that you can't see coming at you is enough to drive anyone mad. And it did.

"Come on Max, I'll take you down to Rahn, I don't think he's scheduled to be here too long today," Bud said as he slid the cuffs on my limp wrists. Staring at my wrists, I am in awe at how weak I had become. Only a little over a year ago, I had slowed my running a bit to focus on weight training. Back when life was good, stable and happy. Back when my biggest problem was worrying about fitting into a mother of the bride dress for Shiloh's upcoming wedding. I was worried about the proverbial bat wings that had decided to grow beneath my over the hill forty-three-year-old arms. I started lifting weights and stuck to running shorter distances. It paid off too! I had actually started to build muscle, had a little form and definition. I was feeling good and strong, the best I had felt in years. Gage went to the gym with me. He wanted to look his best for the wedding too. We were feeling good... and then we got the news that Gage's liver was starting to fail.

So, we did what we always did... we winged it. We went to doctors' appointments, studied cookbooks and looked at outcomes. We manipulated our way of eating to include walking a tightrope of liver friendly foods as well as paying close attention to Gage's diabetic way of eating. We eventually landed in the Mediterranean way of eating lifestyle. That meant a lot of freaking fish, which I *hate*. That meant a lot of cooking from scratch, which I also vehemently hate. I have always felt cooking was such a waste of time and would be equally happy with a bowl of cereal or a waffle. But I did it. I did it out of love. I did it to save Gage. That's what you do for your forever crew. You just do what needs to be done.

"He's right in here, Max," Bud said as we turned the corner to the small room where we would soon discuss what I thought would be my fate. Bud removed my cuffs and helped me to sit on the cold metal stool, at the cold metal table across from my cold-hearted attorney. Just kidding. Rahn was a sweet guy. I have known him my whole life as well.

That's what happens when these small towns trap you and you can't leave. They are charming and quaint, and everyone knows everyone else. Rahn had lived up the road from my grandparents for as long as I could remember. He was who I turned to in high school when I was figuring out what I wanted to do with my life. It was under his advisement that I had decided that being a paralegal was right up my alley. I never wanted to put the years in to be an attorney, but I wanted to do something in law and wanted to do something that felt meaningful yet make a decent wage. So, after going to the local community college, I happened to fall in love with public service. I was lucky enough to intern for a local public health department and then move on to the local department of human services working towards helping get families out of precarious situations. Funny how that turned out.

"Hey Max. You hanging in there kid?" Rahn's eyes met mine briefly with fear and sadness. We both knew why

I was here. He knew me. He was one of my forevers. As he glanced across the table at this pitiful broken woman that I had become, I felt that he not only knew where my head was at and why, but also where I was intending on going. This sweet man, the man that had just danced with Shiloh at her wedding reception only weeks ago, was now clearing his throat trying to grasp his words from thin air that threatened to choke us all.

"That night at the wedding, Max, I knew then that you couldn't take much more. To think that He had shown up like that, after everything that had led to that point. He had already been warned not to show up, yet there He appeared. Like a thief in the night, there He was. It really was amazing the type of self-control that Gage had. I didn't think that kid would make it out of there alive…"

As Rahn kept rambling on out of comfort, or out of limited options of what to say, my drugged mind wandered hazily back to that day only weeks ago. We had been planning Shiloh and Brody's wedding for a year. Amidst all the nightmare that we had been living in, I had been forced to wear two masks and live two lives. While Shiloh was living her dreams, getting ready to marry her greatest forever, graduating college, starting her teaching career, Maisey was being plunged into a dark abyss, struggling not to drown within herself at the hands of *Him*.

And there I was, there Gage and I were, in the middle. One day you would be struggling in the lowest of lows with Maisey, and the next day you donned your mask and proudly went back to wedding planning. It wouldn't be fair for Shiloh to miss out on a second of this fabulous time of her life, so we exhausted ourselves in this way, living two lives, holding the wolves at bay for as long as we could. At some point though, these lives would have to intersect, and intersect they did.

The wedding day was storybook beautiful. It was a warm fall day, and to say the weather was cooperating was an understatement! It was warm and breezy, something that was a rare occurrence in our little Iowa town that tended to either be stifling hot or windy as all hell.

Shiloh and Brody, in their sweet humble way, had wanted a very small wedding at their farmhouse in the rolling hills with their chickens running around and sheep watching from their pens. The guest list to the wedding was kept at a minimum, with a larger guest list invited to the reception at the ballroom about twenty minutes away. Everything Shiloh touched was graceful yet rugged, well-loved and a little worn, just like the love of her life. That's just who they were. One was never on an adventure without the other. There was a simple ease to their relationship and anyone who knew them would tell you that they were better together.

They took wedding photos leaning against their old blue truck, beneath their massive weeping willow tree that stood in their yard. As ducks flew overhead, and their gorgeous young chocolate lab ran circles around them, they posed for a photo in front of the tree with a sign that Brody's dad had made with their initials in it that had been nailed to the tree. It was as simple and perfect as their relationship had been. Group wedding photos were taken with their beloved barn and sunflowers as the backdrop. There was just an easiness to it all, a sense of family and of belonging about the day.

Maisey struggled the whole day, and I tried to keep her close. She had been arguing with *Him* for about a week straight. He hated not being in control any more and He was not only not invited to the wedding, but was told by the local police force that He was strongly encouraged not to show up to either the wedding or the reception. This was in part because we just couldn't deal with the added drama and toxicity that follows Him, but also because his mental stability had deteriorated so badly that Maisey was actually starting to fear Him too.

It didn't help to calm her fears when just a few days prior, He was in the garage, sitting in her car when she was getting ready to leave for work. She still loved Him with a protective fierceness, yet was terrified of Him at the same time. He always found His way back into her heart though, and it was usually through pity. We had gotten used to the suicide threats that He would spew out if He didn't get His way, used to the empty promises that He would call the police and make halfhearted accusations towards us, and even used to His fake anxiety attacks every time He felt that He needed more time with my sweet, kind-hearted Maisey.

She had been His keeper, a task she had never signed up for. She drove Him to his psych appointments, picked up His meds and hauled Him to the emergency room when his anxiety became too much to bear. When He had solely become dependent upon the meds, it was Maisey who would continue to drive Him from doctor to doctor in order to get more meds for fake symptoms.

His dysfunctional family included a wayward suicidal sister that Maisey also ran all over town to appointments, and a mother who was as negligent as she was abusive. A few months back, this woman had weight loss surgery and infection had set in on her open sore. Even though this woman never accepted my daughter and badmouthed our entire family, Maisey with her nurse's heart went against my warnings and changed that woman's bandages and went grocery shopping for them, using her own money of course. My poor girl had become so consumed with saving His lost and broken soul, that she didn't even see the damage that it was doing to her. His pain became her pain, as misery always loves company, and soon she couldn't remember where her reality began and His nightmare ended.

This was the torment that was playing in the back of dear Maisey's mind the day of her sister's wedding. A day they had been so looking forward to for such a long time. At this point, Maisey had given up a lot of things for what she thought was love with Him. She had given up most of her relationships with friends, pushed almost all of her family away, and gave up on herself, choosing to give up on her nursing degree for now and move home because the acceptance into the program of her dreams took her over three hours away and like *He* had said multiple times, He would kill himself if she left Him. (I admit I shouted at the Gods and heaven above on more than one occasion to just let Him make good on this threat so we can have our lives back...)

The asshole terrorized her, stalked her and warped her world hard enough that she finally gave up and moved back... (Actually, it was more of a frantic call in the middle of the night followed by her dad driving to get her and drive her back home, but more on that later on in the confession...)

Her bruises had faded. Just a few weeks before, He and Maisey had gotten into a pretty heated argument and He had hit her. It wasn't the first time, but it was the first time that He had left marks, and the first time that Gage and I had actually become aware of how badly the situation had deteriorated.

We had heard through His previous girlfriends that He was an abusive person, but Maisey had always denied that He had hit her. This time though, because my beautiful girl had actually put makeup on for the first time in months and was going to go hang out with her sister, the asshole accused her of cheating on Him. Then He accused her of sleeping with Moby. He panicked, anxiety and fear getting the best of Him, and right there in His mother's home, while she was on the phone with a terrified Moby, He started laying His fists right into her ribs.

During the struggle, He landed a few blows a little higher while calling her a whore and threatening to kill Himself. While His self-depreciation was settling in, He grabbed her throat and began to choke her. As my baby girl was gasping for her life and clawing at his face, it was like He woke up from whatever drug-induced manic state He had been in and He immediately let go. He began to cry, hysterically. She, for the first time in a long time, sat in silence, evaluating her life, evaluating the situation.

As He soothed himself by taking off His shirt because His anxiety was getting to Him and He couldn't stand His clothes touching Him at that point, Moby had already called the police. He just sat there, in the kitchen of His mother's home, talking to himself, rambling about how sorry He was as she began to walk away, her heart empty, her ribs on fire and her mind numb. I am so thankful that one of the officers Gage has worked with for many years had happened to be the first one responding to the call... It was only his quick thinking and finesse that he was able to get my sweet girl out of there and keep Gage from killing the bastard that night. And although our girl who is trying to save all stray dogs and broken souls refused to press charges, *He* did agree to a stint in the inpatient hospital to try and get His head on a little straighter. But it only lasted a few days and He had the staff all conned into thinking it had just been a poor dose of prescriptions that had caused Him to act out as a monster.

So there we were on that beautiful day, dressed in shades of wine and plum, cowboy boots and adorned with sunflowers. There were hay bales draped with antique quilts to sit on and pumpkins and candles all over. Big metal lanterns holding candles and mums dressed up the area under the wooden archway that Brody had built to say their vows under. To add an element of surprise and family, I officiated the ceremony. I had been officiating weddings for years, but no one thought I would be able to hold it together. I think my mind had been so preoccupied with keeping Maisey safe that I hadn't had the time or space in my heart to get too upset about the ceremony itself. I had written the perfect ceremony, while keeping it short, just like the kids had wanted.

I vividly remember the one snapshot in time that will forever remain engraved in my heart and burned into my soul. As I stood beneath the arch, looking at my girl, my beautiful Shiloh, I was getting prepared to do the giving away of the bride, which would entail me asking my husband if he would give this girl away to this boy. While immediately focusing on Shiloh, Brody and Gage, I could see all of the people we love the most faintly sitting in the backdrop of our story. It was in this moment that I saw my Shiloh, my sweet girl, on her wedding day, mouthing the words, 'Will you be OK', to her sister who was standing directly towards my right, as the maid of honor with a cold look on her face and blue eyes fighting back tears. While my eyes saw in front of me all of the faces who love her, who would fight for her, who would walk through the gates of hell to help her out of the darkness, a frosty chill ran over my arms as I hear a defeated Maisey whisper in a hushed tone to her sister, "I'm trying to be…"

Those two. On Shiloh's wedding day, her heart focused on her sister. They had matching boots with little sunflowers on them, 'Same, same', was the joke because when they were little girls, even though they were three years apart, they would get a kick out of dressing alike or eating the same thing, or doing anything alike. So, they would always grin and say, 'Same, same', and giggle every time the situation presented itself.

The morning of the wedding, after Maisey had argued once more with *Him* and threw her phone down, Shiloh walked by sticking her toe of her boot out from under her dress, lightly kicking Maisey's boot and giggled, "Same, same."

A halfhearted smile crawled across Maisey's lips as she returned in a whisper, choking back tears, "Same, same."

They were close. There was never a time when they weren't each other's biggest cheerleaders, but this past year had been hard on them. Although Maisey had alienated just about everyone else around her, she couldn't find a way to separate from her sister. One thing that kept them together was that while everyone else was battling with Maisey to move on with her life and let *Him* go, Shiloh was always very careful of her words. I found out later that she had a conversation with Moby while dancing at the wedding reception and discovered that they both handled Maisey the same way.

"Although I know *He* is so controlling and awful for her, I have to be careful what I say because I don't want her to cut me out of her life forever." Moby had told Shiloh while they danced slowly under the twinkling fairy lights on the dancefloor. "I love her so much and can't lose her. It would break me if I lost her. So, for now, all I can do is be there if she wants to talk and wait it out."

It was during this dance, during this heart to heart between her sister and her best friend that *He* walked into the reception hall, grinning ear to ear and shouting her name.

Chapter 3

Control

There He was, in all of His chilling giddiness. All six feet two inches, 160 pounds soaking wet of Him. Something wasn't quite right. As He was strolling into the ballroom, dressed like the groomsmen in jeans, white button-down dress shirt and sage green tie, along with cowboy boots that He had never worn a day in His exhausting life, His eyes held a new kind of rage and panic that I had never witnessed before.

"Hey Maisey! Maisey, where are you sweet face?" He was shouting into the air. The music that the DJ was playing was pretty loud at this point, as a slow song had just ended, and people were out there on the dancefloor getting crazy to some country tune that the bridal party had picked out. The lights were dimmed low to catch the full effect of the 500 neon bracelets and necklaces that now adorned everyone on the dance floor. At that point, sweet Maisey hadn't even laid eyes on His sorry self yet. She was playing the part of the good younger sister, trying to make Shiloh's dreams come true, even as her heart was breaking. Maisey was in a circle of younger cousins, dancing and swinging them around while laughing and chatting with the bridal party. My heart just sank the moment I saw that this wolf had made it into our safe space. I ran towards Him.

"What are you doing? You know you can't be here; Gage can't see you!" I was hissing through my teeth as I made my way towards Him. By the time I had met Him, He was standing off to the side of the dancefloor. When my eyes locked with His, what I saw sent pain through my heart and a cold sweat immediately down my back. His little blonde poof of hair that He always had combed oddly on the top of His head was drenched in sweat. Beads of sweat were running down His temples, His shirt was soaked. His eyes though... His eyes told the whole story. They were manic and wide as He grinned that terrifying smile from ear to ear, His wicked grin draped lazily over his soulless face and His eyes void of any emotion like an inky black pit of hell.

Maisey used to say that He smiled like that when He was nervous, or He would smile like that when He was stressed. There was always a reason she would give when I asked about it. All I knew was that it was scary. As a mom, His mannerisms and this joker of a smile always kept me on edge when He was around. It wasn't all right, it was just 'off'. The mannerisms and just vibrations emanating from His body spoke of someone who was either overmedicated or in deep psychotic danger. In the year that they had been together, He had eaten dinner with us only twice, and both times He sat silently grinning ear to ear. Every time we would try to have a conversation with Him, we would get a one-word answer and then He would be back to grinning again. At first, I thought maybe it was shyness or just being awkward in social situations, but this night, at Shiloh's wedding, there was a lost and empty look behind those eyes to accompany the grin.

Nothing good would come of this.

"Awe... come on Mama Max! You didn't think I would let the fabulous Shiloh get hitched without being a part of the *family* celebration, did you?" He spat as His insane eyes met mine on the side of the dancefloor. It was right then that Maisey saw Him. Like a bullet, she shot right over to where we were standing.

"Jesus, what are you doing here?" she shouted at Him, already trembling, half in resentment and half in fear. "You know Dad forbid you to come! You know most of the local police force is here! What the hell?" she cried as she grabbed His arm to try shoving Him towards the door.

"Oohhh... the big... the bad... the *scary* local police. Ha, ha! Sweet face calm down! I came for you! I know it's important for you to have *family* time, and I so want to be part of this fucking family!" He shouted as He brushed her hands away.

"What's wrong with you? Please, let's go outside. Please. Just don't do this here, for God's sake please not here..." Maisey pleaded through tears. At this point, Shiloh had noticed what was going on and was working hard at keeping Brody pulled back, as everyone knew that the hate that Brody had for this guy ran deep. On more than one occasion, my sweet son-in-law had stood up for his sister-in-law and threatened to beat the crap out of this guy. Gage then saw the commotion and headed for where we were, trying to not make a scene.

Gage was followed by most of the town's police force as he made his way to the wolf in too tight of cowboy boots. As Gage got in the asshole's face, Maisey just stood there bawling.

Shoulders dropped, tears flowing from what used to be bright blue eyes, she wrapped her arms around the monster to shield Him from whatever was coming from the wrath of her father.

"Get the fuck out you fucked up piece of shit pedophile! I told you this is a private event and you aren't wanted here!" Gage venomously spat as he was only inches away from the face of the devil himself. Bud stood with his hands on Gage's back, not only for a show of support, but also for restraint. This was a back-and-forth game that had been going on for the better part of the last few months. Gage would try to scare the predator out of our lives and in return, the wolf would try to get Gage fired, thrown in jail or worse.

The response that came from this piece of shits face was classic Him.

He just averted His eyes to Gage and grinned this huge maniacal smile, raised His scrawny pale hand to brush His blond poof of bangs out of His face that were drenched in sweat, and while grabbing Maisey by the arm, said, in a mocking tone, "Well now Gage, you know how badly I want to be a part of this all loving, all accepting, perfect little family unit you have going here! Come on now, stop being so controlling and just accept it! I love her and want to be with her! After all, I'm the one willing to be civil. I'm the one being an adult about it all and wanting to try for the sake of your darling daughter." And then silence as He stood there grasping Maisey's hand, grinning like a Cheshire cat. He wanted Gage to swing at Him. He was aching to feel that beating. But Gage wouldn't bite. He wouldn't let things go down like this. Not here. Not in front of these people, not with his police buddies as accomplices.

"Look dickhead. I don't want a scene. We are not doing this here. This is a family event. Leave now!" Gage ordered under his breath as a crowd started to form around. Shiloh had stopped in the middle of the dancefloor, clinging to Brody who was about to pounce. The music kept playing and there were actually some people who hadn't seen what was going on who were still out there dancing under the soft glow of magical twinkle lights.

"Look kid, you need to leave," Bud started to say as he moved towards Him to lead Him away. Then it happened. I don't know if it was the yelling that struck me first or the sheer horror as this deranged asshole started taking his clothes off. As he wildly peeled off his sweat drenched shirt and dropped it on the floor, He was yelling something about not being able to do this... He can't live without her... how can she do this to Him...... He will die without her... blah... blah... blah.While crying and spitting and choking on his words, there would be a laugh, then gasping for air, then laughing again. The guy had cracked. Or, this was just one of His famed panic attacks. I had heard about these before. Any time Maisey wasn't paying enough attention to Him or He worried she would leave, He would pull off these grand 'panic attacks' or 'psychiatric episodes' He would call them. That's the thing with this guy, He *was* mentally unstable, and years of therapy had done nothing to control His issues, they only gave Him a larger arsenal of psychobabble words to use against Maisey. He knew how to play on her heart just as He knew how to play the crazy card in the emergency room to procure more pills.

As He was standing there, spewing words that made no sense and starting to work on unbuttoning His pants, He dropped Maisey's arm and Bud grabbed Him, in a half bear hug, half 'get your ass outta here' attempt to move the guy. They made it as far as the restroom toward the side entrance of the historic ballroom, where the prick ducked in and locked the door. We were no longer under the illusion that no one saw what had just transpired. As we slowly turned around, we could see the entire ballroom staring at us in awe, and a beautiful bride crying in the middle of the dancefloor. Maisey ran to her and held her.

"Shiloh, my God, I am so sorry!" Maisey choked between tears. "I tried! I tried to keep Him away. He's just better when we are together and He can't do it on his own…" she trailed off.

For her part, Shiloh pushed her sister out at arm's length and said the most haunting and painful thing she has ever had the courage to say, "Maisey, you have traded your life for Him and it's still not enough. I love you sissy. He has controlled you and manipulated you so badly. If you can't get away, He may take you both down with Him." Shiloh grabbed her little sister, hugging her close to her chest, breathing in the smell of her, feeling her heart thumping in her ribs.

Shiloh knew there was nothing left to say. This was the beginning of a new life for her, and as badly as she wanted to have Maisey follow her into this new world, she knew Maisey was stuck, chained to a life she never wanted, holding the reigns of sanity for a person who clawed desperately to her to hang on. She kissed her sister on the cheek.

"Love you Magoo," Shiloh whispered against Maisey's warm cheek, watching her ocean-blue eyes swim in a pool of tears. And she let her go, turned around, and began to dance with Brody.

Maisey was heading back towards the restroom where He was breaking down to try and control some of the damage, when she was stopped by a voice that could talk her off of almost any cliff.

"Hey sexy, you don't want to go over there right now," came Moby's soft voice behind her. She spun around and buried herself into his arms.

"Really asshole? Where were you when that shit was going down?" she asked with her face still buried in his chest.

Moby just stood with his arms around her as she sobbed, body trembling with adrenaline. She cried for herself now, for all of the things that she has given up this year for Him. She cried for Him because she hasn't been able to help Him, save Him, fix Him. She sobbed for Shiloh and how much she missed her. Hell, she even missed Moby.

"Seriously kid? This TikTok famous face can't handle the shit that was about to go down. I mean I love ya and all, but geesh! Can't damage this money maker!" Moby teased. "Anyways, He's gone now."

"What? What the hell? Is he OK? What happened?" Maisey said as she jolted backwards out of Moby's grasp. Moby was not surprised that she was this worked up. It had been a slow descent into hell watching his best friend chase rabbits down dark holes for this loser over the last year. It didn't matter, to Moby she was still perfect. Even if all he could do was stand by her side and be there when she needed him to, that's what he would do. He knew that she was his forever, his ride or die, and he would never leave her behind.

"Girl! Quit trippin! After your boy stripped down to his skivvies, Bud convinced him that going to the hospital would be better than heading to jail, so he got him out of here." Moby threw his arm around her shoulder. "Seriously kid, you OK?"

Maisey sighed, "Let's see, I have destroyed my sister's wedding, failed my family on so many levels, just watched my ex-boyfriend have a mental breakdown and this bridesmaid's dress itches like hell. No asshole, I am so far from OK!" she muttered through tears as she leaned her head into his shoulder watching the party resume on the dancefloor.

"You know what you need, girl?" Moby asked before turning to kiss the top of her head. She looked up at him. She looked into those piercing green eyes, looked at the chiseled jaw of the boy who wasn't 'just a friend', but her very best friend.

"Damn straight son, let's go!" she whispered with a grin as they headed for the door.

"Max. Max, where'd you go there?" Rahn's voice bellowed above me. Shit. I am on the floor. I am not on the cold hard stool at the cold hard table any more. I am now realizing that I am on the cold hard floor. Bud stepped in, putting his hands under my arms to help me back to the stool.

"Jesus Rahn! Between not sleeping for the past forty-eight hours and being drugged repeatedly, I don't know where I am! I don't know where I am! I don't know who I am!" I was babbling, crying, making a pathetic mess of myself again. I put my face down on that cold metal table and wanted to disappear. How in the hell did it come to this?

"Maxine. Max… you have to pull yourself together. The reason I wanted to see you…" Rahn started.

"Yeah, yeah Rahn, I am already working on the statement." I exhaled as I lay there, face on the table. With everything in my empty heart, I wanted to wake up from this hellish existence. How did I not protect her? How did I not keep the wolf at bay?

"No. *No* Max… It's about Maisey," Rahn said in a hushed tone.

My ears started ringing and my heart was pounding so loudly that I couldn't hear. There was a moment where I almost didn't want to know. This fine line I was walking, this hell I was existing in could possibly be better without knowing what came next. At least when I was walking this tightrope, I had hope left that my baby girl was going to be OK. I swallowed a dry hot knot that had wedged itself in my throat and willed my body to sit back up. I just sat there, staring at Rahn with a million thoughts fighting for space in my head.

"Max, she's awake," Rahn blurted out with huge soulful eyes that were bloodshot from lack of sleep. "She's awake. Gage is on his way to her, but Moby was with her when she came out of it."

In that moment, I felt all of the tension lift off of my body. My lungs inflated for the first time in forever and my body just started to shake from crying. I hadn't even realized that I had started bawling, howling really. Life is like that, walking a tightrope one minute and just letting go and bouncing on a trampoline the next. My girl is awake! My heart knew then that she would be OK and that everything leading up to this was worth it. And everything from here on out, well… At least she would have her Moby.

A shaken Rahn reached out to my trembling hand as I was still struggling to breathe and my body trembled with a unified relief and fear.

"Maxine, what she is saying just isn't aligning with the timeline... Of the events..." Rahn began. "Max, she's asking about Him. Moby is in there doing his best to calm her down, and it's hard to distinguish if her panic is coming from a place of fear or anger or just disbelief," he paused and looked down at the table with a stagnant pause, trying to choose the next words he would speak ever so carefully as to not poke the bear that was in a trembling heap on the other side of the table who was clinging on to life by her bleeding fingertips at this point. With a shaky inhale, he then lowered his voice to a hushed tone and muttered at me almost inaudibly, "She is rambling on about how it had been her intent to end it all."

My soul became electrified. Anger raged through my stone-cold veins and felt like fire escaping from my heart. My instant reflex was to recoil, jerking my hand out of Rahn's grasp, I fought the urge to scream. I fought the urge to throw up. I fought the urge to launch into a maniacal tirade about the asshole and incriminate myself any further than I already had. Instead, I fought to swallow against the lump in my throat and forced words to come out of my pursed lips.

"And how much are we telling her about Him at this point?" I let the acidic words escape through clenched teeth as I focused all of my attention on Rahn while angrily gripping the edge of the table, seemingly trying to keep my angry tirades at bay.

"Rahn, what has Moby told her?"

"Max, she knows. She knows very little, but she knows."

I suppose this was the point of the conversation where Rahn was going on to tell me that my daughter, one of the greatest loves of my life, was hurling accusations at me. This must have been the part where she was deliriously screaming into the air towards Moby, ranting about the person that I had become, livid with herself, and me. Her soul had been crushed, her heart had been destroyed and it was just easiest to lay all of the hurt, the anger, the pain, the blame, on me.

I suppose this was the part of the conversation where Rahn began discussing options for not only how she would be treated in the hospital as this moved forward, but also what my options began to shape up looking like. I supposed this is where I should have been alert, should have given a damn, but instead I just let go. I allowed my mind a moment of respite, of peace. I felt myself falling into darkness again, this time every fiber of my being welcoming the warm slumber, reminding myself that she was alive, she was awake, and she still had a fighting chance at a future.

Isn't that all I was fighting for to begin with? To save her from herself, from Him and to hold her sweet little head of bouncing gold curls above the water? Although my mind went to this peaceful trance, my body apparently did not follow suit. According to Rahn, when I spoke to him later, it was as though everything that I had been holding in at that point all tried to escape my body at the same time. What had started with trembling, progressed to bouncing between hysterical crying and laughing. I sobbed deeply until snot was running out of my nose and my eyes were swollen, only to begin laughing and rocking back and forth in my cold hard chair, and then went back into the sobbing again.

Thankfully for us all, the staff was quick to react, and I was administered a sedative at lightning-fast speed. Although I don't remember a thing about this, I do remember right before I was taken back to my tiny cell, as I was sprawled out on the floor (after, I assumed, I had been tackled to the ground) Rahn kneeling and holding my hand. I vaguely remember he was reciting the Lord's Prayer as I was drifting into a drug fueled bliss, thawing the ice in my veins, if only temporarily.

I had a second of clarity, my brain grasping to review this year's events at lightning speed. As the faces of my happy little family passed by in my mind's eye, they soon were replaced with visions of Him, of a daughter crying, a daughter in pain, a daughter turning her back on her family. The destruction of relationships, the missed vacations and holidays, being robbed of what our future could have been.

Somewhere in this slow motion replay of our lives, the sound of Rahn's sweet, rough, familiar voice reciting the Lord's Prayer echoed within my soul and haunted my heart. I had an instant sense that while Rahn was busy trying to save my soul, and pray for my family, that I had already lit a fire to a chain of events that there was no saving us from. My faith had been rocked and my fate had already been sealed. I then let go and drifted off to a deep sleep, letting my weary body rest, if only for a little while. As far as I was concerned, whatever came for me next, I was ready, it was worth it. My job was to save my cub from the wolves, and save her I did.

Chapter 4

Lake Lap

Somewhere in the night, most nights anyways, my mind searches to grasp for better times. I was never an avid dreamer in years past, but I suppose when your world gets so intense, maybe your brain just can't shut off, it just has to keep moving along, working out the matters that lie unresolved in your heart. On this night, under the guise of a warm medicated bliss, my mind took me to the lake. It took me home.

That's the thing about living in a lake town. No matter where you are going, or who you are going to see, you are all connected by the lake. When you are explaining to people how to get somewhere, the directions always start out with, 'You take North Shore', or, 'You head out on South Shore'. The lake is sixteen miles around and if you do the speed limit, the lake lap can take about twenty minutes or so. That's twenty minutes to calm your fears. Twenty minutes to work out problems in your head. Twenty minutes to pretend that your life is something else, something better.

As a kid, there was nothing better than doing a good old lake lap with Grandma and Grandpa either in the old green pickup or burnt-orange Scout. All my grandparents lived out in the country, so coming into town to get groceries and maybe do a lake lap meant you had to get cleaned up first and change clothes. If it was in the height of summer, you may be lucky enough to stop out at the Ice Cream Drive In for a milkshake.

As a teenager, a lake lap could mean a couple of things. You could be just cruising the lake to see where all your buddies were, trying to figure out the plans for the rest of that lazy summer day. You could be driving around to see which cabins and lake homes were unoccupied that weekend so you could fish from their docks. A lake lap could buy you some time on an awkward date night when you were done with the movie, but not quite ready or gutsy enough yet to go to park on either a gravel road or State Park lot to steam up the windows. Or, that twenty-minute lap could just be you and your best friend trying to figure out what to do with your life or mend a broken heart.

As an adult, the term 'lake lap' takes on a whole new meaning. Maybe you just want to cruise in that new car, or old muscle car, reminiscing on summers gone by, years that have flown too fast. You just want to feel the sun against your face and wind licking at your hair as you waved to people walking their dogs, aimlessly watching the boats drift out on the lake.

Maybe that lake lap is the way you take home after a night of drinking because you aren't about to get on the highway, or the place you take your new driver to learn the rules of the road. Or maybe like me, one night when life got to be too much, you grabbed your keys, eyes stinging from crying after arguing with your daughter for the last time, hopped in the Jeep and took off.

It was after midnight and I had to get up for work in four hours, but the lake still called to me.

I vividly remember a numbness in my bones, a clarity as to where I was going. I just kept repeating, "I'm not OK. This is not OK," over and over as I calmly backed out of our driveway, as Gage was blissfully unaware and sleeping downstairs, gun on the nightstand.

My mind was on autopilot as the Jeep found its way to the shoreline. It was June and hot as hell out, but even so, I rolled the windows down to feel the warm lake breeze make its way over my broken soul.

In the dark, radio off, with only your thoughts to keep you company, the lake becomes your guide. It's easy to get lost in her beauty, but just as easy to get lost in her torment and uncertainty. With the drive being highlighted by the lake, and her backdrop of a dark sky and haunting moon following you all the way around, in the middle of the night, your mind starts to wander. I began to wonder how many questionable souls had made this drive. How many people fought off their mental demons by spending twenty minutes winding slowly around her, and how many people made decisions that were life altering while making that same drive.

I am never anything but honest with myself, and I won't lie to you either. That night on that lap, my mind wasn't right. I had reached the end of the proverbial rope with my daughter. A mother should never feel that hopeless. That final argument that we had had in the darkness of night wasn't anything major, I suppose, but was a final nail in my coffin. After everything we had endured, all the arguing, all of the crying and begging and pleading, it all boiled down to two things.

First, at this point, she had been so manipulated by Him, that she believed she had a duty to protect His mother and family. His mother, talk about a manipulative bitch! Keep in mind that when my daughter first started dating her son, she hated my daughter. I always told Maisey that she should never have to work to get anyone to like her because she had such a good soul and caring heart and if someone found fault with her, they weren't meant to be on her path or they would just be holding her back.

His mom didn't like the fact that she was only seventeen and He was twenty-three when they met (neither did we for the record!). She thought this could be trouble, plus she was still good friends with His ex-girlfriend whom He had dated for four years. This woman beat her children and choked her son out when He was fourteen on a regular basis. She had mental issues herself, suffering from anxiety, depression and bipolar disorder. She figured out how to manipulate the system and did so like a champ. She collected disability for disabilities that she invented and stayed in homes she didn't pay for until she was physically removed. She couldn't keep a man and made Him stay living in the basement to help pay rent on their dilapidated slumlord managed housing, as well as to help care for His psychotic sister who dealt with her own mental issues and didn't know where, or if, she fit into this world either.

This woman, who, as the relationship was having major issues, decided to stir the pot and jump on my social media pages calling me psychotic, controlling and abusive. She threatened to call the police on us for stalking her twenty-three-year-old son when we couldn't find our daughter (of course she was with Him, where else would she go when she threatened to run away?). She told everyone who would listen how scared her son was for His life because we were crazy. She loved putting us in the public eye with these accusations because she knew our jobs were at risk and it spread like wildfire through our social circles as well. The woman thought her son could do no wrong and boy did that bitch have a big ugly mouth and hardened soul.

So, on this night, on this final argument that I had with my spawn, my mind snapped. I had asked my daughter to remove that woman from her social media pages so this piranha wouldn't be fed. I didn't want her to be able to see any cracks in our façade, any opening that she could insert her opinions and divide the gaping canyon that had formed in our relationship.

But my dear daughter couldn't see it my way. What was coming out of her mouth was one defense after another towards this woman, this dark soul. She screamed at me, telling me that His mother wouldn't have to be so cruel to us if she didn't feel like she needed to defend herself constantly. (I retaliated by saying I never talk to her or her son, so how would she know what was being said in the privacy of my home... Which led my dear daughter to confess to telling that woman absolutely everything because she 'deserved to know'.) My blood boiled and my heart ached as I watched my daughter defend the woman who claimed that I was a bad mother, that I was unfit, uncaring, abusive. I know in my mind that my daughter had been manipulated into feeling this way and I am sure she was feeling the pressure from Him to stay true to the only thing that He felt mattered, which was Him.

My jaw dropped as she shouted at me, pointing out that she was surprised He hadn't tried to kill Himself yet because of how horribly that I had treated Him. (I did *not* yell in retaliation what was going through my head in that instant, which was, *Let Him make that threat and I will hand Him the fucking gun,* again, just angry words coming from a broken mother's soul with no real threat behind them), but I bit my tongue until it bled, leaving me with nothing but a metallic taste in my heart and angry hot tears forming in my eyes.

So, if the first thing that tore a hole right through my soul that night was listening to my daughter value and defend this woman above and against her own mother, the final blow to my already weakened mental state was the complete lack of respect. I had held my shit together for so long already.

I held my breath when my once sweet, now soulless daughter spent Mother's Day with His mother instead of her own. I winced but remained upright as she ran off on Father's Day with Him because she was worried about His mental health due to the fact that He didn't have an active father to speak of and this day was, 'just so hard on Him and so hard for Him to deal with'.

I didn't lose myself to the dark thoughts that began to choke my heart when I watched her that snowy day in February stand on my front lawn crying hysterically trying to decide if she should run away with the asshole as He locked her crap in His car and sat laughing and smiling at all of the family that had gathered to put up a fight to save her. To save her from Him, from herself and from whatever darkness that was slowly inking its way into all of our lives. He was a snake who slithered in and no matter how we tried, we just couldn't cut His damn head off.

Even as the police pulled up that day, neighbors watching from their windows and my daughter appearing to have an anxiety-induced breakdown on my lawn, I remained strong. But on this night, as we continued to argue and I forbid her from going out yet again with Him because we had fought so hard to get her to pass her college level anatomy class that she needed for her nursing degree and she had put off studying yet again to see Him, it was a few simple words that had stacked together to form a force that was finally strong enough to snap my mind, to batter my heart, to take me to that edge of losing both my faith in her and sanity within myself.

With cold, weathered eyes that peered out at me from where my baby girl's deep ocean blues used to dance, and with a voice that was emotionless and hollow, my defeated shell of a daughter opened her mouth to let her final arrows fly. "Look at yourself, Mother. Why are you getting so mad? I'm not yelling, so why are you being so defensive?" she began to preach, ever so slowly moving her way towards my face.

As she was spewing hatred at me, a strange realization happened. I was watching her movements, hearing her words, and seeing and hearing Him at the same time. This shell of a person, this empty vessel where my beautiful daughter once stood has been reprogrammed to not give a shit any more. Family no longer mattered; her future no longer mattered. Loyalty had been thrown by the wayside and I was one of the only things left standing in her way. So, naturally, I am where all her bitterness and hatred was directed.

When my Magoo, one of my best buddies, my hip rider was inches from my face, she coolly, meticulously looked into my terrified eyes, knowing I was hanging on to her every venomous word, and said in a hushed tone as she put her hands on my shoulders, "Listen Mom... I'm eighteen now. You can't stop me. You don't give a fuck about my happiness and what I need to be happy, and I no longer respect you, so I am fucking walking out of this house. I'm going, and you can't stop me."

She backed up, grinned, turned around and grabbed the doorknob. As she grabbed her keys and walked out the door, she yelled over her shoulder casually, "You chose this Mom, if you would just respect Him..." she trailed off.

71

I know. I know. Trust me, I'm with you all reading this statement, every part of my body wanted to throw that kid out on her spoiled bratty ass! So did my husband! But what you haven't heard was the years of work this kid had put into school and her grades and community service and scholarship applications to get into a top nursing school. St. John's had a 26% acceptance rate and by spending all her sophomore, junior and senior year taking college courses that would transfer over, and me spending months pouring over scholarship applications, we got her in with multiple academic scholarships! We had done everything we possibly could to give her the upper hand, to get her to this point. She was set up perfectly. She would get her RN in two years, finish her bachelors the third year, then work and move on to her masters. Her scholarship money she had been awarded would cover almost all of it. This kid once had a big dream to change the way nurses are treated and to approach hospice care with a more holistic approach.

This kid, for seventeen years, out of all the people I had ever known, has had the biggest heart, and I knew that she was meant to do big things in this world. I could not, would not let her derail here. We were months away from moving her to college, months away from a new life, where I had hoped, she would be too busy making her way in the world, she wouldn't have time to baby Him any more. Instead of saving stray and broken dogs like Him, it was time for her to save herself. I couldn't kick her out and she knew it. That just made the situation more dire.

In my mind, if she left because I threw her out, from that point on in life, any mistake she made would be traced back to that exact moment, pinpointing me forever as the villain in her nightmare. I reasoned with myself that if she left on her own, if she walked out on her own merit, I would be let off the hook. Until that happened, I would keep trying to keep my head above water, trying to reach her with a life preserver, even though our rope was fraying, and the boat was filling with murky undercurrent.

It was at this point, this defining moment when I snapped. Watching my daughter act as if I was nothing, as if I wasn't the one who came to her all those years when she would scream in the night, not the one who held her little body when she was sick or chased the monsters away in the dark. She had forgotten that I was the one who taught her the virtues of patience and grace, the value of family and determination and hard work. It no longer mattered that I held her hair when she puked and cleaned shit out of her clothes. Didn't matter any more that I survived on post it notes and never-ending lists and lay awake at night trying to remember what I had forgotten to do that day. The birthday parties, the loss of friends, the broken hearts. I was there for every glorious, gritty and painful moment of that kid's life and she ended up turning away from me.

This is what broke me. This is what haunted me. This is what I wanted to run from, hide from, and try to find a new way back to her.

And so, with a numb mind and screaming heart, I ended up on that lake lap. As I gripped the wheel, my mind began racing through the slow motion memories that my brain was rapidly firing. All the late-night movies we would watch together, how I would rub her feet, how we would talk late into the night when she had her heart broken, how she would make me laugh.

When she started taking Spanish, she started calling me, 'Madre'.

It just became her thing and when she was trying to get on my good side, she would call out, "Hey, Madre!" And flash that wickedly entrancing smile while those blue eyes would dance. My girls were always with me. We talked all the time, even after Shiloh moved out. I don't know how to lose one of them, how to move on in a world without one.

As the warm summer air blew across my face, I felt a new emptiness in the pit of my stomach. For the first time, I had felt like I had truly lost her. As a mama, I always told my kiddos that I would fight for them forever, I would always do what had to be done. They were protected and forever loved, and I would forever be their shelter and home. But this... This was something that I could have never seen coming. This wolf, this snake that had made His way into our lives and began ripping my family apart, severing relationships one by one. I wasn't equipped to fight that off. I was at a loss as to how to save her. How was I supposed to just let her go? Give her up? Write her off? That was never an option for me.

I succumbed to the powers of the lake lap and just let myself drive. I let the loneliness crawl over my skin like marching ants and felt the sting of the loss and darkness run up my spine. I will not lie. I had thoughts that I don't like to speak of. I think people who have been taken to such extreme lows in their lives would be lying if they said these dark thoughts don't creep in from time to time. I think they dance briefly in your mind because the pain can be so great, and the answers are unknown and happiness seems so far away. So, I drove.

I drove in the darkness up and down hills. I drove by the mini golf as warm tears ran silently down my confused face. At one point, the car seemed to be on rails, or I was driving on autopilot. As towering maple and pine trees passed me by on one side of the lake, and the lake lapped at the shore on the other side, ever so briefly, I wondered what would happen if I just let go. Would the car veer toward a tree or the water? Icy goosebumps flared up on my arms as I asked God, the heavens, or whoever was out there if it would hurt or would it be instant. Would it be peaceful? Peace was all my soul was interested in finding right now. The Jeep rolled to a stop at the seawall. I got out and went down to the water.

There's a peaceful feeling that the little lake brings, glorified even more on a warm summer's night. I could see further down the parking lot there were a couple of fogged up cars and half grinned to myself. How I wished that the least of my worries right now was that my daughter was making out in a parked car by the seawall. Instead, I am left mourning the loss of the living, a concept that I just couldn't wrap my head around yet.

I kicked my flip flops off and walked towards the sandy beach. There were a few streetlights that illuminated the parking area, but the beach area was only set a glow by the moon. There, by the edge of the water, I collapsed in the sand, staring out into the nothingness. Only my feet felt the cold rush of the water as my eyes blankly watched nothing out on the water.

I glanced to the right where the yacht club had their boats on the dock. Without even thinking, I could make out the sail that was illuminated by moonlight that was Steele's old boat. I never really understood how someone who seemed to have it all together was actually so lonely and lost that he could do what he did. I can still see him getting his boat ready, grinning ear to ear. He was always so good with the younger kids, teaching them about boats and water safety. His smile was infectious, and his green eyes were so clear.

"I get it now Steele, I get it," I called into the darkness. The loneliness, the helplessness, the pain, the regrets, I understood it all. If I, as an adult, have trouble keeping these thoughts in the darkness from taking hold of my soul, what chance do these kids have? What chance does my daughter have?

Sometimes, you are your best therapist. I talk to myself a lot, always have. It's not a crazy thing, not like I am talking to someone who isn't there. I think it's just how I process things. Sitting on the damp sand, feet in the cold water, a haunting sailboat to my right. I once again stared at the complete nothingness out on the lake.

"So how does this end?" I sighed to no one. "How do I go on with life without her? How do I give up on her? If there is a God, a creator, anything out there, what do I do? How can you let this happen? What is this hell we are living through?" Questions kept flowing from my lips and the anger began to release from my body. It felt good to question, to process. It felt good to be somewhere other than trapped in my own mind, in a house that is on fire, grasping for the hand of a daughter that was just out of reach.

After sitting there a while, I felt calm. Still alone, still broken, but at least calm. I had talked myself away from the darkness, away from the edge. I still had no real answers, but I no longer felt like joining the great abyss of nothingness. Not tonight.

I stood up and walked back to the Jeep. I threw the flip flops in the back and crawled in. I glanced over at the other end of the parking lot and noticed the cars with the steamed-up windows were gone. Their occupants had probably made their way home after a glorious night of awkward sex in their parents' car. Normal teenage stuff. The stuff you experience and look back on later on in life and smile. I then glanced over at Steele's sailboat, looking as though it was just waiting for him to come back.

Who decided which kids make it out unscathed and which kids don't make it out at all? All I knew at that moment was that I was done putting up a fight. I had another daughter to survive for who actually wanted to be part of my family. I had grandkids to look forward to. If I was going to save my daughter, if I was going to steal her back from the gates of hell, it wasn't going to be by arguing. I would have to come up with a new game plan. I threw the Jeep in reverse, cranked the radio, and sang along all the way home.

Chapter 5

Jaded

Ringing. In. My. Ears. More often than not, once I was able to quiet my screaming soul and block out all the noise in my life, I was left with a deafening high pitch ringing that just became my new normal. Looking back, I suppose it could be attributed to the high blood pressure that has crept up into my world, or maybe it was from years of kids screaming and running through the house and when they left just silence remained. Maybe the ringing filled the void of the silence. Whatever had caused it, I had gotten used to it, until I was left alone in this cell with only the silence as a backdrop to my day-to-day survival. Now, that high pitched yet far away ringing is a pulse that reminds me I am still here, still trying to make sense of all that has happened and get my thoughts out into the world before they consume me or until my time is up, whichever comes first.

Sitting alone in here, I can see how a sane person can go mad. When you are left with nothing but your own thoughts for company, sometimes you are drawn into a darkness that can become so all-consuming that you risk the ability to lead yourself back out. Thoughts become misaligned in here and reality walks a fine line blurred with memories and nightmares. Hell, my whole life has become a nightmare. We weren't always like this. I wasn't always like this. That is something that is so crucial to our story. We were the family next door. Life had been awesome, until it wasn't.

Our kids grew up in a house of love and sacrifice. Gage and I had always worked hard so the girls could have better. We took them on family vacations, hung out at the family cabin, went snowmobiling, four wheeling and boating. Everything that we did in life was done as a family unit of four while they were growing up. Gage and I were always working multiple jobs, trying to save so that our girls would always have every opportunity to learn and grow and live wonderful lives. There had never been an exit plan for us. We had never had visions of our little humble lives going in any other direction than the one that we had painstakingly carved out and built, brick by painstaking and exhausting brick.

Am I jaded? Do I feel slighted? Hell ya I do! I have put my life on the back burner for the better part of the past twenty-two years. That's what a good parent does, right? We work tirelessly into nights and worry around the clock, making calculated trades to ensure that our babies would prosper. I gave my time for their well-being. I traded my dreams to give them life experiences. I would go without so that they could have more. I gave everything of myself to the girls, and in the end, everything still wasn't enough. Is it fair? Fuck no! Do I have time to sit and wallow in all that was lost, the life that we could have had? Also fuck no. All that is left for me now is to once again give everything that I have in my power to put their lives back on track. To get them back onto the paths that they were destined to live before He destroyed our track, before He manipulated her into losing her way.

When you bring little souls into this world, it's a heavy weight to bear. There is an all-consuming burden that is weighted upon your heart at all times, knowing that if these little beings live or die, succeed or fail, give up or prosper it's all based on how you guide them. I thought that I had taught them well, led them towards a path of prosperity and fulfilling lives that would have been entwined with loving family bonds to hold them up. I thought I had done enough, taught them enough, loved them enough to be able to back off once they hit adulthood and sit back a bit and watch them thrive and conquer their dreams.

Instead, I realized that all of those years, all of the pain and the love, the arguments and the hugs could so easily be forgotten by her when He had gotten into her head. She may have blocked us out for a while, may have forgotten us, but I never did. My soul never had forgotten them. Even now, while I am in this solitary world of darkness, my mind still searches for them in the shadows, my ears still think they are calling out for me. As a mother, there is no letting them go.

When my mind wanders as I am writing this, it is easy to go back and get lost in it all, back to when we were so good, to when we thought we knew where we were heading. I like to give my heart a break and let my mind fall back in time, watching her run around chasing cats at the farm, listening for the sound of the both of them giggling from somewhere down the hall, watching them whip laps around the yard on snowmobiles and four-wheelers. I craved to remember the nights when we would hang out watching movies together or spend the afternoons shopping, just listening to every tiny detail about their days. Out of everything that I miss, I miss their voices the most. Their laughter, their chatter, the way they called out for me when they needed help. I close my eyes and can feel her crawl up on the couch next to me in the middle of a cold winter, her well-loved blanket cuddled under her chin. "Rub my feet mom, they're cold," she would say, grinning as she settled in next to me.

My body fills with warmth and gratitude as thoughts and memories flood over my tired body and engulf my weighted down soul. In my heart, they are still riding around out there somewhere in their pink Barbie Jeep Power Wheels, Shiloh at the wheel ripping around in the driveway and Maisey's eyes wide open and laughing her famous full belly laughs. They are still sitting on my counter, no shirts on dyeing Easter eggs and giggling as they yell at the dog to get down from the table. They are still out there running around at the zoo, posing on every stone animal and racing to the ice cream machine.

"It's too hard mom, I can't do this!" I grin as I watch through my mind's eye while Maisey is sitting at the dining room table working on math homework, knowing full well that she had the capability to do it, she just had to sit still long enough to try. I can see her coming home with her first paycheck from working at the local lakeside restaurant at thirteen years old, where she had spent four hours washing dishes, proud and excited that she had money of her own. I can imagine her rummaging through the closet, looking to borrow my shoes, some gloves or a sweatshirt, even though she had never returned the last one. I can feel the pangs of fear in my gut when I think about the first time she walked out the door with her newly obtained driver's license, smiling ear to ear and ready to take on the world. She was always ready to take on the world.

My heart has hung onto it all. Every day of boating, every cabin sleepover, every Barbie and horse that she lovingly clung too, every cotton blanket that she cuddled to rags. Every outfit from every dance recital, every bat swung at softball, every first date, every heart break. They are all held captive within me, and those snippets in time are all that keep me going now. Seeing her laugh, seeing her smile, seeing her thriving, those are the things that I have chosen to fight for.

I can't tell you the exact moment that I knew we were in trouble or when it was that I knew she was slipping away. I can tell you that as her mama, I know she's still in there, still fighting. She's going to be OK. They will all be OK.

She always let her heart lead her. This was her greatest asset, but would also be the thing that would bring her to her knees, her world lit in flames around her. She wasn't a hunter because she could never take another life. She was an empath, she felt when others were in pain. She accepted everyone into her circle, a noble yet reckless way to live life. This would also cause her a great imbalance with me as she was growing up. Because she was so all-loving and all trusting, the way she saw people was different. There was no testing the waters with our Maisey, she was always just diving in.

I remembered when she was in about sixth grade that her friend group had taken a sudden shift, as most middle school kids are known to do. She had let go of some of the more 'reserved' friends and gravitated towards a few that hadn't had the best home lives while they were younger. Parents were rarely at home, or single mamas were working two or three jobs just to keep the lights on and bellies fed. In sixth grade, she was intrigued by this newfound freedom that this group seemed to have and delighted in the idea of running a little freer. Of course, I could see where that road was heading so we did butt heads there for a while. There were houses that Gage and I wouldn't allow her to go to and events that we wouldn't let her attend. We never forced her to give up her friends or told her who to hang around with. Everyone was always welcome in our home, but because we actually gave a shit and had rules and were actually home, certain groups of friends wouldn't exactly like hanging out at our home.

The situation was made worse because Gage was a cop. Our daughters grew up in a world where every time they walked down the street, they knew they would be seen by some acquaintance of ours. They also knew from a very young age that we had already given our parental permission to every police officer, fireman and paramedic in town, as well as city workers and our friends in town hall, that if any of them ever saw our girls being disrespectful or putting themselves into a dangerous situation, they could throw them in the back of their car and drag their asses home. Or to the station, whatever would get the point across. We were a small town and we looked after each other's families.

I can remember both of the girls had stories growing up where they weren't at school for one reason or another and one had been stopped by a fellow police officer and the other had been questioned by a public works official as to why they weren't in school. Neither of them had been skipping school, one was leaving for a doctor's appointment and the other was a senior in high school and had an open campus, so she ran home for lunch. Another time, while Maisey was hanging out with the 'undesirable' group as I like to call them, they got caught being out past curfew messing around in City Park. She was promptly escorted back home by a local firefighter, who also happened to be one of her previous teachers.

But for every inconvenience those girls went through while being so closely guarded growing up, there were also moments of grace that they were also blessed with.

When Shiloh was trying to get to school and her defroster wasn't working on her truck, one of the city's Public Works guys saw her struggling and stopped to help her out, clearing off her car of snow and working on the defroster. When Maisey was at the gas station trying to hurry to get to school in sub-zero weather and a raging wind, a local paramedic ran over from his truck to fill her tank too. For all of the moments growing up that those girls were 'inconvenienced' by our friends trying to keep them on the straight and narrow, there were abundantly more times that these same sweet souls just stepped in to help them, trying to take a little of life's weight off their shoulders, if even for a moment.

Our girls lived a very blessed and protected life. We weren't perfect, no one is. But man, did we love them. We loved the hell out of them and just tried to do everything that we could to bring them up right, teaching them the value of family and the virtue of humbleness. They chose who they hung out with, they chose what they wanted to do with their lives and all we could do was stand by and protect them from the sidelines, armed with only the small army of friends and family that we had assembled. We were blindly trudging forward towards a future that we didn't know we should fear.

Sometimes, however, life just goes to shit and the soldiers all fall down. I can still hear her screaming at me from hundreds of miles away. She had just started college and she was once again upset, once again lashing out at me because I was one of the only ones who could take her wrath and not hate her for it. I think that on that night, she was mad because I had questioned her on how classes were going, if she was looking for a new roommate yet since the initial one decided to move in with her boyfriend and I had been trying to convince her that she really shouldn't buy a dog right now, even though she was lonely because she had clinicals, class and an almost full-time job that she had been juggling while having anxiety, depression and sleep issues. Her little heart was so stressed, and her mind wouldn't stop running at night.

"God dammit Mom! Stop trying to control me!" she began lamenting into the phone.

I could hear her nose stuffing up and could imagine her little face turning crimson as those ocean eyes filled with a confused and terrified pool of tears. Adulting was hard. Adulting while being attached to a bipolar, anxiety ridden, manipulative asshole like Him had to have been hell.

"All you ever do is try to control me! It's my goddamn life and my goddamn choices! I know what I need to be happy. You don't even care about my own happiness!" She sobbed into the phone, no anger actually in her voice, just self-pity and sadness.

She had moved away to a place to go to school where she knew no one. Then the roommate moved out, so she was alone. She was a person who has always craved human affection and interaction and would be so depressed without it. He had been using this to His advantage, urging her to get a dog (He knew that we said we would stop paying her rent if she did, we knew she couldn't handle the anxiety owning a dog was going to cause her at that point...) teasing her with the idea of Him moving in with her, never to follow through with it. I believe that He was doing everything within His twisted power to get her to fail at living out there alone and get her back home where He could better control her. It's hard to ride the coattails of someone from so far away.

I didn't bristle as she rambled on and on about how she was just great at pretending to be OK before He came along and that she was just really great at acting, but she was never happy before Him. I listened as she told story after story about seeing different therapists because her depression and anxiety had gotten so bad that she was now on higher doses of sleeping medication and anti-depression drugs. Terror crawled up my spine as she told me she worried that the drugs weren't doing enough and that she woke up one morning with her eyes swollen shut from what was perceived to be an allergic reaction to a new dose of new medication. She only grumbled as I reminded her that she was born with a heart murmur and excess unwarranted medications aren't good for the heart, that I wish she would look into other options than overmedicating herself.

Out of nowhere the subject turned and she blurted out into the night, "Why can't you at least be civil to Him, Mom? You know... He has said He can find it in his heart to be civil to you... even after everything..."

My mind had to somersault, and I had to choke back vomit in my throat in order to form a coherent answer to her. This asshole, this person that weaved His way into our daughter's life and crippled a family, this manipulative little dick who preys on young girls, drains their savings accounts, uses them for a good time and moves on while living in His psychotic mama's basement had the audacity to act like *He* was willing to hand an olive branch to *us*?

At that point, I couldn't believe that this was my actual life, that these words were actually coming out of my sweet (or used to be sweet) daughter's mouth. I wanted to say a thousand things. I wanted to continue shouting at her into the night, hoping that some part of what I was saying would pierce the shroud that He had draped over her soul. But I knew I couldn't. I knew there was no defense, nothing to say that would make its way into her stoned-up heart.

"Maze... I have told you. I can love any animal that you may bring into your life. I can love any baby that you may bring into this world. But I, and your father, will not allow that toxic piece of shit to cause any more havoc in our lives. He will never be allowed in our home, around our family, never be invited to any holiday or vacation. If you choose to live alongside that toxic lifestyle, you are right, it's your choice. But you will be living two separate lives because that son of a cunt is dead to us. Dead," I calmly spit the words into the phone while my heart hovered behind its shield and my soul prepared for the repercussions that were sure to be hurled my way.

There is a place that I have learned to go to when I have to shield myself from her. She's my daughter, like my own heart beating outside of my body. She has a heart of gold, but He has taught her to have a cunning soul and manipulative mind. Her tongue had become a knife and she had become a master in wounding me with it.

In order to survive the pain, in order to not let her completely reduce my heart to ash, I had learned to find the silence. I focused on the intense ringing in my ears, listening to my blood course through my heart. I closed my eyes and searched the darkness until I could see her and her sister, arm in arm, sitting on the front porch with the dog, laughing and waiting to have their picture taken. I attached my mind to her smile, to the life that radiated off the both of them. I let my heart take in that love and allowed my mind to hold on to the not-so-distant memory of who she was, who she still is. I then held my breath to slow my breathing and sat in a calm, dazed silence while waiting for the storm to pass.

And with all of the fury and hatred that she could summon, she began to hurl insults at me one after another, trying to break me, trying to get me to feel the pain that she was living in. It wasn't lost on me that she was merely in survival mode, and although she was an eighteen-year-old adult, she was still my terrified little girl who feared things she couldn't see and placed her trust in people she shouldn't. She still welcomed everyone into her circle, hell-bent on fixing the broken, even if it was her who would break in the aftermath.

"Mom, I am so sick of this! So sick of it all. You are just pissed because for once in my life, I'm not doing exactly what you want me to do! I am an adult and I am making my own choices!" she bellowed out, sounding like a terrified and pissed off three-year-old stomping her feet trying to get her way. She really was exhausting.

But I stayed in my shield, stayed below in the quiet and darkness as I responded in an almost monotone voice, "Maze... You have always called your own shots! Your little bullet head came ripping into this world five weeks early and you have never slowed down since. There have been plenty of friends and boyfriends and decisions that you have made that we may not have liked, but we let you do you. If you need a reminder that you are living your own life and it has nothing to do with what we want, just look down at your own arm kid," I breathlessly finished, and could hear the faintest of maniacal giggle coming from her end of the line.

I knew then that she looked down at the half sleeve tattoo on her lower inner left forearm of sunflowers and dragonflies that she ran out to get the second that she turned eighteen. She always called her own shots and she knew it. Maybe that factored into her pain then, somewhere within her soul, maybe she knew that He was calling the shots now.

Her small giggle was short lived as she once again gripped the edge of reality, hand picking memories and skewing them to make them fit her misguided narrative. Still, as she continued to release all of her pent-up fury at me, the only person in her life who could take it, I clung to my dark abyss, shielding my heart as though I was hidden underwater somewhere in the lake, where it was silent and calm, dark and warm.

I remained at peace while she continued, "All you know how to do is control me, *Mom!* And I have had enough! Remember in sixth grade, you wouldn't let me hang out at certain people's houses (yes, she *really* pulled out the sixth grade card here...) just because you didn't like their parents. I was one of the first ones to have a tracking device for Christ's sake! (Because we gave her a cell phone and the whole family was on the life protection app...) Well, you can't control me any more and you can't stand it!" She had abruptly stopped and I could hear her sobbing.

I wanted to tell her that I knew. I knew she didn't want to be saying these things to me. I knew there was no one else to vent to.

I knew being an adult absolutely sucked sometimes and that I was still there for her. I wanted to tell her all of this, but from where I was sitting all I could muster was half whispering, "I won't apologize for caring about you. I won't apologize for being a mom who gave a shit."

I can remember the emptiness that I felt sitting alone at the kitchen table, clinging to the phone like a lifeline to another time.

I was alone, but not because Gage had moved out yet, this was just before then. We had been fighting nonstop and were at a place where we were both so broken, that he decided that he needed a break. A break from me, a break from her, a break from life. So, without much warning, he booked a trip to visit his parents who were wintering in Florida, and he left me.

He left me at a time when I myself was lost and scared and pissed and dealing with all of her shit. I remember being so angry at him for leaving me like that, just expecting me to be the one to pay the bills, feed the animals and keep our lives rolling on. Like he had no responsibilities, he felt free. I distinctly remember envying that freedom while I sat at that kitchen table that night. The urge to want to be free from it all, to not have to hurt any more, to not have to worry or try to fix things any more. This is what was clouding my mind when she let the hammer fall, and I had been too preoccupied to keep my shield up and protect myself.

"You know, Mom," she began in a much calmer, quieter tone than previously. "I have talked to people here at school and at work and they tell me that they have been in my situation and what I should do, because it worked for them, I should just cut you all out of my life for one or two years and you will miss me so much that you won't care about Him any more... we could be happy again!"

There was no trying to hold back my anger or watch what I said. This wasn't coming from any 'friends' or coworkers or people at school. This was directly from His filthy lips to her naive ears. I remember her saying when they first started dating that the only time that He had moved out of His mother's house was when she was yelling at Him all the time, so He moved out and stayed gone for six months and she practically was begging Him to come home. This was the same tactic that he tried convincing her with when he convinced Maze to run away her senior year of high school.

"Seriously kid?" I shouted into the phone, gloves off, shield down and heart raw from her words. "You are threatening to cut us out of your life? Do you understand how much life happens in a year or two? Why would you do that? Why would you listen to Him and that advice? Come on. I…" but she cut me off before I could even finish the plea that my heart was making.

"*Mother!*" she screamed into the phone, a voice that I no longer recognized. It was a voice that had been forced from fear, from anger, from regrets. A voice that was scared, pissed off and offended at the same time. "*He* makes me happy. *He* is the life that I want and I will not choose. It's not a choice, I want both," she yelled and then abruptly stopped. There was silence on the line.

As she sat, no doubt contemplating her next words, I sat alone at my kitchen table, tears freely falling down my face, the safe place that I had been storing my heart in, yanked out from beneath me, now fully exposed. I had mistakenly let her get to me. I had stopped focusing on remaining calm for just long enough to let down my guard and let her dance with heavy boots upon my heart. I gasped for a breath as my mind went blank, no clue as to what to say to her, no ideas of how to fix what has been broken.

A funny thing happens when your shields are down. The loneliness that you are exposed to is much like the dark all-consuming coldness of depression, yet your heart lies fully exposed, yearning for the love that it once knew, holding out hope for one kind word, one glimmer of hope that she still exists, that she is still somewhere within herself, struggling to hold on, searching for a way out of it all. There is a weakness to it all, a bitterness that is singed at the soul's edge, yet a hollowness beneath the thin veil of hope.

"By the way, where the hell is my scholarship money? Why can't I have access to it? You know that it is only causing me more anxiety worrying about where it is and if you have spent it! That is *my* money and it's illegal for you to keep me from it! Mom! Are you even listening to me?" Stunned, I now sat with my jaw hanging open, dropping the phone to the table. She couldn't have just said that. She couldn't have just accused me, her mama, of spending her scholarship money. This was Him talking. For fuck's sake, what does He want now? A car? A motorcycle? Some new half ass business idea like the one He had with His ex-girlfriend to sell some counterfeit watches, which He still owed her over four grand for. I snapped out of it, put the phone to my ear and hissed right back with all of the fierceness that I could muster.

"You listen here little girl! (Mom, I hate it when you call me that!) When you gave up on yourself in high school, when you ran away and moved in with him, stopped caring about school, stopped caring about

95

yourself, where was I? I was the one working on scholarship applications in the middle of the night. I was the one making sure all of your deadlines were met, fees were paid, and homework was done. I was the one contacting teachers to see what you could make up to protect your GPA! It was *me* that submitted your damn essays, *me* that spent hours in the middle of the night scouring the internet searching for more scholarship opportunities and *me* that didn't give up on your ass. So, tell me why then would I spend that money? You have enough people who believe in you that you shouldn't have to take a loan out at all! You do realize that if I spent that money, I would have to take out loans to help you pay for school then? Listen to yourself! Damn it kid… you aren't making any sense! We don't give you access to that account because we have watched *Him* convince you to blow through all of your savings account… over five grand in the course of three damn months! I will not…"

But I was cut off mid tirade by a voice that sounded like my daughters, but was controlled by another. A voice that used to call to me in the middle of the night when she thought there were monsters in her room, a voice that would carry the best belly laughs across the spring air as a toddler, a voice that whispered, 'Don't leave mama', as I left to work early on a Saturday morning. The beloved voice that always used to end every one of our phone conversations with, 'Love you, Mom', now spoke to me with no other intention than to lash out and hurt me, to make me feel the pain and misery that she has been manipulated into, to make me feel the hate.

I sat at that kitchen table, alone, in the dark now as the sun had set, and only the glow of the TV illuminated the room. My skin was so cold, I had goosebumps of loneliness slowly crawling up my arms and a hollowness made its way into my chest. I felt alone and empty. I was exhausted from the fight. I looked down at the floor towards my feet where the little fluff ball dog was lying and heard the cat rolling over on the couch. At least they loved me. At least they needed me. I wasn't truly alone.

I could hear her take in a deep breath, as if she had finally calculated her last words and fished them out of the suffocating air, just wanting this conversation to be over and wanting to make me feel pain just one more time. Slowly, her soft voice formed the words that would be my final downfall, the words that would drive me to end it all.

As I pressed the phone to my ear, tears pouring down my face, staring at my pets and trying to search the darkness of my mind for those safe quiet spaces and a snapshot of who she used to be, I heard her voice. "You know Mom, when I hug you, I don't even feel anything any more," and the line went dead.

Chapter 6

Fear

There is a certain type of fear that just hangs on like an echo in your mind. It's like knowing how a horror movie is going to end, and so no matter how much that you try to pay attention and enjoy the rest of the movie, you know that ending is coming, that excitement, that heart pounding fear and anticipation. No matter what you do, those echoes call your name, causing you to lose focus on what you are doing, what you are really trying to pay attention to. In life, this fear is palpable, it's all-consuming, and it starts to blur the line in your mind's eye between reality and what the perceived future may look like.

This type of fear, the mind numbing, day-to-day ache in the chest. The obsession of thoughts that begin with, *Maybe,* and *If,* and *In the end....* The fear that chokes you in the middle of the night as you struggle to find peaceful sleep and to let your mind rest for a few blissful hours. This type of fear that weighs so heavy on your soul and leads you into a rabbit hole of worries and doubts. This life robbing, soul-sucking, adrenaline pumping, mind fucking fear is what I have wrestled with over the past year. It's paralyzing, relationship destroying and toxic. Once this fear has wormed its way into your world, you are left with no other option than to live with it, day in and monotonous yet terrifying day out, letting it fester and destroy everything that you are trying to protect. It will destroy your every dream, every relationship, every thought. You will become completely consumed with chasing the ending, trying to rewrite it. Until, that is, your tired soul and exhausted heart convince your slipping mind to hang on to reality just a little bit longer, to grip that ledge with bleeding nails just a little bit tighter... in order to rewrite that ending, slay the monster and save the princess just one more time...

I was having a hard time getting any sleep in my cell, tossing and turning as my brain couldn't differentiate between when I was writing and when I was trying to rest and let my body give in to sleep. Much like the last few months of my life, the constant exhaustion led to never-ending nightmares, not only when I was asleep, but when I was awake as well. If I could just relax enough to find some peace... To catch just a few minutes of sleep in this cold room... I lay down on the old thin mattress and threw the stained sheet over one leg.

It was completely dark and cold, just how we liked it. I cannot stand to sleep in a hot room, so when we moved into this home, which was the ninth home we have had since we have been married twenty-three years ago, but I digress, we built our bedroom in the basement. Built is perhaps the wrong word. Reconfigured the basement, I suppose, as we first had to rip out the walnut wood and

Formica orange small kitchen that had been where our bedroom now stands. My husband had etched out a corner of our basement to turn into a cute little room for us, dark and quiet, attached to a pretty big closet and behind the bathroom that we had torn out and started over with. This little bedroom was directly underneath Maisey's room.

We had gotten lucky with this house, in all of her 940 square feet of glory. Before this little crown jewel of a home that was quietly tucked away from the world, just a few blocks from the lake, we lived right on Main Ave, in a fabulous two-story with a huge front porch and swing.

Loved that house, the old original wood and the history that it held. What we did not love was the corner lot that left you on display constantly, so you could never have a relaxing moment of peace. Every time we were outside, we had to put on a happy face and entertain anyone who happened to wander by. It was awesome for watching the Fourth of July parade and Christmas by the Lake parade as the festivities rolled on by, great for hosting get togethers. We did not, however, love her heftier house payment and tiny one stall garage.

As we were trying to decide if we should build a four stall on her side lot; an old friend of my dad's was debating on putting our crown jewel up for sale. His mom had lived there as only the second owner of the house, which had been built in the 1940's. After she passed away, he stayed there as a bachelor, alone with all of her memories. He had been thinking about getting away from town, always the hunter and fisherman, wanting to move to his cabin up north on a more permanent basis.

This little slice of heaven was the type of home that sold as soon as it hit the market. Houses in this little resort town, especially ones that are single level homes, sell fast and sell high. We did the math and figured that instead of taking out a loan to invest at least thirty thousand into the home we had, we could sell it as is, cut our mortgage from a thirty year to a fifteen, and build the garage for cash. My husband was always good at looking towards our future back then, and pointed out that it would be relatively easy to get our little home paid off in record time, allowing us to retire earlier and travel more. I was sold! Although it would take a couple years for the little house to truly become our little crown jewel as she stands today.

When we first stopped in to take a look at her, our daughters cried. They didn't understand why they had to give up their big bedrooms and porch swing for this tiny home that had been well loved since the 40's but never updated. They couldn't see what we saw. We knew it could be something great. We knew it would get us to our end goal quicker. We knew we could turn it into a home and be happy there.

Although they were less than thrilled, the girls did help with some of the renovations. Shiloh helped with running the Bobcat, digging and leveling the backyard to pour the foundation for the garage. She would also end up helping shingle and side that garage before she moved off to school. Maisey was more of an inside worker. She liked things like painting walls and sanding floors, trimming out cupboard doors and polishing the old oak paneled walls. OK. Maybe she didn't like it, but she did it. And our little home became loved once again. A home that was inviting and small, snug and safe.

As I lay there that night, snug in my bed that was in the center of the cold dark corner bedroom in the basement, the fear still snuck in. I lay there thinking about where we were in our lives, rolling over to an empty space where my husband no longer resided. I missed the noise of his sleep apnea machine and the warmth of his leg when my feet were cold. I missed knowing he was next to me, knowing it was us against the world. As I lay there in the dark, covers pulled up under my neck, dog between my legs and cat firmly into my side, I heard movement above me. The 1940's wood floors creaked with her every step as she walked from her room towards the bathroom. But on this night, the creek with every footstep didn't stop in the bathroom hallway. Instead, they softly made their way towards the sliding glass door in the living room.

Immediately, my heart began to pound and move up into my throat. My six-pound dog was silently dreaming at my feet, so there is no reason for her to be heading for that sliding glass door. My mind raced with anticipation as I recalled all of the arguing over the past few days. So many times, she shouted in rage at me, telling me how little I meant to her any more and how wrong I had been to disrespect *Him*. It wasn't until I heard a few more footsteps and a male's voice laughing maniacally that I knew my fate had been sealed. We had become that Lifetime movie. We had become the family down the street that looks great from an outsider's view, but who was seriously trashy behind closed doors.

As I lay there, my body trembled and I ached for a time when I had felt safe. I froze in fear as the laughing had stopped and I heard the click of the latch on the sliding door close once again. There were no more voices as the 1940's floors kept creaking underfoot. It wasn't one set, but two sets of feet that I could hear slowly bumping into walls and making their way down the older basement stairs that we hadn't replaced yet. I knew once they reached the foot of the base of the stairs, I would hear nothing further in the darkness, as the water sealed and epoxied cement floors would make no noise, giving me no hint as to where they were, or when they would be coming.

I lay there for a few seconds, unable to stifle the heavy breaths that were heaving in and out of my chest. My heart was pounding in my ears and my mouth was as dry as dirt. I couldn't swallow and just lie there shaking. All at once, my brain kicked into survival mode, and with hands still trembling, I lowered my covers and reached one hand out to my bedside table to grab my 9mm. (At this point in my life, I didn't even bother tucking it away any more, she just sat there, loaded and ready to fire on my side table, next to my bottle of water, cough drops and mint Chapstick.) The dog had gotten annoyed and moved up towards the vacant pillow that now rests to my right, where my husband used to lie. The cat was irritated by us both and jumped down to the floor, retreating under the bed, unaware that there was an imminent threat lurking its way through the darkness.

It was her voice first who cut the silence in the dark. "Madre," she half hissed and half sang on the other side of the door. "Mom, are you awake yet?" she asked softly with an undertone of sarcasm. The few seconds that followed felt like an eternity. The panic that rang in my ears and fear that gripped my heart were no match for the live stream of electric memories that flashed in my brain like old snapshots in a family photo album. I saw visions of the way we were, stills in time of my girls laughing and running through leaves in the yard on a fall day, one dressed as a princess and the other as a puppy with ringlets of curls and a little black nose as I was trying to get a good shot with them next to their beloved and faithful ninety-five pounds of love lab cross, Timber. Memories of the cabin and boating and fishing. Our little family lined up on the seawall breathlessly looking up at a sky full of fireworks, silly faces on carnival rides and the agonizing wait for the parade to begin on a curb somewhere. The girls in a bucket of a skid loader, grinning and looking at their dad like he was their hero. Christmas tree after tree with them posed with family and cousins in front of it, showing their age progression. Disney pictures, cruise photos and a particular favorite of us standing in front of the retired space shuttle, Atlantis.

It was in these few seconds, while my brain was short circuiting, trying to juxtapose these sweet, precious snap shots of time against the terror that we were now living, that one memory stopped my heart. It had been a long time since I had even thought about it, but there it was, crystal clear in front of me, blinding me momentarily from the devastation our lives had become.

When you mention my younger daughter's name, this is the image that forever comes to my mind, steals my heart and makes me lower all of my armor. It's her at about 3 three in the back seat of my 1993 Chevy Blazer (Side note, my most favorite vehicle ever! It was the Pro-Am Classic package with wood grain effects on the interior and a pink pinstripe down the side that faded to purple. Damn I loved that big blue beast that was made for garage saling, not so great for lifting kids in and out of car seats out of the back...) Anyway, it was in this setting that I will always remember her. The way she was. The way we were.

Shiloh was in her car seat, about six years old, blonde hair just glowing in the summer sun in her long pigtails, chomping on a nugget out of her happy meal and throwing fries through the grate that kept our big old dog from climbing over and eating everything. As the dog would either successfully make the catch or just drool and miss the fry by a mile, our lovable goofy girl Maisey would giggle and throw her head back in her car seat, releasing a glorious belly laugh, kicking her little feet that were adorned with little flip flops that had the straps across the heal so they stayed in place. Her curls were a crazy mess after a day of boating at the cabin with Mamo and Papo (affectionate names for the grandparents, picked out by

Shiloh herself, as she was the original only grandchild) and she was getting tired.

Her three-year-old self has her soft cotton blanket balled up under her chin and she is watching her big sister with big, tired ocean eyes. Shiloh, of course, loved seeing her sissy giggle and performed this trick over and over as I drove.

I drove a lot during that time, especially in the summers. Gage was working long shifts and picking up extra shifts to help to make payments on our home, which was our fourth home in just a few years of marriage and was completely out of our league. We were drowning in debt for a house that we bought because we had wanted the land, and between him working all of the time and me working a couple of jobs, we didn't see each other too much. I missed him. I missed us.

I was lonely, so I would take the kids on nice weekends and make the two-hour drive back 'home', to where my family was, the cabin was, and the lake called our name. For those forty-eight hours, I wasn't alone. We laughed, had fun and just lived. It was me and my girls. They were raised in cabins and boats, snowmobiles and golf carts. They survived on smores and mac and cheese, during a time when there were no rules at the cabin, no bedtimes, and family was always welcome. They were raised by everyone from their great grandparents, grandparents, to second and third cousins. I hope they can say it was an idyllic way to grow up, that they always felt the love.

On this particular snapshot in time, I can hear my sweet, soft-spoken six-year-old Shiloh speaking to Maisey in her little Kermit the frog voice that I can still hear when I close my eyes. She's singing to her now, the little song we made up when Maisey was a baby. (I'm *that* mama, both of the girls have their own songs, and even now, when I am missing them and just need to remember them in my heart, I will occasionally sing them aloud, letting the words rip a little at my heart to remind my soul of a time that wasn't so long ago, a time that flew by when no one was paying attention.)

She was staring at her little sissy singing, "Maisey Alexis in the deep blue sea, swam so high and she swam so free, with the heavens above, and the valleys below and her little fishy tail on the go."

Then Maisey giggled and wanted to sing the Shiloh song, "Shiloh Lee in her flying machine, up she goes... up she goes... Where she stops, nobody knows... stinky toes!" Ending in crazy little giggles.

It was after a few rounds of 'their' songs that the car settled down and sleep was wrestling with heavy eyelids in the backseat. I glanced in the rearview to see Shiloh passed out, her poor blanket hanging from her mouth, disgusting I know. Never a pacifier for either of them, but Shiloh would suck on the satin edge of her 'Mimi' which was a blanket that had floppy arms and an almost detached elephant head from six years of rough love and laundry room time. Her sweet blonde head was flopped towards the window, bug bitten legs dangling over the edge of the car seat with bare feet flopping, as always. Maisey was still fighting sleep, cuddled up towards the side of the car seat, her blanket wadded up into a ball, being held under her sweet little chin below her round little face. The weekend of boating and cabin fun had been exhausting and the road was calling us home.

As her ocean eyes grew heavy and she stared out the side window at the rows of corn that flew by in the orange glow of the setting summer sun, I heard her small voice pipe up from behind me. "Mama, I remembered when I picked you," my sweet girl said as her eyelids grew heavy.

I remember half laughing and asking my Ms. Magoo what she had said, "What do you mean, you picked me Magoo?" What she said next caught my breath and warmed my soul all at once.

"Before I was a real baby and I was swimming around in the air, I had to find you. I looked through all kinds of mama's and I saw you and said, 'That's mine, that's my mama', and I picked you and went into your belly." As I glanced into my rearview, there sat my three-year-old angel, grinning ear to ear, blanket tucked under her chin, eyes heavily crashing down. I will never, ever in my lifetime forget that face, forget that glow of evening sun, smell of the fries wafting up from the back seat, forget her sister peacefully sleeping next to her or the dog panting from behind her. If I was never blessed with another moment of peace while my soul traveled the earth in this body, my heart was full. In this snapshot, in this exact place in time, in this old Chevy Blazer with the wood trim interior on our way home to my husband who was eagerly waiting for us, I had everything. This is how I keep her in my heart.

As I lay there clutching my gun, a few thoughts began to swirl in my mind. If He came through that door first and I fired, she may be behind him. (First rule of gun safety, know what is directly behind your target.) If she came through first, then what? If He were to attack me, then run, do I still shoot? (Second rule of gun safety, if you shoot someone in the back, that meant they were trying to get away so you most definitely would be in trouble, shoot them when they are facing you.) If I shoot and they run, do I chase him out of the house? (Third rule of gun safety, shoot the intruder in your home, if you shoot them in the garage or outside, you are in trouble again.) And if I can fight my corrupted angel off to shoot at Him, is that still considered defense or too much use of deadly force? (Final rule of gun safety, remember, if you shoot someone you will be arrested... *where did I put that attorney's card?*)

Although I could barely see the door opening in my dark basement from the sliver of moonlight shining in around the edge of our blackout curtains, I could hear the knob turn and I could feel the dog stir at my feet. Although she was startled, she didn't growl, a clear indicator that it was Maisey that had entered this tomb of hell, or at least she who entered first. That dog, and all animals loved that girl. She was a natural with animals and always had such a pure heart.

"Mom," her soulless voice whispered with a sharpness that cut the darkness and made me stifle that last inhalation of fear that I had just sucked into a set of lungs that seemed to have stopped working out of fear. I was still laying there, frozen, gun in my right hand as she crawled onto my bed and cuddled into my side.

For a moment, time fell away again, and here was my girl, cuddled up next to me, waiting for me to tell her a story of how the scary things under the bed could be fought off by the valiant Timber dog, how the castle is always protected by the king and how she would always be safe in her own bed. Every part of my body could sense her lying next to me, and in my confusion, I imagined her as she once was, sleepy ocean eyes, sun-kissed little face and tangled blonde curls. I could feel her dry little hands, covered in eczema cream as they brushed against the skin on my arm, just wanting reassurance that I was there. The most exhilarating part was her smell. Like a Mama Bear, I knew her scent, even in the cold darkness of night. She was a clean, flowery smell with a hint of warm vanilla. Always has been. (Her sister was always a bold vanilla and sugar cookie smell, it's the only way I can really explain it.)

But on this night of terror, I was tired of fighting the monsters in the darkness. I had grown lonely, soulless and tired. I had lost my faith long ago and was living on the brink of insanity. The fight was gone. The battle was over. I was intoxicated by this perfect soul that I had brought into this world, and just wanted to lay here with her a little while longer before the monster came to take her away.

My tired and trembling fingers released the gun. I finally exhaled the breath that had been fiercely trying to escape my lungs. As I rolled my head to face where she was laying, she spoke.

"Mom, I love you, but I have to live my life for me now. I'm tired of living my life for everyone else, tired of trying to make everyone else happy and worrying about what people might be thinking of me," she spoke in a voice that was not her own, it was a medicated flat tone. There was no emotion, no tears, just matter-of-fact and calculated. She was close now; I could feel her hot breath in my face and smell the lilac shampoo in her hair. "I am living my life for me, and you never respected Him. I am tired of the guilt trip. I am making my choice."

At least I think those were the last words because I felt the searing pain before my brain could comprehend what was happening. It was a sharp pain in the center of my chest, but it was the crushing force that I could feel breaking through ribs first. It was the stab and ache of a lung being deflated and a heart beginning to drain that I felt before I heard Him laughing standing over me. He's laughing and she's crying. But it's calm. So calm. No lights, still complete darkness. I can't breathe, but I feel her pull me close, hugging me. I feel her heart beating in her chest while mine is slowing down. Somewhere in the darkness, I heard a small sniffle and something wet fell from her face onto my cheek. He's still giggling like a maniac in the darkness, but she weeps. I never lost her at all. He may have clouded her judgment, but she was still in there.

"I love you, Mama," she's whispering to me so that He can't hear, "I love you and I will choose you again, in another world, I will choose you, Mama."

Why is it so wet? Why am I so cold? Jesus, my back is killing me! I open one eye to see the cinder block wall across from me and the glow from the hall light falling across the foot of the bed, exposing the old blue blanket.

"Fuck," I say out loud as I realize that I had pissed myself in fear once again. Damn these drugs that they keep giving me in here and damn the life that has left my mind in shambles, sentencing me to vivid nightmares, nightmares that seem to have been based on what my greatest fears used to be.

Ironically, the way it all played out was worse than any nightmare that stalked my sleep. They say that my mind has been having manic episodes, that I am still in shock. They say that I am unsure as to the sequence of events leading up to the confrontation of the asshole, and seem to dance between a perceived reality and what really happened. That's why they have been drugging me the last few days. They say I need it to calm down, to focus on the questioning, to focus on my story, my deposition. They sure have a lot to say and a lot of opinions for people who didn't have to keep treading water while balancing their kids on their backs to keep their heads above water.

I kick off the old blue blanket that smells like a mothball and shuffle towards the cell door. The floor is damp and cold, and my bare feet made sticking sounds as I walked across it. It's a small town with a small-town jail. Not luxurious, not awful, just a place to exist.

"Hey Bud, you out there?" I hollered into the hall, "Bud?" A sense of deep loneliness was beginning to take hold of me. How small I felt yelling into this empty hallway, like a rescued cat crying from its shelter cage. Begging for water, begging for food, begging for help. I hadn't even realized that tears were streaming down my cheeks as I had a death grip on the green cold metal bars in front of me.

"Bud?" I whimpered one last time. I slid down onto the floor and crumpled into a heap. I curled my numb, wet, cold body into the fetal position and hugged my legs into my chest. This was a new loneliness, deeper than the kind that finds you when you are depressed, more suffocating than the kind you feel in the middle of the night when you realize that your life had fallen apart, your kids are gone and your husband left you. This loneliness, I realized, was my heart and soul just wanting to be done. This loneliness was finally myself giving in and giving up on me.

The cold damp floor felt welcoming to my face, and my body was less cold as I hugged myself. A million thoughts go through your mind when there is no one left to talk to, no one left to blame, no one left to fantasize about saving... or killing. As I lay there, still covered in my own pee, coming down off of the drugged haze I had been in, I began to think about my girls. I thought about their lives, our lives and what they still had to look forward to. I thought about Gage and what could still be salvaged of his life. I knew where my road was about to lead, but as badly as I wanted to give up the badge of warrior, I knew I still had a story to tell. For them. For her. For all the girls that had been her or would have been her in the future.

With a deep breath, followed by a guttural and weighty sigh, I sat back up. Getting back up off the floor was a little harder than I had imagined. At only forty-four, I had done more harm to my body exercising over the last few years than good. I had given myself multiple stress fractures in my legs from overdoing it when running for too long and too far. I had hurt my left hip running hills and now I just deal with it when it pops in and out of position. I had an external hernia by my belly button that was repaired, only to give myself an internal one while lifting weights. That's me, deciding to do something and then diving right in, most times overdoing it, just like my dad. When we want something bad enough, we just go for it, oftentimes not even seeing what we are doing to ourselves in the process. But we lead with our heart, and oftentimes the drive of what we want just blocks out our own pain and self-destruction.

I stood up and gave my hip a quick second to be able to bear weight again, kind of like an old dog getting up off of the floor, all stiff and needing to stretch those old bones. I slowly walked over to the little sink in the corner by the toilet. Not needing to pee, obviously, I decided that there was no way in hell I was going to sit in these pee-drenched clothes until morning. I had one tiny washcloth, a bar of soap and a little towel. *Fine. A whore bath it will be.* I giggled at the thought of it. That's a term I learned from a friend of my brother in law's. Exactly as it sounds, a whore would only bother washing where her next lover was going to poke around.

For whatever insane reason, as I stood there peeling off my peed-on clothes, I giggled at the sound of him saying, *You know Max, pits, tits, ass and cooch.* I turned the faucet on and with lukewarm water, a bar of soap and a tiny washcloth, I got the job done.

It was almost an out of body experience standing in that little jail cell, completely naked and exposed after toweling off. I stood there for a moment, feeling the obscure exhilaration of it. I am in a cage, and there is nowhere to hide. I am always fully on display, yet unless I finish writing my side of the story, no one will ever know what we have been through, what I have done or why. I walked the few feet back over to my cot, grabbed the mostly dry top blanket of itchy wool, wrapped it around my tired wounded body, and sat down at the little desk to finish writing what I had started. Let's go back to the lake.

Chapter 7

Hope

It was a few days after Shiloh's wedding that I had talked to Moby about what had happened that night when they left the wedding reception. My sweet boy had stopped by the house because he was picking up some flowers and vases and lanterns left over from the wedding to take to his sister, who was a jaw droppingly gifted photographer. (She had taken the pictures of Moby and Maisey at their senior prom, the one time that she stood up against Him because He was too old to be admitted to prom and she wasn't going to miss it. So, her best friend, her soulmate, happily took her. Looking back, knowing how much he has always loved her, it had to kill him to go as 'just friends', had to hurt like hell through time to watch her descend so far into a madness that was her hell.) It was on this visit with this dear soul that I would learn the depths of their conversation and come to understand Moby's devotion to her, and just how sweet that final lake lap must have been for them both.

I had been sorting through the massive stockpile of wedding decor that had been used and returned into unorganized piles in the room that once housed my Shiloh.

As I sat in the center of the room with lanterns, candles, silk flowers and unused bubble containers all around me, I glanced around quickly at the walls. I remember not allowing myself to linger in a stare for too long, as these days my emotions are raw and most days, I feel like it takes nothing to make me fall apart. There was a sweetness though as I quickly glanced around. Shiloh had only been moved out of the house for two years, just long enough to finish college and get married, and even though I had started to turn her room into a spare room by adding a sleek mid-century modern futon and mounted a TV on the wall, remnants of my daughter still graced the room.

There was her stuffed animal net that still lifelessly hung from the ceiling in one corner, long after her old beloved stuffies had been taken down and packed away. A spooky looking, frozen in time, puffer fish still hung from the ceiling in another corner, a gift from Grandpa that we were all too scared to crawl up on a step stool and remove. By the time my eyes hit on the little wooden surfboard that hung above the light switch on the wall that my little girl had to bring home from one of our Florida vacations, I knew my heart was on shaky ground, so I returned to the task at hand.

Sorting through all the silk flowers, foam pumpkins and fall decor was daunting, but by forcing myself to just get in there and get the job done, I was graced with a flood of warm emotions from that day that crawled out of the recesses of the now dark part of my heart. Too often the darkness that consumed the end of that evening overshadowed the sheer brilliance of Shiloh's dream come true. Looking at the silk sunflowers and tattered burgundy roses, my mind was able to catch a breathtaking glimpse of her walking down that aisle. With her flowing blonde hair gently blowing in the breeze, I could see her walking arm in arm with her dad, while he had a small sign that hung from his arm on twine that simply said, 'I loved her first'. I could see that famous three-year-old ear to ear grin she gets when she's a little bit nervous and yet expecting something super exciting to happen. Staring at the lanterns and battery-operated candles, I was reminded of her face during their first dance, when she stared up into his face and the smile that he shot back at her told the whole story. Shiloh had written her happy ending; she had found her forever.

So, I kept sorting these things, just keeping busy, trying not to think about the dark things that had consumed us for so long. Besides, Moby's sister Beth, was so excited to take a lot of these things off my hands. As a new photographer, props are expensive, and I was thrilled to be able to bring a little light into someone's life, if you want me to be quite honest. I think that when I am feeling at my absolute worst, sometimes a good deed gives me a little bump in my soul. (Although at this point, I could do more charity work than Mother Teresa and I don't think I could save the direction that my soul is headed in now... Come on, kind of funny, you have to laugh when things are this bad...) My actual mantra over the past few months had been, 'There's a special place in hell just for me', when things would take a turn from bad to even worse and I had very little faith left in anything, God, humanity, myself.

Moby, the unassuming sweet soul that he was, had no problem at all volunteering to come over and box this stuff up and grab it for his big sister. He had no qualms with stopping by the house, the place that felt like a second home to him for so long to help me. He had no issues spilling his guts to me, because that's just what families do, or what we did anyways. On this day, I would learn what I already knew, just how deep feelings ran between these two and just how much of himself he was willing to sacrifice in order to hold her head above the swirling, suffocating tide.

"Hey Mama Max!" I heard him holler as he came bounding through the side kitchen door of the little crown jewel of a home. Without seeing it, I knew his routine. He would kick off his shoes and head to the fridge for a sweet tea and something to eat. Then, on his way through the living room, he would stop to scratch the cat behind the ears and rub the dog's belly. Respect and kindness had always been main driving forces in this sweet soul's DNA. I never thought he had a dark side. Never thought he had a cruel bone in his skinny, yet tall body.

"I'm back here kiddo!" I shouted from where I was still sitting amongst the piles. I think by that time, I had fallen back into being sad and had stopped sorting momentarily as a few more memories in that room flooded my heart. I think when your world falls off its axle and literally goes hurling through the galaxy at gravity defying speeds making you puke, that it must be natural to try and think about softer times and gentler memories. As I allowed myself a few more stolen glances around the room, I remembered what used to be here.

At one point the walls were covered in fireflies and beach themed decor. Where a giant bright orange stuffed puffer fish once sat on a bedside table, an adult, lonely desk now stood empty. In the opposite corner is the cat box, adorned with a little sign that Shiloh had mounted to the top that read, 'I'm a cat, I don't have owners, I have staff'.

Maisey was always the animal lover, where Shiloh really wasn't. It's why we were all shocked when the girls went to volunteer at the local humane society in order to receive volunteer credit for school, and Shiloh fell in love with a little black cat prenamed Tapanaga. She was a junior in high school who got great grades, worked hard and stayed out of trouble, so when she made the call home that she just had to have this little cat, I was sold. Gage took some convincing, as he is more of a one pet at a time type of guy, but he came around. So, T-Pain, as we call her now, made her way home. Then Shiloh headed off to her new life and the cat bedded down with Maisey. Once Maisey walked out on her life, Panga was stuck with me. It seems like most lost souls find their way home to me one way or another.

But here's the thing about this little cat. Remember how I said that there are forever souls that we meet and just feel like we have known them forever or that they are just familiar and homey to us? That's Tapanga. Now I have never been a cat person myself, but since the girls have left the house, this chunky black furball and I have put in quality hours together. In fact, I can safely say that my two little furballs are who have kept me going this long. They follow me around the house and we have daily routines. They want nothing but kindness and love, and chunky Panga has a little magic about her too.

You see, I seem to have taken to crying a lot before I go to sleep at night. (That started even before Gage moved out.) Sometimes it's just silent tears that roll down my cheeks as my brain struggles to shut off and my heart wrestles to find peace. Sometimes it is a gut-wrenching cry that makes the snot run from your nose and your eyelids swell up. Sometimes it's more of a peaceful cry, like when you are mourning someone and thinking of them and just trying to make the pain go away. No matter what kind of tears fall, this little magical beast climbs up onto the bed, avoiding the sleeping eleven-year-old crabby six pounds of fur who sleeps at my feet, and gently climbs onto my chest. It doesn't matter if I am still or my chest is heaving trying to swallow air and flush out the pain, she stays true to her post, calmly purring into my heart until my soul is calm and settled again. At some point when I am sleeping, she hops down to her pillow on the floor and goes to sleep herself. Who would have ever known that this little copper-eyed rescue that Shiloh had dragged home a few years ago and was then left behind by not one, but both girls, would end up being my saving grace and one of the few reasons that I open my eyes and try again each day.

"Geeze Max! I didn't think there'd be this much junk left!" Moby laughed as he made his way into the packed yet empty room. As he flopped into the desk chair, eating what looked like half a taco that must have been in the fridge, and holding the cat hostage under an arm, he just looked at me and grinned. I was in awe of this boy who sat before me, such an old soul who was so full of life and hope. Oh, how I missed having hope.

"I know, I know." I exhaled. "Gage thought we really overdid it on the sunflowers, pumpkins and candles, but boy was it worth it! To stand there in that field, with the sun setting between the trees, surrounded by the people they love and seeing her marry her very best friend like that, Moby, it was so worth it!"

He shot me a glance as a wicked little grin crawled across his lips and laughter danced in his eyes. That squared off jaw tensed just a tad and only briefly. I know exactly what little nerve I had just danced on. I know where that boy's heart will always lead him.

"Isn't that the way it should be though, Max? On that day of all days, when a person is committing their hopes and dreams to someone else... who better to attach your forever to than your best friend?" Moby chirped rather matter-of-factly.

"I hear ya kiddo, I hear ya," I said, half grinning back as I started to pack some flowers into a box and putting bubble wrap around the lanterns.

I remember that the cat had had enough of Moby's rough love and launched out of his arms with a nice fat thud on the floor, taking off to undoubtedly see what the dog was up to and to be sure she hadn't missed anything from her window spot in the living room where she watches the days go by. Moby had stood up and begun moving around the room, working swiftly and not in silence as he helped me pack the odds and ends up. Moby being Moby, began talking as he worked, telling me bits and pieces of what went on that night, the events of their last lake lap, and what he didn't tell me, my heart was able to figure it out.

This lazy Saturday afternoon with my boy, with the kid from down the street who I know will be in our lives forever, filled me with hope. That afternoon, I honestly believed that maybe there was another way out, that maybe things weren't as bleak as I had believed them to be. Moby had definitely believed it. After everything we had witnessed the past year, he still believed in her.

What neither of us could have known that afternoon as we packed, as I listened to him tell stories of her and daydreamt of a world that was so close, yet so far away, was what was lurking right around the corner. We had no way of knowing what was about to happen or the steep price that I would have to pay.

But on that lazy fall afternoon, I also listened, truly listened to this boy as he explained how devoted he was to his best friend, my Maisey. He loved her so much and had such big plans for his future, and his future always included her. I knew then, just as I do now while I am writing this, that Moby will never give up on her. He would be patient and kind and lift her gently out of every gutter she may fall into. He would sacrifice things of himself to protect them both, always moving gently within her world, even when voices were echoing in her darkness, and she was battling hard-fought wars that she never saw coming.

I listened as he spoke about her greatness, her passions, her goofiness. I understood his heart that afternoon as he reminisced over old times, lost lake laps and an innocence lost. He was a new high school graduate, nervous to take on this new world, yet excited to think about what his future might hold. In this sliver of time, I understood him, I understood it all. This boy, this soul that is one of the good ones, one of the ones that I have known in multiple lives on multiple levels, will always be connected to her. After he had told me most of the details of that final lake lap that happened after the wedding, he told me something else that took all the air out of my lungs.

"You know Max, she's my best friend. If she can't love me as anything more than that, I'll be OK, I just don't ever want her to love me any less than that either. I will love her always, no matter what." And that dear boy, is where I handed you her heart for safe keeping… I told you, he's the epitome of class.

This is how I knew that whatever I had to do… However, this would all end, he had her. He would never let her fall. He would protect her always and love her forever. He would take care of her and be her safety net, even when I couldn't.

It's that final lake lap with her best friend that hugs my heart, even as I sit here in this cell that smells of urine, sitting on this cold stool writing on this cold table so that you will all know the story that led up to what I did. It's that final sliver of time that rolls around in the dark edges of my frantic mind, reminding me of her youth, her hope, her heart. Reminding me of who she was before Him and that there will be a her after Him. The gift of the story of the lake lap that Moby had given me is where my mind retreats at night when the gravity of pain and the desolation of fear threaten to drag me under the tide. When I start to panic and my breath gets harder and harder to squeeze back into my lungs, I close my eyes, breathe deeply and daydream of a simpler time and of the ease of youth.

And so, the story goes… (At least this is where my mind picks it back up every time I think about it…)

"Come on then girl, let's bounce," Moby whispered back, looking into her tired panic filled eyes. He flashed her that toothy smile that made him TikTok famous, the ornery grin that played well with his carefree persona. As he grabbed her hand in his playful, carefree way, he took one last look back around the place.

Shiloh and Brody had carried on, surrounded by friends and family, smiles across their faces while they danced. Gage and Mama Max were arguing in hushed tones over in the corner behind the table where the three layered marble wedding cake with buttercream frosting stood that Brody's grandma had made. The wedding party had resumed taking shots of Fireball over at the bar. Life was just moving on after the chaos, as it always does. It seems to move on for everyone but Maisey, who cannot seem to escape His grasp.

Moby looked back down into the eyes of his best friend once more. Her ocean eyes stared back up at him. She was still trembling, shocked from the horror of what had just happened as well as just from being down right pissed. He knew she was hurting, scared and was angry at the world right now, but that wasn't what Moby saw in her. All he saw that night was what he always saw when he looked at his girl: beauty and a heart of grace with a stubborn attitude. Resisting every urge that he had in that moment to just kiss her, instead, he just pulled her towards him as they headed towards the side door.

He half shouted over his shoulder, "They are all half lit, they ain't gonna miss us anyways." He grinned and grabbed a bottle of champagne off the table as they ran for his car.

The lake seems to be a healer of all things... broken hearts, poor decisions and shattered minds. It calls to the tired and rejoices with new life. Riding around her in the dark, windows down, warm air licking at your face while weighing life's problems almost seems to be a rite of passage. All local kids did it, hell, we all did. She calls out to you to settle your heart and calm your soul. There's just something about the loneliness of the night and the absolute solitude of the lake that wraps around your heart, forcing your lungs to take in one painful last breath although your body is so tired and you have let your will to survive fall by the wayside. She calls out to you like an old girlfriend and then seduces you into a lake lap or even a skinny dip, when that had never been your intention.

But that's what this lake does, what this town does. It has a way of knowing what you need, knowing where you are headed, and then lulls you into the darkness, leaving your mind swirling in the abyss. Thoughts and ideas, stories and prayers all intermingling into the night, confused in a web of realities and fears and half-truths. But by the time you finish those laps, somehow, the world is righted again, even if only for one night.

She was a crumpled mess of wine-colored taffeta ballgown in the passenger seat of his red 1973 Chevy Monte Carlo. Moby loved that car, almost as much as the crying mess of a person that was taking a lake lap with him in it. She was hunched over in the seat and he could hear her sobbing again.

"Hey Maze, scootch your butt in a little more, I'll shut the door," Moby gently said as he grabbed at the door handle, pretending not to notice the fingerprints she had already left all over the side of the door. He just shook his head and grinned as she popped her head up from her lap and began to berate him over insinuating that she had a fat ass.

"Girl, your ass ain't fat like F-A-T, it's fine as hell like P-H-A-T!" he told her, trying to get her to laugh. Instead, as he went to close the door, all he could see were those ocean blues looking at him, and it hurt him to see how empty they seemed to be now, how broken she had become. She said nothing, made no motion to even attempt to laugh. This just crushed him, weighing so heavy on his soul. This woman, this soul mate, this best friend… To see that she had become so lost, so lonely…

"Maze… I just didn't want to catch your dress in the door. Just scoot over OK," he pleaded softly. In return, she half grinned at him, pulled her dress into the car a little further, and he closed the door.

He told me that as he walked around to his side of the car, all he could think about was that this was the first time in all the time that he had known her that he wasn't able to make her laugh. All at once, he felt panicked. He had never imagined a world without her, yet in that brief interaction, he could feel her slipping away. He had to save her, had to help her find her road back home.

He carefully opened the trunk and cradled the stolen bottle of champagne between his basketball shoes and the stack of books he was supposed to be studying from this weekend, the books that he knew he would be blowing off for forty-eight hours because the only place he had wanted to be was at her side for the wedding, scholarships be damned. He then slid into the driver's seat and brought the engine to life. He didn't have to ask her where she wanted to go, he knew. As he backed out of the parking lot, he glanced towards the infamous Surf Ballroom. A flash of a smile danced across his lips as he remembered dancing with her there, just months ago at their senior prom. Sure, she was still with Him at that point, but He was too old to be allowed at the prom, so Moby got to go by default. He didn't care what the circumstances were, he was just happy to have been there, having fun and being young, with her.

Pulling away from the lot, Moby felt like they had aged twenty years in the last few months, how far away Prom had felt to him now. Within just a few months' time, she had gotten accepted into her college, moved over three hours away from home (but only an hour away from Moby's school), had a nervous breakdown brought on by Him, quit school (moved back home, over four hours away from Moby), had the crap beat out of her by Him, and finally broke free of Him. During this time, Moby just held on, by phone in the middle of the night, by text in the middle of class, by driving to the hospital over four hours away to be with her. He balanced it all: school, sports, her.

He was exhausted. They were exhausted. It wasn't supposed to be this hard. It never is.

As he flipped the headlights on and pulled out onto the road, heading down to South Shore, he went to reach for the radio. Out of the darkness, her small cold hand grabbed his before he reached the knob.

"I just want to hear your voice Mobe's... just talk to me," she nearly whispered, leaning his way now, resting her sweet head on his shoulder. It was in these moments that his heart raced. He could smell her shampoo as her head rested on his shoulder. That girl always smelled like mint and rosemary, her favorite lavender shampoo. That smell lingered in his mind and tugged at his heart even when he was almost five hours away at school.

This girl was why he drove those almost five hours home and back most weekends when he was able to sneak away from his school and sports schedule. This girl was the reason he didn't sleep well any more, laying there worrying at night about how she was doing and if she was holding on until the next time he could be with her again. This was the girl that made his life just feel better knowing she was in his corner, no matter what their relationship was classified as. He felt more confident with her, more secure with her in his life. It wasn't just about Moby taking care of Maisey, he needed her too. As he pulled the car out into the darkness and she snuggled in beside him, his mind raced back to just a few years ago before he met her.

Moby came from a home where his biological parents just didn't work out as a unit. They were great homes, that wasn't the point. Because his parents lived in towns across school boundaries, he had to decide where to live and which school to go to. He chose to go to school one town over while living with his mom. It was a much bigger school system in a much bigger town than our little lakeside community.

When Moby was younger, everything went well. As he grew though, and advanced in sports and found his love of theater, he also found that the people he had thought were his friends weren't so much. By high school, his friends were determined by which sport he happened to be playing or which play he was in. He no longer felt connected to anyone and began to fight his own lonely battle with depression. I didn't know him during this time, and I really have a difficult time picturing this charming goofy guy as not being able to connect with anyone and drifting into such a dark place. I suppose humanity can do that to anyone.

This world has become littered by people who unknowingly destroy other human beings' self-worth solely because they couldn't figure out how to make them fit into the square box they have decided we all must fit into. These same people want to use you when you are at your best, then discard you as you start to slip. This is where Moby was at in his life when he had made the life changing decision to move to town with his dad and bonus mom. She's a bonus mom because that woman couldn't love him any more if he was her own. In fact, when you see her around town, she's just as quick to tell you about what Moby is up to as she is about her biological son and daughter. Moby comes from a line of good people with equally good hearts, and it shows.

So, Moby had come to town right before his sophomore year of high school. Although he knew a couple of guys from playing football, I think it was a pretty big adjustment. Just the size of the school itself was so small. He went from a graduating class of about 450 to a graduating class of about ninety-eight. There was no place to hide, leaving him exposed to everyone. Our ever-jubilant comedian was actually pretty subdued when school started that fall of his sophomore year. He was looking for his place, trying to form his circle. Immediately he clicked with his football guys and track guys and baseball guys, but he couldn't just relax and be who he was with them. His older sister worked at the local daycare up the street and got him a job there working in the school age room. He loved that job and was great at it! He exuded comedy and the kids loved him for it. This is where he first met our Maisey girl.

Apparently, she met him at work before she ever saw him at school because believe it or not, they didn't have any classes together that fall of sophomore year, even though the school was that small. This is because Maisey was already dead set on her future and gave up a lot of her high school classes in order to start taking general education classes at the local community college. The funny part is, as Moby tells it, she completely snubbed him in the beginning. He tried for weeks just to get her phone number. She kept shooting him down. But they would work together and laugh and just be kids. Finally, she caved. His charismatic smile and gentle style had won her over. And that was all it took…

Moby flashed back to their beginning while he crept down the dark road. All the texts back and forth, all the petty disagreements and middle of the night phone calls and SnapChats and Instagram wars. He thought back to when she was so angry about his choice of who he was dating at the time (as she was dating someone else, mind you…) that she would go on and on at night lecturing him about what a great person he was and how he deserved so much more than the types of girls that he was settling for.

But that was the thing, compared to dating her, anyone else would be just settling in his mind. He couldn't tell her that though. It was too much of a risk at the time. So, their relationship just bumbled along as buddies, friends who flirted but never crossed the line. He would build her up when she would call him with a broken heart, and he would come up with creative ways to excuse himself from dates when she needed his shoulder to cry on. But he also knew this act of love went both ways...

Glancing quickly down at this precious soul with her mess of blonde curls on his shoulder, he knew that she had saved him too. When his mind was fighting demons in the darkness who were lulling him to give up, when he was feeling alone and that cold aching feeling of depression began to nip at his soul and cloud his mind, it was her that he turned to. It was her who he would text in the middle of the night in tears just wanting to talk, wanting to vent, wanting to find redemption through. It was this girl that would console him and take his pieces to build him back up into the generous, funny determined man that he was. This is what they did. This is who they were. They really didn't know what they were supposed to be classified as in each other's worlds, but they just knew that life was better when they were fighting the battles together, the world didn't seem as harsh, and there was an underlying friendship and love that was easy and comfortable.

Thinking back at where they had been, Moby laughed into the darkness.

"Hey, Maze... remember when you gave me a ride to school in the winter and then I did something to piss you off and you wouldn't let me in the car in the parking lot?"

He loved that memory because he could clearly see her through the window in her grandpa's truck, trying to keep a straight face, acting pissed, locking him out of the car. She then proceeded to act like she was slowly driving away as it began to snow. There were kids all over getting into their cars, and there he was, making a bigger scene than he needed to, trying to win her all over again. He could remember when she stopped the truck and he could see her through the passenger side window that he had previously scraped the ice off for her, how beautiful and full of life she had looked, and how his heart just paused for a minute looking at her. For a moment, she grinned at him and he swore there was more behind that grin.

But then she reached over, unlocked the old truck's door, giggling like a child and said, "Well, come on butt-head, get in!" Of course, as he actually went to grab the old truck door's handle, she laughed and crept ahead. Again and again, she would do this, and Moby, of course, would feed right into her game, making a scene for the entire school parking lot to have a good laugh at.

Maisey let a small laugh escape from her tired heart somewhere into the night as she thought about it. "I've had some of the best times of my life with you, Mobe's..." she said in an exhausted tone that seemed to trail off somewhere else. "And you have also been with me through some of the worst…" What was her poor beautiful head thinking about? Moby hated to hear the underlying sadness escape from whatever dark corners of her mind that she likes to keep it hidden in. Seeing her like this, moving around in a world as a fragment of the energetic force that she once had been, broke him. It infuriated him. It hurt him.

They rode along a little longer in the darkness like this, her head on his shoulder, just two kids out on a lake lap. Except they weren't kids any more. Their spirits had been broken and they have had to endure a year of hell, brought on by the narcissistic asshole that had crept into their lives when they had their guards down. He had only made His way in, Moby had decided, because at the time, Maisey had pushed Moby out of her life a little, if only for a couple of months because she said she was having 'trust' issues, as she called it. At the time, they both had come out of relationships that were going nowhere and found themselves spending most of their free time together. It was also around this time that Moby was focusing a lot of effort trying to become what the kids call, 'TikTok famous'.

So, the story goes that on this one night, while they were watching a movie in the basement at Maisey's house for the gazillionth time (I am guessing something like *Cheaper by the Dozen* or *Grownups*, or some goofy thing like that, which is Maisey's taste…), Moby tried to kiss her.

Apparently, he just kept looking at her and kept thinking he was so tired of wasting time dating all these dead-end girls when he knew that he loved his best friend. So, he went for it. Nothing forceful, nothing harsh, just leaned in for a quick kiss. This took poor Maisey by shock all right, and maybe the whole thing would have had a completely different outcome, but our dear Moby had been holding his phone to record the whole thing and she was furious! Moby said that there was a TikTok challenge going around where you kiss your best friend and film their reaction.

Now, maybe this had been true, but it ignited a fire in Maisey's heart that made her shut down for a while. Moby had done everything he could think of to apologize for a kiss that he was never sorry for, but she was still hurt.

When Maisey had told me about the incident, she had said that it wasn't that she didn't want to kiss him, it was that she was terrified that in the end she would lose him. She worried that if they tried to go past the safe carefree boundaries of friendship and failed, she would never get him back, and she couldn't imagine a world without him. Oh, and she was pissed that he had filmed it and intended to post it online. (I still don't buy into that, I think it was just his cover up for the kiss to begin with, a way to come out of the awkward situation unscathed.) After this incident, she pushed him away for a while. This is where Moby's blame lies. He thinks that if he had still been around during those few months, he may have been able to stop this disastrous relationship of hers from even getting off the ground. Maybe he could have been there to save her in the beginning, before she lost herself.

By the time Maisey had let him back into her world, the demon had already latched on to her. Moby had been patient though, answering the phone when she called, responding to every text and SnapChat. Things got really interesting when Maisey asked him to go to their senior prom. He was stunned! Mostly he was miffed because had he known she was willing to go with him, he would have pulled off a social media worthy way of proposing prom to her. Basically though, it was just a girl wanting to go to her senior prom and her boyfriend was too old to go. (Twenty-three to be exact, a fact that we were never thrilled with, as made clear when Gage would stand in the driveway yelling, "Go home pedophile," towards his car after things got bad. Made even worse by the fact that the asshole had told my eighteen-year-old nephew that the best way to find a piece of ass was to troll the local high school like He had done...)

I was honestly shocked that she stood her ground against the asshole and went to prom. He had to have been pissed. I mean, He knew about how close the two of them were and I am sure didn't like it one bit that they would be together all night. In fact, before she could take her prom pictures, she had to get all dressed up and head over to the asshole's house for a few pictures that He would then make her splash all over her social media with stupid quotes like, 'You were the best part of prom', and 'My special day wouldn't have meant anything without you being part of it', *puke*. But Moby took it all in stride. After all, he was the one dancing with her all night, going to dinner with her, taking prom pictures and making memories all night.

And although all during pictures, they were laughing as she would tease him by saying things like, "We are working out our trust issues." They were just happy to be together. She was smiling from ear to ear and his heart was full. There was no way to know that warm May evening that within just weeks, this pathetic excuse for a human would get so entrenched into her mind that she would run away from home. This is the guilt that Moby carries now, the guilt that he wasn't there, that he couldn't stop it.

As the car rolled to a stop out in the parking lot at McIntosh Park, all these thoughts were still swimming in Moby's mind. There was one streetlight holding its own against the darkness in the lot. Maisey sat up, then slumped back over in her seat, head in her hands, the rumpled taffeta creation of a dress forming a pillow around her. She spoke into the darkness, with her words reaching for Moby's heart.

"For so long I couldn't see it Mobe's. I couldn't see what he was doing to me. Not when I pushed my friends away, not when I ran out on my parents, not when I gave up school, not even when I ended up on the psych floor. I didn't see myself changing for him. I completely, whole heartedly bought into the thought process he fed me of, 'It's you and me against the world, babe', and it makes me sick to see it now. I became dependent on him! Oh my

God... how could I have been so stupid, so weak?" She began to cry, slow tears building up in her ocean eyes, finding their way down her hot cheeks and dripping onto the wine-colored taffeta.

In the darkness, with only one lonely streetlight illuminating their way, Moby turned towards her in the car and held her. She had changed so much. She seemed so frail, so weak and scared. The bastard had stolen the light from her ocean blues and robbed her of her confidence. Moby didn't know what happened next. He didn't know how to fix all that had been broken or fully understand all that she needed from him. In that moment, in that Monte Carlo, all he knew was that she needed him. He knew that her shaking body being held together in his arms felt good.

And he knew damn well that he was fighting every last urge he had in his body to kiss her. Instead, he just held on, his long yet muscly arms wrapped gently around this beautiful weak soul wrapped in crumpled wine-colored taffeta. She turned in her seat towards him, wrapping her arms around his shoulders, nuzzling her face into his neck, beneath his chiseled chin.

He could feel her warm breath against his neck as she spoke, "I'm just so tired Moby. So tired of being so sad and alone." This was too much for him, the feeling of her warm body pressed against his, her arms now embracing his shoulders, her breath on his neck, I mean *my God!* So, he did what he always did, got out of a precarious situation by cutting the tension...

"This is like the koala thing, huh?" Moby asked her and as soon as his words hit the air, she was giggling and pushing him away, which for the moment was a good thing for this young guy trying so hard to fight the urge to kiss her.

"Seriously Mobes? You bring that up now?" It had felt good to hear her giggle, no matter how small of a giggle it may have been. She half-heartedly slugged him in the arm.

"Ow! Hey, it's not my fault that your biggest dream in life is to fly to Australia to hold a koala bear and..."

He paused and she joined in unison, "Feel its heartbeat beat with my heartbeat." She was laughing now, a good, full bellied laugh, which made Moby feel good too.

"Yeah, I don't think that was the answer that they were looking for on that particular part of the written section of the SATs, Maze," Moby laughed as he started to get out of the car.

"It was just the practice exam, and I was nervous!" Maisey shouted after him as her eyes followed him around to the back of the car. Moby disappeared beneath the trunk lid, then reappeared at her passenger side door. Ever the gentleman, he opened her door and reached for her hand.

"My lady," he said, overly dramatic and full of the sarcasm that she adored. She took his hand and willed her rumpled body of taffeta out of the car.

"What do we have here?" she asked, eyeing the stolen bottle of booze peeking out of the oversized blanket emblazoned with a giant M, a gift she gave Moby when he went away to college just a short time ago.

"A little medicine for the soul girl! A little fizz to fix your flat. A little stroke to your ego." He giggled and kept going, forever a character, "A little Yin for your Yang, a little hop for your step, a little booze for the cruise, a little…"

She was still laughing at him while she playfully interrupted, "OK, OK I got it, I got it. Let's go." And with that, she kicked off those wretchedly high heels that had been digging into her ankles and blistering her littlest toes, leaving them by the side of the car. Not to be outdone, Moby kicked his off as well, threw one arm around her shoulders while clutching the stolen champagne with the other, and they set off barefoot in crumpled formal wear down the short trail to the beach.

Even in the glow of the one lonely working light in the lot, they could see the playground to the left of them as they slowly walked the trail up and then down the short hill that led to their favorite spot, the spot that they always ended up at when they made their lake laps.

The spot that grounded their souls and made them feel safe. This was their spot.

Chapter 8

Letting Her Run

They weren't like the average kids who came out to McIntosh beach to swim, lay in the sun and try to entice local boaters to come in close enough so they could hitch rides. The beach wasn't your average beach either. The little lake in our little town had multiple beaches to hang out on, but this one was run and maintained by the DNR and the set up was a little unique. To even get to where the beach area was, you had to follow a winding road, past a campground and then park in a boat lot where the boats launched. Then, it was a short hike up a dirt path, past an old playground that was usually overgrown with weeds and accompanied by a bathroom that was usually locked, and you were at the small sandy beach. But this main beach isn't the best part of McIntosh.

Maisey and Moby were more about the magic of the smaller part of the beach, only accessible when the water was a little lower. If you walked clear to the end of the sand beach, you could then walk in ankle-deep water over to what these two always called Koala Island. Really, it was just a little extension of the original beach that had been eroded, but it was surrounded by all kinds of rocks that were great to explore if you were just looking for a way to let your mind wander for a little while. The kids called it Koala Beach simply because that had been Maisey's biggest dream, so it was fitting that the beach that they hung out at all the time had a name likened to a beach of dreams.

Now over on the beach at nighttime, all you had for light was the glow of the moon, and your phone, of course. The parking lot was too far away for the lonely streetlight to lend much of a glow. This was perfect for kids making out, skinny dipping and getting drunk or high, except that the cars in the lot would eventually tip off a DNR officer, who may or may not meander up the beach just depending on if the mood struck him or not. (I say him because we only have two DNR officers around here, both of which are men, so don't judge. I told you, small town vibes here.)

It was here, towards this magical little piece of land that they were headed. Once they hit the sand, Maisey just froze, standing staring out into the water. "Maze, come on," Moby hollered at her as he ventured onwards towards Koala Beach. But Maisey just stood there, entranced by the reflection of the moon over the still water. There was a faint breeze in the air that rolled over her, reminding her of the aching loneliness that she had been drowning in for so long. She drew in a breath deeper than what her lungs were expecting her to and began to cough. She then inhaled a slower, more shallow breath of the lake air. The elixir of all ailments, somehow that breeze coming off the lake always found a way into your soul, breathing life back into the hollow passageways of the heart again. She hadn't felt alive, truly alive in what felt like forever…

She stood there, staring at the still water, fighting back tears again until Moby interrupted her once more. "Maze, get moving or I am going to drink it myself!" he shouted from across the beach. She turned to see the faint outline of his silhouette in the distance and let out one small breathy laugh as she saw his lanky shadow dancing some kind of goofy dance. There he was. Her Moby. Her best friend that she had treated so badly this past year, but he was still here fighting for her, never ready to give her up. With the damp sand squishing beneath her toes, she ran to him. In truth, she will always run to him.

I have to believe that as she was running across that damp sandy beach, with only the moonlight illuminating her path towards her dearest friend, that she must have felt lighter, like she had made her way out of the darkness, out from under the heaviness that was *Him* for so long. She had to have felt like her life was moving towards something better, something worth hanging around a little longer for. Although this account of what happens next is based on what a lovestruck boy had confided in me, my mama's heart is quick to fill in the missing tidbits of information here and there, although I do hold all the events in this memo to be completely accurate and here to serve as a background to our story, to my admission as to what I have done and why…

By the time Maisey had made her way over to Moby, he had already begun tapping the top of the bottle against a sheared off rock, trying to release the cork. Maisey let the mayhem ensue for a few more minutes and then spoke up.

"Mobes, dear, don't break the damn bottle! Although it's a complete shitshow of hilarity to watch you attempt this, I think I can handle it. Back off son…" She grinned and swiped the bottle from his hands. Ever the comedian, Moby made grand gestures of disgust and parked his butt in the sand, watching her beneath the moon. He flashed his toothy smile at her as she grabbed a couple of bobby pins out of the top of her head, which allowed her unruly, and at this point, sweaty, curls to fall around her face, landing gracefully on her bare shoulders. She too plopped down into the sand, a heap of wrinkled wine-colored taffeta falling into her lap. She laid the bottle down, fashioning some type of a crude corkscrew concoction from the bobby pins, and then began stabbing them into the cork. Although she pulled with all she had, the damn thing wouldn't budge. Moby moved towards her in the night, and as he grabbed for the bottle, his face was eye level to hers.

"All right smarty pants, let me try," he said, and before he even could pull the bottle away, she leaned in and kissed him. No movement, no hands, no breathing. She just leaned into her safety net, and without thinking about it, softly pressed her lonely soft lips against his. To hear him tell the story, there were fireworks and his heart was exploding and it lasted forever. He would tell you that her hair smelled like the rosemary and mint shampoo that he had come to love and her lips tasted like raspberry lip gloss. He would say he could hear her heart beating in perfect sync with his and that all he could think about was what their kids were going to look like someday. In this moment, for a few seconds, Moby had won the battle. It was as if all the questions and uncertainty in his life had just fallen away, and his direction and purpose had never been more aligned.

Later, after talking with Maze myself, she told me what really had happened. She had said that when he leaned in towards her, she had never felt so safe, so loved and so free. It was an honest reaction of the soul, to just reach out for the thing that makes you happy, the thing that will make you feel good in that moment, after feeling like she was alone and dying inside for so long. So she leaned in and kissed him. According to her, he didn't move. He didn't breathe. And after she pulled her face away, he actually laughed. Not a cynical or cruel laugh, but more of a giggle of surprise.

And without missing a beat, without wanting to make the situation awkward for her, he blurted out, "Well, I guess our trust issues have worked themselves out now, haven't they?" And then his hands touched hers as he took the bottle away and pulled out the cork.

They talked a lot that night, and I think Maisey was really at a crossroads in her life, maybe even at some point of an awakening and didn't want the night to end, didn't want to let him go. She knew that within the next few days her best friend would be packing his bags to make the long trek back to college, leaving her here, unsure of where she was heading in her future. His future was solid, he had a plan. He had sports and scholarships and college. He had everything that she had given up only weeks ago to follow the Joker down a rabbit hole that ended in His mother's basement with no greater plans.

As she sat in the sand, looking out over the still water, clutching the champagne bottle in her hand by its neck, huddled beneath the blanket with the emblazoned M on the front, resting her head once again on Moby's shoulder she whispered into the darkness, "What the fuck have I done? How did I fall so far?" Her heart must have been so heavy as she silently let tears roll down her face.

Moby grabbed the bottle, took another drink, and sat for just a moment, trying to gauge what he should say to her. Everything around her had become such a precarious dance these days. He tried to make her happy, tried not to overstep. He would listen, but she never actually wanted his advice. But the hardest part for him had been watching this girl fall so completely in love (or so she thought, dependent upon may be a better phrase than love) with a person whose intentions were so cruel, so vile. To watch her sparkle slowly fade to a low dim and lose all confidence in herself, lose her footing in this world. So, he chose his words painstakingly carefully, made even harder under the influence of cheap champagne.

As she reached to take the bottle back, he found the courage to finally let his voice escape his heart.

"Maze, you have always had the best heart, and the best of intentions. I mean hell, look at us! I know when we first met you only started talking to me because I was the new guy and you didn't want me to feel alone in an already unkind world. That's your heart, kid. It's why your path is and always will be being a caregiver, nurse, hell I don't know, maybe a doctor someday! It's what you do. It's all your heart knows how to do. So when you met Him, all you saw was a quiet broken soul. And you being you, wanted to help at first, but then helping turned into fixing Him," he began before she interrupted him.

"Mobes stop! I don't want to talk about Him. I can't go there with you right now. It's like I have been trying to live in two different worlds for so long, trying to keep Him happy, while trying to live a separate life and keeping everyone else happy at the same time. I'm so damn tired, I just can't..." she interjected before Moby cut her off again.

"Maze, I just need you to understand that it was never you. Do you hear what I am telling you? He was a master manipulator, He set you up to fail, winding you up like a toy and knocking you over when He felt like it." Moby started. He stopped himself though as he noticed she had fallen silent and was just staring at him beneath the moonlight with those ocean blues wide open and tears falling from her cheeks. His heart ached for her. This was not something they were going to solve tonight. She had already dealt with the pain of seeing Him tonight at the reception, in all His raging glory. This was not why Moby had brought her here. This was not what his buddy needed right now. He wiped the tears from her cheeks and grabbed the bottle back once more.

"Two truths and a lie!" he shouted out at no one. He wiggled out of his suit jacket and laid it behind her. "Come on, let's play." He grinned a half-hearted grin, hoping it would lift her mood. She took a deep breath in and let out a huge sigh, almost as if she was trying to release all the negative energy from her body.

"OK, Mobe's, I'm in," she said as she laid back in the sand and stared up at the night sky. The only noise that they could hear was the water lapping at the boats tied on the dock as she lay there on his jacket in the sand, a mound of crumpled wine-colored taffeta.

Moby laid back too, stared up at the sky and took her hand. "Me first," he began.

"Let's see... Umm..." he began while staring up towards the darkened sky that was illuminated with just a sprinkling of shy stars, twinkling so far off. "I got lost in a mall when I was seven and ended up on the back of a security cart shouting through a megaphone for my mom, a company reached out to me a few weeks ago to offer me a sponsorship on my social media account and I kissed a girl during rush week my first week at Maryville," he spoke while trying to keep a straight face.

Maisey giggled a low maniacal and disapproving tone while debating the proposed options as she tried to figure out which was the lie. She wanted more than anything for him to be successful as a social media influencer, as he always thought that would be the thing that would break him into the acting side of life. She had hoped against every feeling in her heart that he didn't kiss the girl at school, and she could actually see him as a goofy young kid riding on the back of a security cart. "The lie is the girl!" she blurted out into the darkness. Her answer hung in the air as it was met by an awkward silence.

"Actually, Maze, I never got lost in a security mall when I was seven," Moby said to the stars, a grin crawling across his lips. She had immediately jumped to the next point in wild excitement.

"Shut up! When did they contact you about an influencer sponsorship?" she shouted out turning her face towards his in the darkness.

"A couple of weeks ago. They said they had been watching my content trend and noticing the millions of views I have been getting and wanted to bring me under their wings. Kind of cool! I will get some products shipped to me to promote and who knows where it might lead? It's pretty badass!"

Her excitement fell as fast as it had risen when she made two immediate discoveries that almost collided into her exhausted head.

"Wait Mobes, a few weeks ago? You had this incredible offer a few weeks ago and didn't say anything? Why? Why wouldn't you share that with me?" As she questioned him, he had told me later that you could hear her heart just free falling once again, as though she had been cast aside and left out by him.

"Maze, I said it was a couple of weeks ago…" Moby started again, calmly and choosing his words very carefully, as to not detonate the mine that now laid between them.

"Yeah, I know, you said that already! That doesn't explain why you would leave me out of something so huge! It doesn't explain why you wouldn't want to shout from the top of every mountain to your very best friend that your dreams are starting to happen!" She was rambling, not angry, but the agitation in her voice was walking a line between bitchy and condescending right now so Moby thought he had better jump in here to calm her down.

Very quietly, and with the grace and patience of a saint he asked her one question, "Maze, Hon, where were you a couple of weeks ago?"

The realization of the words that were now slowly tumbling out of Moby's mouth took a couple of seconds to connect with her champagne clouded brain. It was as if suddenly all the numbers on the combination of the safe to her brain spun and clicked all at once, unleashing memories at a violent speed. This was something they hadn't spoken of yet.

"Oh," a meek answer exhaled from her heart into the dark sky and floated out over the still water. "Sorry, Mobes. Of course, you couldn't have told me about it then."

Five East. That's what they call the inpatient mental floor in our local hospital, just one town over. It's such common knowledge around here that it almost became verbiage or slang in the way the locals spoke.

If you had a rough day you might say, "They are going to haul me over to Five East." Or if the neighbor is acting batshit crazy, you might tell your best friend that she, "Needed to take a vacation to the lovely Five East." The part that weighs on my heart is that until you have watched someone fall to their lowest point and you find yourself pacing those desolate mint-green halls waiting for answers, Five East is just a thing of legend and nightmares.

Unfortunately for my family, Five East was no stranger to us, more like a mistress that you wanted when she could give you what you needed, but joked about her and ignored her when she wasn't a part of your world. My dear Aunt was a manic-depressive schizophrenic. When I was about nine years old, my sister about four, and my aunt would have been in her early thirties, she was watching a movie with us and very calmly turned towards my sister and I and said we had to hide because the robot in the movie was coming for us. She also believed our parents were trying to hurt us. She quickly moved us under the stairs, in her mind she was protecting us. This was her first onset of the disease.

She would go on for another thirty years, battling this monster that would show up out of nowhere and rob her of her sanity, never returning quite the same after each hospital stay. The look of fear in her eyes, the confusion that fell on her face when the police showed up to try and take her to the hospital was something that has stayed with me all these years, pinned to my heart. So, unfortunately, when I saw my sweet daughter falling further and further into the abyss, the lights dimming in her eyes, and her body defeated with mental and physical exhaustion, I knew it was time.

There had been a year's worth of events that had led up to my daughter mentally coming unraveled, and they all led back to the asshole. The joker. The nightmare that He was. I had already witnessed her first breakdown, or mental episode, right in my front yard months earlier. Actually, most of my neighbors and family were right in the middle of the storm. She had wanted to leave Him then, wanted to get back to her old life. He showed up at our home to pick her up, angry that she didn't know what she wanted any more.

You have to understand the scene... It's lightly snowing. My daughter has half-haphazardly thrown random belongings into the asshole's car. He is now sitting in the front seat grinning the creepiest smile that will haunt your nightmares from this point forward. She is now sitting in the backseat of His car while He took breaks from grinning at all of us that had congregated in the front yard long enough to yell at her. We were helpless watching from the outside of the frosty windows of the car. We could see her bawling, hair was a mess, face was beat red... But she wasn't answering Him.

It was my dad, her grandpa, who had walked over to the car and convinced her to get out so we could talk. He then walked around to the asshole's driver's side door, where He had rolled his window down just a crack. My dad had asked this low life to please leave, it's a family matter and we had some things to discuss.

He just looked up at my dad with soulless eyes and said, "Nope! I think I am fine right here." Proceeding to lock the doors so she couldn't get her things back out of the car, and went right back to that drug-induced or manic grin.

It was at this point, my newly eighteen-year-old daughter stood in the cold, in the snow, face in her hands while everyone she loved begged her to come inside. We begged her to end all of this. We begged her to find the will to be strong and move on. Through hysterical tears she dropped to her knees and said she didn't know what she wanted any more, that she just wanted it all to end.

I can tell you as a mom, there are no worse words to hear come from your child's lips than that they feel they have been defeated in life. When it happens, it feels as though the world has opened beneath your feet and you are walking a precarious ledge over a fiery inferno. You spend their whole childhood preaching about good choices, praising them for all the good they put into the world, telling them how wonderful their souls are. You hug them and love them and try to make life easier for them. You are a vigilant parent; you lay awake at night in their teen years imagining all the worst-case scenarios that then lead to future late-night talks with them to ease your troubled heart.

When suicide reaches its gnarly claws into your kids' classmates, you cling to your kids a little tighter and foolishly wonder why those parents didn't see it coming? Is there more you should be doing? Are there things we hadn't talked about? I know there are the kids who have mental histories that make them more susceptible to letting the darkness come after their souls, and there are kids who just were given the seriously shitty end of the stick in life and are exhausted from trying to survive. There are the kids who have been abused, ignored, picked on and humiliated.

Kids whose parents place bars so high that failure is all they feel capable of achieving. These are the dangers that are laid out in black and white. These are the dangers that we knew to watch for.

What no one could have prepared me for was that in the course of just a little over a year, my beautiful daughter with such life in her eyes and a smile that can reach into hearts to heal would find herself letting go little by little, losing her fight a little more each day. This once energetic teenager now sat in the darkness of His basement almost every night while He gamed and smoked pot and popped God knows what pills. His anxiety had become her anxiety and suddenly she found depression to be her ally. She stopped wearing makeup, stopped doing her hair, and dressed down to go to school. We found out later this was because He would always accuse her of flirting with people at school like His ex-girlfriend used to. He was all about control. Over the months, He had cut her off from her friends and family, and even took her phone when they were together. He would access her social media and delete her friends and limit who had access to her phone. Everything was her fault, no matter how small, and He blamed her when his anxiety and depression flew off the rails and there was no one else to blame. Many an argument was silenced by His plea of, "But I will kill myself…" She was trapped.

Adding to this trap that He had so finely crafted, was her need to defend Him, to save Him. He fed her this bullshit hero story of the two of them facing the world together, that He would save them both. Through enough of His games and manipulation, my poor kid didn't have a fighting chance. At certain points, He had convinced her to run away and stay at His house for weeks at a time during her senior year of high school, holed up in his dismal basement doing who knows what. (There are some things that a mother's heart doesn't want to know, because the things that I do know are already enough to make me insane myself… No mom needs to know that He has drugged her, that He has hit her, choked her, shoved her around, screamed at her, that He has abused His own dog to get back at her, blew through her $5,000 in savings, that He has threatened suicide, accused her father and myself of stalking Him and making death threats, that He has helped to destroy every relationship she has with her friends and family, He has rumored to have made a sex tape with her and holds that over her head, and even threatened to kill us all.)

So, on that particular day, when I am watching my daughter fall apart on the cold snow-covered ground and hearing Him laugh in the car as He watched the drama unfold that He had created, all I saw in her face was fear and defeat. Gone was her confidence. Gone was her pride and love for life. Her glow had dimmed to a smoldering coal, and she had finally had enough. Although she was eighteen now, my heart saw a scared little three-year-old trembling in the snow with this look on her face like, 'This hurts mom, help me. It's too hard, make it all stop'.

That's the thing. They can act like they hate you, don't need you, like you are the worst human on the planet. But if you are lucky, when they are scared and hurt, you might be one of the lucky ones that gets another shot with them because they just might scrape the last little bit of fight and courage that they have left to show up broken and exhausted from the battle asking you for help.

It took two squad cars and four officers to convince Him to drive away that day. That was only after they retrieved what was hers from the car because she was too terrified to reach back in and get her things.

As the police officers were talking to her, He just kept yelling at her from the car, "Just come with me, let's just go!" He wasn't just giving up without a fight, and even as I watched His car roll down the street, I knew then that this wouldn't be the last of Him.

Narcissistic manipulators don't just give up their victims. (We later found out that it took His previous victim almost four years to find her way out of the darkness with Him, and she only found her way out when my daughter came along… What a gut punch that is to think that the only way out for her may be to hope that some poor innocent minor might catch His soulless eye and He would become interested in someone else.)

After He had gone, we had determined that she wasn't in a stable frame of mind. The police officers had tried to convince her to stay with my grandmother or another friend, but I believe she knew that He would still be able to get to her like that. I believe that her body and mind were so exhausted from being manipulated and trying to protect both sides, that she was confused and honestly didn't know what she wanted.

I knew just by looking at the terrified and broken expression on her face that she needed to go to Five East, but here's a fun fact: unless a person is an immediate threat to themselves, you can't force them to go. I mean they have to be a viable threat to be forced to go. Like most things in the medical and governmental systems, it's all about red tape, insurance claims and lawsuits. This little fact pisses me off almost as much as the bullshit laws that prevent us as her parents from being able to protect her against Him in any way because she is the magic age of eighteen now, which apparently means she magically has all the answers in life and is able to protect herself. Such bullshit. She could show up at my house beaten and bruised, but if she wouldn't press charges, there was nothing that we could do. And He knew it.

Freezing in the front yard that day, she would only agree to go stay at my grandmother's house. She was so close to my grandmother, a woman who had eighty-seven years of life experience. Although my grandmother was no fan of the situation, Maisey knew that she could rest her heart there and that Great Grams would listen without standing in judgment. She told me how she was so tired from it all, that she didn't know what she wanted any more. Her body was run down, her head hurt all the time, and all she wanted was to sleep. It was to a point that sleeping was all she wanted to do, which really scared me because I knew this was a sign of depression, and this had never been who she was.

My heart broke as she cried on the way over to my grandmother's home, telling me she can't keep arguing with us, with Him, with her family and friends, she felt like she was trying to keep everyone happy, yet no one ever was. There was just no good way to live two lives, and she had burnt out trying. In that few minute car ride, I knew that I had failed her. By fighting to protect her, fighting to try and get her away from Him, I had only added to the insanity. She had come home to me broken and tired, ready to either give up on her life or fight to get it back, but it had to go one of the two ways because her body couldn't keep up any more.

After about a month of staying with my grandmother, she was ready to try coming home again. Although she still was unsure about living at home again and she left half of her belongings at my grandmother's home, she came back for a little while. She started to care a little more about herself again. She wore makeup every now and then and dressed up to go back to school. (Although I found out later that even this would piss Him off and he would accuse her of only doing this to try and get attention from guys at school, supposedly like His ex had done…) She even went out with her friends a couple of times. It was around this time that she took the job working as a CNA at the local care center, which she loved so much. She once again found purpose to her life, some small type of balance. The only thing that we had to change to get to this point was that we never discussed *Him*. We just were at a standstill and no longer wanted to fight any more.

So, life just continued for a few quiet weeks, no fighting, no anxiety, just existing and wedding planning. It was during this time that our smart girl got some news that would shake up her world. Maisey had always known that she wanted to be a nurse. She had applied at several different schools, including the local community college that was just a half hour from home.

One day she was just hanging out in the living room and I had brought the mail in after getting home from another day of working to save other families. I threw her a couple of pieces of mail that were addressed to her, without thinking much of it because as a new to the world eighteen-year-old, there were always plentiful credit card offers, school mailings and convincing letters asking you to consider joining the service.

As she was flipping through the mail, she stopped on a thin white envelope from St. John's. This was a school that was notorious for training the best hospital nurses around. She had applied on a wing and a prayer, figuring at least she gave it a shot.

"Oh no," she said in a disappointed voice. "It's such a small envelope. That can't be good," Maisey said in a shaky voice as she sat staring at the slim paper that was meticulously folded and placed inside of the crisp envelope.

"Come on kid, you have to open it!" I said in excitement while crossing my fingers behind my back and silently praying to every entity that would listen in my head. After all, this was one of my last hopes of her getting on with her life and away from this one that had been suffocating her for the past six months at that point.

I sat in the recliner with my stomach in absolute knots, ready to throw up as she opened the envelope that may or may not hold her golden ticket. I cannot even put into words the feeling that gripped my heart as my eyes watched this little beaten down soul open that envelope and find her hope inside.

With a smile crawling across her lips like an old friend that had been missing for far too long and hot tears slowly spilling down her pale cheeks, she began to read, "Dear Ms. Anderson, we are honored to announce your acceptance into the fall 2021 semester of the nursing program at St. John's College of Hospital Nursing…" We cried. We hugged. I told her how proud we were of her and how she was going to make such an amazing nurse. We even got the video camera out (yes, I still like to record on a disc) and acted like she hadn't opened it to reenact it all over again. She called Gage at work and cried as he told her how proud he was of her. The future was so close and so good.

The excitement lasted for about an hour. That's when *He* called. I could hear the conversation and see her face fall. Where once stood an excited eighteen-year-old who was proud and held her head high as she was already planning for the fall, a fragile and scared soul then emerged after being questioned by Him on the phone. I remember the very first thing that He asked her when she told Him she was accepted. He asked her if she was going to accept the acceptance, was she planning on going.

When she said she was planning on it and trying to tell Him how awesome of an opportunity it was, all He said to her was, "Well, we'll see where we are at in our relationship by then." There were no congratulations from Him, no telling her how great she was. It was immediately turned into a poor Him thing and how would He make it without her. (Side note here, even though she and Moby weren't talking as much at this point, the first thing that Moby told her when he found out she was accepted was, "Of course they wanted you in their program! Who wouldn't.")

From that point on, the relationship between Maisey and the Joker just intensified on a destructive path. It was during these few months that He convinced her to run away from home and live with Him in His mother's basement, slowly eating their way through the savings account that she had built for herself since she was fourteen. It was during this time that His mental illness intensified, and He clung to the only thing that made Him feel alive, even though it was quite literally killing her.

Chapter 9

Five East

As I am writing this, the irony doesn't escape me that I have come to a point in our story where I am talking about the slipping sanity of my daughter, yet I am the one sitting in this cell, waiting for the charges to come, waiting for my next dose of God knows what to keep my brain lucid enough to tell the tale and recall the events of the last few days. There is a perplexing calm that has come about me now, as I sit here, getting the story right, getting it down on paper. For so long over that past year, I have spent quite literally all my free time worrying about her future while aching for the past. What I wouldn't give to be at the lake now with the girls and Gage, for one more boat ride, one more summer of innocence. I came close though, to getting it all back.

Or at least thinking that I was close. Actually, in my mind we had saved her many times. We always had an illusion that things were getting better, then the next week they would be worse again.

We did get her to go off to school, which was no easy feat, believe me. Gage and I had figured that if we could just get her there, get her away, she could escape the hold that He had on her. What we didn't account for was just how destructive He was capable of being and to what lengths His obsession with her would go.

Hanging on to her has always been easy, it was when *I had* to let her fly on her own, struggle a little with her own choices that annihilated my soul and made me find a strength in my fragile world that I didn't know I had. Before Gage had brought her home from school, things would run lukewarm and cold between her and I. At one point, I had traveled to see her, loaded down with all kinds of things that she needed since her initial move to school had been so rushed. My sister had made the trip with me, because she hadn't seen Maisey in a while and had bought her some things for starting school, just like she had with Shiloh when she went off to college.

We knew that as soon as we showed up, something wasn't right with her. She was distant, almost pissed that we were even there. Yet, she maintained a fragile smile, even though her mind was hundreds of miles away. Our plan had been to work on her apartment since she had to work at the care center that she had just taken a position at part-time while going to school. While she was at work, we busted ass to sew and hang curtains so she felt warmer and safer in her apartment until she could get a new roommate (the first one had already flunked out of school just a few short weeks in and had dropped out). We also put plastic on the windows to help keep the heat in and her heating bill down. My sister and I were laughing as we worked, while running back and forth to the laundry room on the floor below us to get her caught up with the six loads of laundry that she either couldn't afford to do or was too terrified to run down alone and do it. We bought her groceries to get her though the next couple of weeks and I hemmed the cute shower curtain that Maisey had hung but was puddled on the floor because it was too long.

Although we hadn't got to visit her a lot while we were there for that visit, I knew that someone was running through her thoughts, putting pressure onto her already very fragile world. It had become apparent that although she was so attention starved and wanted our company so badly, she also couldn't wait for us to leave because she needed to deal with other issues that were going on in her world.

So, my sister and I did all that we could do for this child of mine, this scared little human that had summoned all her bravery to move so far away from home at eighteen to chase dreams that were written on her soul. We cooked for her, cleaned for her and took her out to dinner. We bought her new scrubs and helped hang up decor in her apartment that she had picked out. I should have seen the trouble brewing when she became embarrassingly hostile in the uniform shop. We had picked out a new nursing lab coat and a few more scrub sets, along with a few more pairs of compression socks. I had made my way to the checkout line as she was standing by, flipping through messages on her phone, the phone that I paid for as well. I went to write a check and the cashier apologized and let me know they don't accept checks. I said no problem, I would just use my debit card and then told Maisey that I would then transfer the money from her school expense account back to myself to cover the costs.

This child, this young woman who was barely out of my house, the kid that gave up on herself to run away with Him the latter part of her senior year, leaving me to be sure all of the scholarship applications got submitted on time and essays were written, spun her angry face towards mine in front of the nice sales lady and spit out, "Well, if you would just give me access to that account, you wouldn't have to move money around! That's *my* money you know. I don't understand why you think you have any right to control it!"

The stunned saleswoman proceeded to calmly and quietly put our purchases in the bags as I melted into the floor of embarrassment right then and there. "Seriously? You are going to do this here, now?" I hissed beneath the smile that I had so fakely yet delicately forced upon my face. "Maze, you know the reason I haven't given you control over that money. That's over sixteen thousand dollars, and I told you, if you played your cards right, along with the renewable scholarships, you will be out of school in three years with your RN, bachelors in nursing and no school loans. I can't risk you blowing it all," I said as I smiled and handed the cashier my card.

Maisey lashed out in anger once more, quietly, yet with the razor-sharp tongue that she has developed under the misguided influence of Him, "God damn it Mom! I wouldn't be stupid enough to spend that money. It's *my* money anyways!" she said as she headed for the door.

My sister followed her out, and the last that I could hear within an earshot was my dear sister asking my kid why she was being such a bitch today. I swallowed that familiar lump that had once again taken residence in the back of my throat and looked back at the sweet cashier with all knowing eyes, whispering a meek, "Thanks," as I took the bag and began to walk away.

"It's hard at first when they go," she said in a motherly all-knowing tone. "But she will find her wings."

I grabbed my bag and with a heart full of defeat, turned towards the door. "Thanks," I called over my shoulder. "I hope you're right."

Back in the car, we rode in a deafening silence over to the restaurant that we had previously picked out for a late lunch before she had to head off to work again, knowing that there was trouble brewing right beneath the surface. I refused to let the tears fall that had built up in my eyes on the drive back. Arguing with her had become exhausting at that point. There was nothing that would come out of my mouth that would ease her mind right now, and nothing that came out of her mouth that I had any faith in any more.

At lunch, she loosened up again a little bit and began to tell my sister and I about all the classmates that she had started to become quite close with at school. She talked about the cafeteria at the hospital, the artistic young guy who worked there and how she wanted to ask him what he was majoring in, but hadn't gotten up the nerve.

There was the older lady that also worked in the cafeteria who knew her order every time that she walked in. She told us about doctors and surgeons that she had met, and which floor of the teaching hospital had the nice nurses versus the bitchy ones. She even laughed as she was telling us about her little crew of three girls that she had met within the nursing program, and how they study together and make up silly little songs to remember things for tests. She said that these girls were quickly replacing the friends that she had left back home, and that she had hoped she could convince one to move in with her.

Everything about that lunch that day was civil, yet unemotional. It was as if we were having lunch with a neighbor, not my daughter. Not the child that I had raised and loved for 18 eighteen years. This was different. This was one of the first times that I had truly felt threatened that we as a family may lose her, that He had wormed His way into her mind and soul to the point that she didn't feel anything any more, that we were just a formality now, a business transaction.

I felt His effects even more when we loaded the car that afternoon so that we could get out of there before she left for work. All the pleasantries were there, she smiled as she threw her arms around us, but her arms were empty. Her soul felt cold. She didn't really hold us, didn't really connect with us. And when she pulled away, she was unable to hide the tears that had built up in her eyes.

There is a really soul darkening effect that a mother feels when you go to hug your child and feel as though a barricade has been erected. I couldn't reach her now. I couldn't connect with her heart any more. Her eyes had darkened and although she thanked us for what we had done, it was as if she held on to the feeling that we owed her more. Suddenly, there was never enough that I could give her, buy her or do for her to fill the dark hole that had begun to erode in her heart. But for just a second, as I was looking into the eyes of my second born wild child, my kiddo who was born calling her own destiny, I saw a small flicker in her ocean blues.

A small glimmer of hope, of pleading. With her half-hearted smile and face fighting to stay strong, she couldn't hide from her mom what I already knew. She may have been caught up into something that she didn't know how to get out of, she may have been manipulated into believing everything that He told her, she may have felt she had no choice but to turn on her own family, but she was still in there. That old caring soul, that belly laugh, that smile that radiates across the darkest night sky, she was still in there. I just had to figure out how to get her back.

Even though I saw that little glimmer of life in her eyes, begging desperately for me to hold space for her in my heart, I still wasn't prepared for the next call that she would make home, the call that made me take a very hard road for her and for myself. I had been back at home for a couple of days from our visit. Gage was out of town (he took a much-needed break from his life, and from me and helped to drive his parents to Florida, the first time we had ever vacationed separately in twenty-five years of marriage and twenty-eight years together...) and I was holding down the fort so to speak.

Although I still got scared with every bump in the night and locked myself in my bedroom at night, I had been getting used to being alone, used to being brave, used to trying to stay sane alone despite my circumstances. I remember that night well, the night that was the beginning of me shutting down and reevaluating my plans. I had just gotten out of the shower and had sat down to watch something brainless and scary on the computer with my animals when my phone rang. I thought nothing of it when I saw Maisey's name pop up because it was a Tuesday night and I knew that she didn't work. I just figured she either needed something or was lonely, as she frequently was.

The conversation started out nicely, she was telling me all about her study group girls and the patients that she had met and cared for at the care center. After about twenty minutes of niceties, the conversation took a sharp and painful turn.

"Well, at least I won't be so lonely in a few weeks." I could hear the grin on her face as she said the words. She knew exactly what that red-hot dagger would do when she chose to poke me with it.

"What are you talking about, Maze?" I calmly asked while swallowing that lump of fear that had once again begun to set up residence in my throat and begin suffocating me. I could hear my heartbeat in my ears. This was the way it usually went down; she would poke the beast and my body would start to get its fight response brewing. Damn it. I hated that feeling.

I hated it worse because it was my own flesh and blood, my little Magoo who would turn on me and bring it on. All too often, I walked a fine line between heart attack and stroke, my blood pressure was raging and my heart was skipping beats before she even responded. I knew this dance. I knew what came next, and there would be no shielding myself from the blows. When you get used to the roller coaster that we had been riding, you learn to recognize when the highs are building up and when the tracks are about to be ripped out from beneath you. She was almost nineteen, she had destroyed a lot of tracks.

"I will pick up my dog in a couple of weeks," she stated, very calmly and matter-of-factly. And there it was. Our latest point of contention on a seemingly mile long list. The damn dog. Asshole had bought a dog a few months back, and had intended to buy her one as well. I knew what He was up to. I was on to the bastard. There sat my lonely daughter in an apartment, hours away whose roommate had just moved out on her. He decided to appear to step up and save her again by offering to help her buy a puppy from the same breeder. Looks great to an outsider, right?

Looked great to an impressionable eighteen-year-old girl too. She didn't understand the bigger picture, what was at risk.

"Jesus Maze, you are going through with it? After everything we have discussed, everything we have fought over? Dad and I had set you up so good there at school. We paid your rent, you didn't have to take out loans, and if you played your cards right, you wouldn't have even had to have worked the first year in school!" I could hear the anger build within my body, my arms and shoulders tensing up, just wanting to shake her from hundreds of miles away.

"Mom, I am so lonely though! My anxiety is through the roof. I know what I need to try and keep me from becoming more depressed, to try and keep me from that ledge, and I don't get why you don't see it! All you are doing is causing me more anxiety and pushing me deeper into depression because you are threatening to not pay my rent!" she lashed out, beneath a thin veil of tears that I could hear as she kept sniffling into the phone.

She absolutely couldn't see the manipulation, His bigger plan. That asshole knew that we didn't want her to get a dog. We told her a dog would be too much, it would limit hanging out with her newly found friends, cause anxiety when her work and clinic and classroom hours changed, and cost money that she didn't have. I begged her to get a cat with a litter box, something that she could cuddle and love on but yet still have her freedom. I mentioned that if she ended up breaking up with Him, could she stand to look at the poor dog, or would it be a constant reminder of His psychotic face. He knew that we had threatened to stop paying her rent if she got a dog. He promised her that He would help pay her rent if it came to that. At this point, the girl had little to no money left, as He had blown through her precious savings account that had held her life's savings of years of hard work as a young teenager of over five thousand dollars. He knew if we weren't paying her rent, she couldn't make it and she would have to move back. With Him. Exactly as He had planned.

I knew that I would never stop paying her rent while she was in school, I would never help Him get her to quit and come home. But she couldn't know that. She needed to believe that what she was about to do would have stressful consequences.

"I know you are lonely kid, but so are all of the other kiddos that just moved off to college. You have to give it time, Maze. A dog isn't the answer right now. If you would just stop and think."

I began to try and be the voice of reason before she cut me off with her razor-sharp yet newly formed tongue, stemming from a body that was trying to appear confident in the shakiest of situations.

"Damn it Mom! Just trust me! Why don't you ever trust me? This is just like when I was in sixth grade and you controlled who my friends were! You wouldn't let me go anywhere! I was the only kid with a tracker on their phone at the time! Why can't you just let me make my own decisions and live with my consequences? Why do you have to be such a controlling bitch all of the time? You are only pissed at me now because I am finally making choices that you can't control. Just because I am not living life and doing things the way you want me to, doesn't mean that you can control me any more!" She began to descend into her tirade of swirling emotion, gathering all of the hurt, anger and fear and hurling it all at the only person who was standing in her way,   her mom.

I held that phone to my ear and listened as my daughter, my soul that glides effortlessly outside of my body, my everything, began a tirade of insults that lasted another hour. As I listened to her weep and scream and cough and gag and start all over again, I discovered that after a few minutes, it didn't hurt as bad as it used to. My heart had formed a callus that year, trying to protect itself from the darkness that was threatening to suffocate us all.

As she went on and on about what an awful mother I had been, how wonderful He was, and how I deserved all the awful things that His mother had said about me within the community, I had a moment of clarity. She was a scared and wounded child. Her age may be almost nineteen, but she was fighting and lashing out like a frightened ten-year-old. There was no defending myself with her. What was the point? She no longer saw the world through her own eyes any more. She wanted so badly to believe that He was her destiny that she was willing to walk over her entire family to get to Him. It was around the point when she was talking about trust and began screaming at me about her scholarship money that I once again really tried to focus back in on what the tirade was being directed towards. She was so angry. I was so done.

As I listened to her vent, I felt that cold dark shroud run up every hair on my arms, the coldness chilling me to the bone. Depression is an absolute bitch and while I sat listening to my daughter's heart break into thousands of pieces all over again from hundreds of miles away, I realized that I was no longer the strong mama that I had started out as. She had worn me down. She had pulled my life out from beneath me and rattled my cage. Yet there I sat, lonely and scared, depression licking at my soul, much like the position that she was perched in.

"And another thing!" She spouted off through tears, grasping at every point that she was trying to make, sharpening every stone that she threw. "What you are doing with my scholarship money is illegal, you know! That's *my* money, Mom. I don't see why I can't have full access to it!" Aghhhhhhh. Again with the damn money. I had had enough of it by now and could no longer sit biting my lip until it bled.

"Maisey Alexis!," I shouted a little louder than I had really meant to. "Let me remind you of a few things…" I began, in a tone very calm and slow, yet I knew she would take as condescending. "Look at your fucking track record kid! That asshole helped you blow through your own savings account! I can show you the bank statements! You spent over a grand on a weekend in Wisconsin Dells right before you moved! While you stayed at His mom's house, you bought the groceries and got into the habit of door-dashing food two or three times a day! If you think that I am going to give you access to the money that is supposed

176

to get you through school over the next three years just to watch you 'loan' it out to him, you are nuts! Remember, He 'borrowed' four grand from his last girlfriend and she hasn't gotten that back either!" I wielded my words hotly out of my mouth, only pausing because I thought that I was going to pass out or puke.

"Oh again with the ex, Mom! Seriously! Why would you ever believe that bitch? She obviously wants Him back; you should hear the awful things that she has said about me!" she screamed with equal force back through the phone.

"Don't forget Maze, you broke them up. You went after Him while He was still with her. You broke the girl code. She was your friend, you deserve every awful word that she calls you.

"Yet, she still tried to warn you of what you were getting yourself into! Remember when I spoke with her and she said it took her four years, losing all of her family, friends and money, and *you* coming along just to get away from Him? Wake the fuck up!" The words escaped my soul without much thought. They had hit their intended target and there was no reeling them back in. I knew I had hit a nerve. I knew she was building up into a blinding rage right now, planning out her next assault. I knew we were so broken that there was no looking back. She just didn't want to hear it yet.

But here I am tending to lose my focus on looking back. The point was that finally, she did admit herself to inpatient therapy, but it wasn't until He had already scared her so badly that she moved home from school. It wasn't until He had threatened to kill Himself one too many times, taking His dog with Him. It wasn't until she was completely pushed by Him to the brink of sanity that she realized how exhausted she was, that she needed help. With the support of her family and her best friend, she finally did end up admitting herself to inpatient therapy, but it wasn't until she was living back at home and just weeks away from her sister's wedding.

Part of this therapy meant that she would have no visitors for the first seven days, and when I walked away from that hospital after dropping her off that day, I would be lying if I said I didn't feel like the most incompetent mother in the world. I cried all the way home, and on and off for most of that first week. I would flip flop between praying to God and screaming out in pain that there was no God. But I made it. We all did.

When Gage and I went on the seventh day to visit her, there was a different person who sat before us. She still wasn't the same person that she had been in the past, but she looked better, rested. She even laughed while we were talking. She had been diagnosed with anxiety and a mild form of depression, but the more concerning thing was that the toxicology panel showed that she had, in fact, been taking a concoction of His Prozac and antipsychotic medications, some of which He was prescribed, others of which He stole. Whether she had been taking these on her own free will or if He had been slipping them to her, like

He had with drugs in the past, we weren't sure, but didn't want to press the issue.

So she 'did her time', as she likes to put it, and came home. We had toyed around with the possibility of getting a restraining order put into place as far as the asshole was concerned, but we honestly didn't have enough evidence to do anything with. At that point, the best course of action was to just live our lives and get through the wedding that was a week away at that point. My hope was that He just wouldn't know that she was back home yet. Maybe we could buy ourselves some time. Maybe she could heal her soul and move on.

The week that we had her at home before the wedding, she became more and more like herself. She would laugh with her sister, play with the dog and visit family. I noticed that she liked to stay busy and around people, I was assuming that it was so she didn't have time to let her mind wander back to the abyss. I hadn't known that He was already trying to worm his way back into her world, texting her, messaging her, begging her to see Him. I didn't know that He had also begun His own downward spiral, frantically trying to develop a plan to keep her close. A plan that included beating her into submission to the point that she would attempt suicide so that He could once again be her savior. But as I am writing this, my mind falls back to the beach on that night before the beginning of the end of it all, the last lake lap that had led Maisey and Moby to their beloved Koala Beach...

"Maze, we don't have to talk about Five East tonight, really. You went through some shit. You worked through it, are still working through it, I know…" Moby spoke once again in a hushed tone.

"When I was in there, I had many nights where I would just violently shake and cry, trying to will myself to fall asleep, trying to get my brain to stop haunting me, to stop chanting threats into my ears," she began, no longer looking towards Moby, but staring back up at the night sky. "And you know what got me through it?" she asked.

"Girl, I have no idea what you thought about in there…" he replied, rolling over onto his side in the damp sand to stare at the silhouette of her face, the face only a few weeks ago he was terrified of losing. He slung his left arm over her belly, propping his head with his right arm in the sand.

"All of the times when we were in school and you would come flying down a hallway, or into the locker bays shouting out, 'Hey! There's my girl'! All of the football games that I would march at with the band and you would push your face up to the fence yelling, 'That's my girl'! Countless times that I would be so pissed about something and you would make me laugh and as soon as I would you would grin and say, 'Hey, there she is, my girl's back'. It was your voice Mobes. Your voice in my brain every time something was hard, every time I was scared. It was your voice that chased all of the other dark echoes away," she explained as she managed a grin against the darkness.

Moby's heart was so proud of her, all that she had been through, all that she had overcome. And here they were, yet again. When danger reared its ugly face at them once again tonight, they end up like this, together, just talking each other through the shit that sometimes was life. It's just what they did.

Never one to let a moment get too serious, he flashed her a huge Moby smile and said, "Awe girl, you know I always have your back. You know you are always my girl! Speaking of girls, umm…" he kind of trailed off…

"Wait, what the hell? That was a truth too then? You kissed a freaking girl your first week at college? You know she will never be good enough for you…" Maisey said and tacked on an evil little laugh at the end for good measure.

Moby laughed. "Oh come on, it was during Warrior Games and it was just one stupid kiss. And I know, Maze… no one else would ever be good enough for me," he said before burying his face into her shoulder.

They continued playing Two Truths and a Lie for another hour. He learned that she stepped on a snake barefoot once, and she learned that he fell off a dock once while filming for his social media right in front of a couple of girls that he was trying to impress. He learned that she doesn't actually wear mascara, her lashes are just naturally that dark and long, and she learned that he has, indeed, tried to apply makeup for his social media appearances.

The biggest thing that they had learned that night though, was even when things change, they actually still stay the same. Those two just keep orbiting around each other, in and out of circles of friends, different classes, life changes. They discovered what they already knew, they were each other's 'home'. This would be a fact that I would hold close to my heart soon, knowing that no matter what, these two would be all right together.

Chapter 10

Hello Me

As I sat on the toilet in my cell, cold and alone, I couldn't help but escape the thought that my daughter had many different facets of this story to tell, many different dominoes that had to be set for the whole thing to go down the way that it did. I stared down at my toes, old calluses dry from running and brittle toenails that still carry the faint deep purple color that I wore just a few weeks ago for Shiloh's wedding. Those worn feet are a reminder to myself that I was strong once, I had direction in my life. I sat there for a few minutes, lost in time, thinking about the letter that showed up at the house shortly after Maisey had gone into treatment. I had read it over and over so many times that my heart could easily recite it word for word. One thing about that kid, she was good at getting people to believe what they needed to if it meant coming out ahead of the game.

"They told me that in order to own up to where my faults lie and to face what I have become, where my mental illness has led me to, I am supposed to write a letter to myself explaining where I have come from and how I wound up here, on Five East. I think this is the stupidest exercise on earth, if I am being bluntly and brutally honest, but I have to jump through the hoops in order to get out of here. I have to prove that I am no longer a threat to myself. The truth is, that although I may have no well thought out intentions to harm myself, I am scared of who I have become. I no longer know what I am capable of, and that just feeds my depression. So here I go...

"Dear me,

"How the hell are ya? Just kidding... I know that's an empty question that only has loaded answers. So self, how are you really? Well, a year ago I had an entirely different life, along with an entirely different outlook on my life and future. I like to tell mom that I was just good at pretending that I was happy, but I think that the spring and summer before my senior year, I was really coming into who I was supposed to be. Sure, I had been crushed when I broke up with the boyfriend that I had been with for the previous year, and that was kind of a mindfuck because I really thought he was going to be the one. Although Mom and Dad thought he was kind of quiet, I guess they liked him enough. He was cute and kind. He had a cow farm and I loved spending time out there. He listened to my dreams and was proud of who I was. We were proud of who we were becoming. But as life would play out, his family life turned on a dime. His father found out his mother was cheating on him, but stayed with her. This threw my ex into a tailspin, as an only child he now doubted everything that he knew to be true in his life. This had a crushing effect on our relationship. The end came when he (incorrectly) accused me of cheating on him with some random guy in my grade. To make matters worse, the guy kind of was flattered by the accusation and did nothing to defend me. So, he left me. And once again, I was alone. Once again, I had put all of my faith and heart into a relationship that had run out of steam.

"But for the next six months, I really spent time with my younger cousins and family. I hung out with my friends again and went on adventures. I focused on school and worked hard because I knew what I wanted out of life. The truth is, maybe I worked too hard. I was either always at work or working on college courses, so the time that I spent just goofing around like an average high school kid was whittled away and replaced with happy little slices of time instead. Although I like to tell my mom when we're arguing that I was always depressed, it's not true. Look at me then, you can see in photos alone that I was in a better place. I was finally learning how to like myself and learn how to function on my own, without a Prince Charming.

"That's my problem though, isn't it? I crave affection, hate being alone. For a while, I had my best friend Moby by my side, until he wanted to move further into a relationship and I had the living shit scared out of me. I know the whole world wants to see us together, but what people don't understand is that he and I are each other's security. No matter how bad things get, we have each other to run to. What do you do if you take the relationship too far and lose each other forever? I can't cross that line. I can't lose that lifeline.

"So anyways, there I was the summer before senior year and this guy reached out and started to talk to me on social media. To be fair, I recognized the name because he had dated a girl from my school for about four years and was also a grade ahead of my sister in school. Not going to lie, at seventeen when a twenty-three-year-old shows interest in you, it does a little something to your self-esteem. It felt good to be sought after. It felt good to be admired. Hell, I even liked it when His ex-girlfriend freaked out on social media and I took it as a sign of jealousy. (Didn't know it at the time, but they were still together when I came along. Not the story He fed me, but whatever...)

"Dad was pissed at first. I mean, I can see now why a father wouldn't want his seventeen-year-old daughter dating an almost twenty-four-year-old guy, but like hell was I going to admit that back then. Mom actually went to bat for me in the beginning, saying she trusted me and my judge of character and all of that shit. That woman, I tell you. Love her with all of my heart but she is where I get my stubbornness from, although she likes to blame my dad for that.

"I don't really know at what point I started focusing on His life and world and letting my dreams and family go. It wasn't a planned thing. All I knew when we first started dating was that I loved being loved. I loved someone paying attention to me. I also loved His timid character.

He wasn't a showoff, not loud and boisterous and kind of kept to Himself. He loved animals and although He had a shitty situation growing up, He seemed to really try to help His mom out and try to be there for His younger sister. In the beginning, it was cool being the high school kid with the older guy paying attention to her. And after a while, I truly believed that I loved Him.

"What I didn't love was all of the arguing. Arguing at home about Him and arguing with Him about my family. Arguing with His family about my family and on and on it went. One issue was my age. Right from the get-go His mom wasn't happy. She knew the implications of an older guy dating an underage girl. It also didn't help that she loved His ex-girlfriend, so much so that they still lunched together. He didn't understand that I still had rules at home to follow, hell I still had a curfew. Which He thought was hilarious. A couple weeks after we started dating, He purposely wasn't taking me home in time to make curfew, just to see what would happen. He laughed and laughed as I stormed out of His house and began walking the mile and a half home, calling my mom in tears at the time. I guess that would be where the defiance against my parents really began. When you have this guy who you think is your whole world telling you how much He misses you, how much He needs you, how fragile His emotions and mental stability are, you start putting His needs first. So that's what I did.

"I began showing up late all of the time, sometimes not coming home at all. My parents were furious, how could they not be? What they didn't know was most of the time I was late because He was in the middle of panic or anxiety attacks or threatening to kill himself, accusing me of not loving Him if I left. It became harder and harder to escape, just to go home. Then I stopped coming home. (Fun fact, when you turn eighteen you can run away and your family can't really do much except call in to have a welfare check done if they know where you are staying, which they did. Repeatedly.) One night I went to work, He picked me up and I didn't go back home. Looking back, I am ashamed. I will never know what that did to Mom and Dad's hearts that night. But hell, when you are in so deep and just trying to survive, you take the easier road.

"Believe it or not, the easier road at the time for me was buying into His bullshit. I just point blank was exhausted from my family. Mom kept saying they were fighting for me, but all it felt like was they were trying to dictate my life. It was my life; these were my choices, damn it. Only I could make those choices, only I was responsible for where those paths would lead me.

"While I was living with Him in His mom's basement, I experienced a different kind of lifestyle than what I had known my whole life. This woman didn't cook and had the mentality of 'if it's in her house, it's hers'. I never told mom that the reason my grades slipped during that time was because that bitch was using my computer to work from home. I think that she considered it rent. I started to spend my own money just to survive. I bought groceries. This was an odd concept to that family though because they mostly ate out. I was expected to pay for them all to eat out if I was eating out, so I did. And that is where I began to lose all of the money that I had saved from working so hard for the previous four years of my life. I had no other options. Of course, my boyfriend would tell me that He would pay me back, and when I got to college, He would help pay for things if Mom and Dad cut me off. I was so flipping naive.

"So, we might as well talk about the first of the elephants in the room. Drugs. No, I am not a druggie. By all definitions of the word, He really wasn't a druggie either. I saw His chemical dependency more of a way to quiet the panic in His heart and the monsters that attack His thoughts. They calmed Him, kept Him sane, and made Him seem more like Himself. In some ways though, He was a product of a failed mental health system in this country. Drugs were the Band-Aid that most practitioners handed out and when they didn't work, the answer was always more drugs. It doesn't take long for a person to become dependent on what made them feel more normal, and dependent He became. Many nights I spent driving Him to the emergency room as He faked an anxiety attack just so He could trick the system and walk away with a fresh prescription.

"One night when I couldn't sleep, I tried one of His meds. And I slept. And I liked it. So, I started taking whatever He had lying around whenever I needed to calm down. Then I got wise and decided to get my own prescriptions. It started innocently enough though... Mom had offered to pay for me seeing a therapist in the middle of the nightmare. I told her sure, it would be good to talk to someone as I was feeling so depressed. I know that triggers my mom. Again, I'm not proud and I hate what I have done to her, but it's in the past now and there is no going back. So yes, although the biggest fear in my mother's life is and always has been suicide, I played that card. And boy did I play it. I fed that therapist such lines of bullshit on what my life was like growing up. Really it was easy to do, I just told His story instead of mine. I had that therapist convinced that my mom was dealing with being an empty nester and dealing with her own marital issues and I just couldn't cope. So, the free-flowing med river began. I would try some, say they wouldn't work and she would prescribe me more. This kept happening every three weeks because that is all the longer she said I had to try something before I could get a new prescription. But guess what? It's not like they ask for the old half-full bottles back. So, I began to stockpile. Prozac, Zoloft, Lexapro coupled with Trazodone and Halcion and I was good to go. I would sleep my way through the lonely days that I didn't have class and was at His house alone with His half strung out mom if He decided to work that day. This was working in my favor until my mom offered to see the same therapist for family therapy and I freaked the shit out. I mean, I get patient client confidentiality and all, but there was no way I could pull off seeing her with them knowing all of the lies that I had already told. So just like that, I was cured from my 'depression' and stopped going.

Mom's no dummy, she works for DHS, she knew what I was up to.

"The thing is though, although she knew at the time, she was so programmed to protect my future that she was limited in ways to help me. She knew that no one could find out about my drug use. I had college coming up, scholarships, nursing school that was *if* she could hang on and get me there. Plus, when your dad is the town cop people are just waiting for you to fuck up and pounce on you. Mom knew it. Her hands were tied. So what did I do? Hate her all the more. Hate may not be the right word though. I don't think that consciously I have ever hated my Mom. She was just the thing that stood in my way for a while, the one thing in the world that pissed Him off, and I was finding out, when He was pissed, He took it out on me. So I was caught in a cycle of trying to survive.

"So that's my story. I fell in love with an older guy who knew how to push buttons and drag me down with Him. I lost sight of what I wanted out of my life. I burned every bridge. I fucked up my life and now I'm not sure how to fix that, but I know that I need a clear head to try."

Chapter 11

RUN

After sitting on that toilet in a daze for way too long, I tried to stand to walk back over to the little table in the corner of the cage. I had sat for too long in a funk daydreaming because it was now painful to try and bear weight on my now fragile legs. I looked down at my body. Oh, how I have failed myself. Not long ago these pale thin legs were tanned and full of lean muscle, ready to run me wherever I may have needed to go. The exhilaration of a good runner's high is something that I was late to learn about in life, but man… there is nothing that compares to it. There is nothing better than the searing, painful burn that chokes your lungs when you are on your first long run out around the lake in a while. When your body is completely fighting against you, yet you force your exhausted and out of shape legs to keep moving forward. One step at a time.

That's what I used to tell myself on long runs when I didn't think I could go any further, just one foot in front of the other. one step at a time. I couldn't have known back then how I would cling to that mantra and that some days, it would be all that I could do to just wake up, force myself out of bed one more time and head in to work, off to help save other families, even though I had failed so miserably at saving my own.

The thing with running is that there really isn't anyone that you are competing against but yourself unless you are an elite runner, you will never enter a marathon with the intent to win.

Most of us hobby runners are just in it for the adrenaline rush that we get when we are put into a position where there is no way out other than pushing your body past the extreme that you had thought was possible. Eventually, you figure out that the border of madness, the edge of extreme, keeps getting a little further away every time you are pushed a little more towards her reach. For example, I started with three-mile runs. (Most people would start walking, then run a mile at a time and build up, but I am more of a go for it all in and pay the price later type of girl...) Then I wanted faster times for those three-mile runs. Then three miles wasn't enough so I would do six miles nightly. I then threw in a thirteen miler every other weekend. Then decided to run around the whole damn lake. When simply beating your body to run on a flat surface didn't give me that rush any more, I began looking into off road runs and extreme adventure marathons. The end goal for a long time, the thing that kept me pushing forward was wanting to run the Great Wall Challenge in China with my dad. But life just sucks sometimes and goals shatter and dreams are suffocated.

Dad and my running times were getting pretty good, our endurance was strong. We figured most people that we had checked out and followed on social media who had run that adventure series, basically ran until they got to the wall, then the wall portion of the run was more grueling and was more walking and climbing for about four hours. We knew we could make the time for the actual running portion, but really had no way to test our ability to work our way across the thousands of uneven steps along that wall. That was the exhilarating part. We just kept thinking of what that glorious feeling would feel like to cross that finish line. And my God, if we could survive that adrenaline rush and be able to tell people that we were finishers of the Great Wall Marathon, what would be the next adventure beyond that? We didn't know, but it was the rush of chasing that dream that kept us going. Until it didn't.

I have no idea why these memories are seeping into this story, this confession, the thoughts that stand in silence in the corner of my mind until I am chasing a few moments of quiet solitude to quiet my panic and terror, then they twirl into my head with a dizzying euphoria, making me miss what I had, making me homesick for the past. I suppose that the events of training for that run kind of collided with the rest of my life falling apart, and it was during those training runs around the lake that I could sort out my soul and quiet myself.

It was also late in the summer that my dad's training runs were cut abruptly short. Dad was a guy who always liked to run in the cooler part of the day, which in Iowa in mid-August, meant primarily at night. In the dark. And he ran alone. (As did I actually... I have never understood the people who can happily run along next to someone while still being able to focus on their own cadence and breaths and pace. Also, there is an insanely healing solitude that comes from just being in your own head for so many treacherous miles, working out life's problems as you happily bob along the edge of the road, randomly hitting the shuffle button on your old iPod, hoping to get a sudden burst of energy from the next song, or at least unlock a memory from the tune that will keep you focusing on anything but the stinging pain in your feet and cramping in your legs...) He was as safe as he could be. He wore a bright safety vest, stayed beneath streetlamps when possible and always faced oncoming traffic in order to jump out of the way.

Even though my parents lived on the end of the lake that didn't see as much traffic, we still had to be careful. Many times, while I have been out running, I have had to hop out of the way because either someone looked down for two seconds and swerved, swerved because they were drunk, or young kids swerved just to be assholes.

On one particular night, Dad had set out to do a shorter run, three miles down and three miles back. He suited up with his gear, told Mom he was going and took off.

I had been on the phone with her discussing all of the latest pains in my life when she glanced at the counter and blurted into the phone, "Well crap, he didn't take his phone." And made a note on a post it to document the time that he had taken off. She figured he should be back in an hour and fifteen minutes, absolutely no longer than an hour and a half if he was cramping up. But he had his reflective vest on and it was a nice night in the middle of the week, so she really didn't think too much more about it. My dad hated having to carry a phone. In the age of smartphones, he still carried an ancient flip phone so that it wouldn't get dirty or broken if he dropped it while working outside or in the garage. He also wasn't on board with my fanny pack idea unless he was running a long distance and he had no other choice to carry his snacks for fuel, endurance electrolyte powder and Band-Aids.

I remember that I had been talking to Mom that night about my daughters, about Shiloh's upcoming wedding and of course, about Maisey. This was right before she went to Five East and was still in a mental battle with herself and lashing out at everyone and everything, but predominantly it was me she aimed the flames of her tongue towards. I had argued with her, yet again, and this time it was over how she had felt that I had never trusted her enough to let her make her own choices in life. She ranted over not being able to hang out with certain kids from way back in sixth grade, and screamed with fury about why she had to have a tracking device on her phone. (Fun fact, we all did! I needed to know if a car broke down, or if someone beat them over the head and dragged them away or worse...)'

In her manipulated and broken state, she then ranted on and on, inches from my face about how terrified He was of us, how I am lucky He hadn't killed himself yet because

196

of how awful I had been. According to her, I was an awful, cruel mother who just wanted to control her and I had no affinity towards her actually being happy. I had finally just let go of my anger as she slammed the door behind her once again, running down the driveway to jump into the Devil's car, and I picked up the phone to hear my mom's voice tell me one more time that it was going to be OK.

It wasn't until later in the evening, after I had tried to take a hot bath, (but the water heater wasn't working right...) tried to have a bowl of cereal (but the milk was old) and tried to go to sleep (but Gage was already gone and the house stood in an unbearable state of silence, so I got up and started to rewrite my ceremony for Shiloh's wedding), after I had tried all of these things to quiet the loneliness, that the phone rang, jolting me out of the chair. No one calls that late at night with good news. The number was a random one on my ID.

As I held my breath and half whispered a half-hearted, "Hello?"

(The thought of, *What happened to her this time* running through my mind...) My body felt an electric surge of panic jolting through my veins. A new heaviness found its way into the pit of my belly as I thought about the last things that Maisey had yelled at me, the last things that we had said to each other. You never know when the last time will really be the last time, but I was terrified that this would be the way it all would end, and my heart would be perpetually broken, stuck in a time that had been so unkind to this mama, a time when my littlest cub had pushed me out, leaving me unable to save her, unable to keep the beast at bay.

"Max! It's mom!" I snapped out of my funk as I heard my mom's calm but tearful voice slowly make its way across the line. The thing with life is that just when you think you know where you are going, just when you think your hell couldn't burn any hotter, you get the rug pulled out from under you once again, to be left tumbling backwards into that dark pit that you had been slowly climbing out of on your hands and knees, bloodying your nails to do so.

Dad had made it his three miles and was on the return run. He had actually made it only a few blocks from home when a brand new full-size Ford truck, in candy-apple red with huge side mirrors swerved right into him beneath the streetlamp. He saw it coming and it was moving so fast and aiming right for him, that he couldn't get out of the way. When he opened his eyes (after being struck in the side of the head and shoulder with the mirror and his hip and mid-thigh with the front fender, he passed out on a side lawn), he was staring out at the shadowy asphalt in front of him. That truck had hit him with enough force to throw him towards a yard, hitting his head on the curb in the process.

He told me later that as he was staring at a broken mirror laying in the middle of the road, the only thing he could think, the only thing that he could scream out into the night was, "That fucker hit me and took off!"

Now, why would someone in our sleepy little lakeside town do such a thing you may wonder? Was it a drunk rich farmer headed out to the country after a night at the VFW? Was it a stupid young kid not paying attention while driving daddy's new ride? Or, was something a little more sinister beneath the surface? Have I mentioned that I was in the middle of fighting with my daughter about Him? Did I tell you that He worked for a body shop in town and had access to a multitude of vehicles plus full access to repair damaged ones? Did I leave out the part where my daughter's asshole of a human has made no secret of His disdain for my father because my dad won't stop fighting for her either? How about the fact that the little prick had already tried to run me off the road? No? Well then let me stop here and back up just a little…

I was on my way to work one day on the one long highway that leads over to the next town. It was a pretty early commute, not many cars on the road. I always have to pass where He works at the auto shop on my way into the office, *when* He works, and aside from waving the bird high in my window every time that I drive by, hoping He was actually working that day and hoping that He would actually see me, I didn't think too much about it.

On that day, however, I remember that it had been a pretty awful week at home with Maisey, this was before she moved into His mama's basement, before she had attempted to move away to college. We had been arguing again about Him, and things had escalated to a point where I was scared that He was overmedicating Himself again.

When they would talk face-to-face on the computer, I would see His haunting pale face with empty eyes while passing through the room, and although that damn face instantly gave me the urge to throw up every time that I saw it, I did notice that He was grinning a little too wide, His eyes were a little too big and His pupils were like black soulless saucers. He was in a once again very clingy stage, putting pressure on Maisey because He, 'didn't know how he could handle her graduating and going off to school'… what if He couldn't handle it? What if His dog missed her too much? What if He had a major panic attack and she wasn't here? His guilt trips that He would hurl upon her never stopped. They were the pressure that He used, knowing full well that her heart would never want to cause Him harm.

I tried telling her, tried reasoning with her. I begged her to at least take a break from Him to clear her head and really think about what she wanted in life. I screamed at her telling her what a thoughtless child she was being and raged at her when she acted like her future was disposable if it didn't include Him in it. She would purposely have Him on the computer screen when we would argue, just so He could hear everything I was saying, and I supposed after a while, my hatred grew to a point where I didn't care what He heard. I didn't care what He felt. At that point of complete parental desperation, I didn't give a shit if He *did* try to kill himself. It would bring her one step closer back to safety, back to home, and back to her old life.

The things that He was telling her, the way she let Him seep into her head like a strung-out druggie holding on for that next fix, that next glimmer of hope, the chance to feel whole again. I had raised a strong daughter, but in the wrong sense of the world. For she may have been strong enough to stand her ground against her own mother, but she had no backbone when it came to Him. Her world revolved around Him at that point, and she was willing to give anything for Him, which scared the living shit out of me. Her dependency came with a price for us all.

Anyways, on that particular day as I was heading into work, I wasn't really paying too much attention to the cars around me. Like I said, there was hardly any traffic, so I was just in the slow lane, kind of just doing that thing where you have traveled the same path so many times that your body and mind are just on autopilot. So there I am in the early morning sun, just driving along trying to think about anything other than where my life was at in that moment, when suddenly, the car in front of me abruptly tapped its brakes. We had been going about 60mph and although I was still a few car lengths behind the car, it woke me up and I got into the other lane.

I had a fleeting thought of, *Dang, they must have almost hit a cat or racoon or something,* before I glanced back over at the car that had now slowed and was directly next to me. There, out in the murky depths of my peripheral vision, was His smiling, snarling face, grasping the wheel tightly on the top of the steering column and almost hunching over it to lean in and look at me. He must have been on His way to work, (shock and surprise that He woke up that day...) driving His mama's car because all of the five or six pieces of crap foreign cars that He owned didn't work. (Comical seeing as how He worked in an auto shop, then again, He's only a buffer, a detailer and doesn't actually know shit about cars, but I digress...)

The single most terrifying thing about Him was what He doesn't do. As a master manipulator, He knows how to play against your fears. I wasn't good at being stoic like Gage. I was one to panic and start swearing like a sailor. So, as I stared at the soulless eyes coming from the blonde-haired man-child that was grinning a wide maniacal smile in the vehicle just inches from my passenger side window, I could feel the fear and anger raging up from the pit of my stomach and making my heart beat loudly and at a terrifyingly fast rhythm in my ears.

With one hand fumbling at the steering wheel with a grip so tight it was as if I was willing myself to stay on the road, I raised my right hand into the air, towards the window, giving him the bird while slowly letting the words, 'Fuck you psycho', escape from my lips with such force that He instantly became enraged and the smile fell from His face and was instantly replaced with a look of anger, a look of resentment and insanity.

There were still no other vehicles around us when He sped up to get in front of me and began to slow down, tap His brakes and speed up again. Panicked, I had started to cry and scream from the inside of my car, frantically glancing around before jumping back into the right-hand lane. I was terrified. This was no longer just arguing with a twenty-four-year-old kid in the street or screaming at Him through a computer screen. I had feared that I may have finally pushed Him too far at the wrong time. What if He *was* undermedicated? Overmedicated? Or just so emotionally broken that He just wanted to take out the one thing that stood in the way of His perceived happiness... *me*.

I didn't want to glance over at His mama's car. I didn't want to see that face, those soulless eyes hunting me down. Suddenly, out of my periphery, I could see that He was close. Too close. I glanced in my rearview and there was traffic coming up behind me, so I knew that there was no way to safely stop, and during this stress, there really was no shoulder to pull over. He methodically would veer towards my car, inching ever so close to tapping my side and pull back over, just trying to scare me. He continued to do this until the traffic behind us caught up to where we were, then He sped up and pulled in front of me. For about another half mile, I was stuck behind the asshole, surrounded by the cars that were just innocently surrounding us on their way to work. He would randomly tap his brakes, as if letting me know that once again, He was in control, He decided who lived or died.

Finally, as we made our way to the corner where He turned off to go to work, He made a point of slowing way down and holding His hand out the window to give me the bird, screaming, 'Fuck you'! out of His window as He pulled off the roadway.

So let me ask you this one more time... In a world where my family sleeps with loaded guns next to their beds and our hearts freeze every time the phone rings in the middle of the night, in a time when my own daughter has stared into the eyes of her own grandfather when he was begging her to walk away from all of this and her response was, "Don't guilt me... I don't know what I want any more..."

In a place where our realities have begun to walk a line of perceived intentions, is it just possible that the boy with access to a body shop and any car he wanted who knew my dad's training schedule and held an immense hatred for our family may have just been over or undermedicated just enough to scare my dad as a warning, but perhaps got just a little too close?

This is the shit I think about in the middle of the night.

Chapter 12

Statement

I could hear him shuffling towards my cage, his left leg stepping a little more pronounced and louder than his right, as it always had, which was just an after effect of his days of working in a quarry when I was a kid and he slipped into a rock crusher. How Bud ever survived that was always a mystery to me, the damn machine almost completely severed his leg at the knee. He's a fighter though, tough and strong. He never says a whole lot, but he never needs to, you can read his pale blue eyes easy enough. When he stopped in front of my cage, I could read him easy enough.

"Come on kid, Gage is here to see you," Bud said in a tone that you could hear the pity in. As I looked up from where I had been sitting at the little desk in my cage, I could read his eyes from there. Pity, despair and disbelief. They were all right there brewing beneath the surface. I was sure that this sweet man spent many nights internally wrestling with his thoughts on my current situation.

It's easy to sit in judgment when the person to be judged is a nameless face. When the accused is as close as family and you have known them forever, there has to be an internal struggle between the heart and mind. On one hand, the heart knows what the accused has been through, what they may or may not be capable of. On the other hand, logic and evidence lobby to prevail. This was what was going on internally that afternoon when Bud came to retrieve me. His eyes tattled on his soul.

I must have been painful to look at because after a quick glance, those cool-blue eyes darted to the floor and dear old Bud took his hat off with one hand and rubbed the top of his half bald head with the other. He didn't want to look into my eyes for fear he would see answers that his heart couldn't handle.

With a deep breath I glanced down at myself, unable to recognize my own body any more. I fixed my gaze on my hands, which mostly just trembled now, I think an effect of stress and meds. It shocked me as to how old they suddenly looked. A dry smile cracked across my lips as I thought of how suddenly they looked like a witch's hands, and honestly maybe that analysis wasn't far from the truth any more. Witches have hard hearts and an intent to change a person's free will, an intent to change the events that they foresee, and isn't that what I had done? Didn't I risk everything in order to change the perceived outcome and to hell with whatever was in my way? Actually, there was only one thing, one monster in my way and I really was hoping that I had sent Him straight to the fiery depths of hell, or at least into a murky cold eternal resting spot full of worms and rot and disease and...

"Maxine, let's go," Bud calmly said as he opened the cage door. I slowly padded over to Bud, no threat there. To the man I had only weeks ago spent time dancing with at my daughter's wedding reception, I now gave him my hands so that he could shackle them together.

"Gage seems OK today, Max. Just try to stay calm when you are talking with him this time. You two have been through so much and I really don't want to see you injected with any more meds. It's not good for you, Kid," Bud was telling me as we made our way down the short corridor to where Gage was waiting.

As we stopped outside of the door so that Bud could key in the entry, I could see him sitting in there, waiting for me. For just a moment, I had butterflies in my soul, just like when we were kids. For a half of a second, time stood still and right before me sat my everything.

We were so much older now, but he still caught my breath every damn time, even when he never knew it. His golden hair had darkened with time, allowing a little trickle of silver to trail through his hair and into his beard. And his eyes, my God, it's where the girls had inherited their stunning eyes from. They can pierce you with one glance, they show pain, they show fear, they show love. Right now though, as he glanced towards the door, all I saw in his eyes, on his face, was pain. Where love used to rest, only loss now resides. He forgot how to care about six months ago. He forgot how to fight. He had forgotten how to love.

To be absolutely fair, it wasn't his fault. We had both become so wrapped up in saving our daughter, and still trying to be there for Shiloh, that as we stumbled along through the hard parts in life, we kind of just let go of our grip on each other. Sometimes I don't think it's really anyone's fault, you just let go to try and save yourself.

As Bud opened the door and we wandered into the room, Gage looked up at me from where he was sitting at that damn cold metal table on that damn cold metal stool. There was no smile, no hint of emotion in his eyes. When he began to speak, it was in hushed undertones and straight to the point.

"Maxine, you have to know what you are up against. Have you thought about how you're going to plead?" an exasperated man who sat calmly across from me rattled out in one breath without looking up.

My heart just ripped while watching this good man try to find the words that he was searching for. This man who I had spent twenty-four years of marriage and twenty-eight years of my life with, bought multiple houses and turned them into homes with, had babies and raised a family with… this man that now was so broken that all he could do was stare downwards towards the table. He couldn't bring his heart, or what was left of it, to capture the memory of this point in time. I can't blame him. I wouldn't want to see myself like this. I wouldn't want to have a face to haunt my dreams to remind me of how far we have fallen, of what had become of us as a family.

"Gage, what choice do I have, you know what I have done. I know what I have done. There is no getting around that one..." I trailed off, again lost in thought. As I shamefully stared down at the checkerboard black and white tiled floor, scuffed with time, I felt like my head was in a fog, almost like a dream. I was trying to remember in my heart what we used to be like.

This wasn't always us. We had so many good years. Sure, it was a struggle being young and having babies. He worked a lot; I worked a lot and we just dug our heels in and did it. The irony is that this year was supposed to have been the start of what we had hoped would have been the greatest chapters of our lives. Our kids were out of the house, one was supposed to be off at college, one was married and successfully starting her teaching career, the financial struggle of hosting a wedding was behind us, we were succeeding in our careers and had found that sweet spot where we could just kind of glide through for another ten-fifteen years until retirement. We had bought our cute little retirement home and planned on buying a boat this year to spend more time in the summers with the kids and our families. All the dreams and hard work that we had put into building our lives for twenty-eight years had come crashing down around us, with only one asshole to blame. We never saw it coming.

"They may have enough evidence to charge you with Murder one Maxine, Murder two if not, either way, there's no way out. Plead insanity," Gage muttered, without even looking up.

Insanity. Not really too far off from the truth at this point in my life. Am I insane? Does wanting your child to have the best life make you insane? Does protecting them against all types of evil make you insane? Does wanting someone out of your world so you can have your life back insane? Maybe not, but the aftermath of what I have done and the weight of the entire last year has definitely altered my sense of normalcy within my reality. For fuck's sake… are there any sane people sitting in cages?

Somewhere in the center of the whirlwind of thoughts that had begun swimming in my mind, something that my estranged husband said suddenly pulled me out of the swirling dark abyss.

"Gage! Murder… you said murder! Does that mean… oh God! Does that mean.?" I was fumbling over my words trying to get them to align with the thoughts that had now begun to make my broken heart race with an angry fury. I could feel the blood, now hot in my cheeks and I could actually hear my heart pounding within my chest. There was a loud ringing that was drowning out my heartbeat and I began to view things through a long dark scope. I had the sudden urge to throw up. I think all of the excitement and terror had attacked my weakened body on all fronts and the choice was puke or pass out, so puke I did.

"Awe Christ Max!" Gage shouted as he jumped up and away from where I sat. I had the sense left in me to at least turn away from the table as I began heaving over the side. Between heaves I would try and form words, but my breathing had become so chaotic that I couldn't speak. At this point, I was coherently trying not to hyperventilate or pass out. I could hear Gage dry heaving against the wall. As strong as he was, even after all the years he has served on the police force, he still can't stomach seeing someone he loves sick or in pain. My heart knew, while heaving, snot running out of my nose and tears streaming down my face, that somewhere in there, he would love me always despite all of this. Despite the failure, despite the pain, despite how things ended, I was always his forever. You can't change that. You can't change the past no matter how much you may try to forget it.

"Max," Gage began in the same hushed tone that he had started out with only moments before. "His mom took him off of the respirator after the doctors had determined there was no more brain function. He's gone."

This was where I was supposed to feel relief. This is where I was supposed to be able to breathe again. This is where the weight was supposed to lift off my heavy heart and life was supposed to be good again. Instead of feeling relieved that my daughter would be safe, that I had won the epic battle that had left us war-torn and scarred and divided, I had a reaction that I wasn't prepared for.

Maybe it was for His family. Maybe it was for His poor psychotic bitch of a mother that had to make that choice to turn off His life support, that mama who sat vigil next to her only son and held His hand, oblivious as to what kind of monster lay beneath His sweet façade. Maybe it was for myself. Maybe it was for Him. Whatever the reason, I felt the darkest cloud form in my heart and

211

strangle my chest. My lungs began to heave as they struggled to find air. My eyes stung with hot tears and I began to cry. This was a new grief. This was a sadness that engulfed me, took over my spirit. I couldn't help but be sad for a life lost, no matter what the circumstances, and it was His mother's face that I saw when I closed my eyes.

We never know how others see our kids. We know how we hope that they are being projected in the world, but we are never at a privilege to really know if they are treading gently through other people's lives or not. As awful as His mama had been to me and my family, as horrible as she had treated my daughter in the past, she is still a mama. We share a common bond if for no other reason than we both brought life into this world, raised them the best that we could, and hoped above all else that they would find their way. So, I sat there and cried for this woman that I despised. The woman who just had to let her baby boy go. I knew that although my reasoning for what I had done was sound and was done in order to protect my own child, it didn't lessen the pain for her. To her, I was the monster now. I was the monster in her nightmares, and it would now be my face that woke her up in the middle of the night.

"I'm not crazy, Gage. There is no plea that will make it OK. There is nothing that can save me from myself now." I cried into my hands. I didn't look up, but could hear him sniffling. I knew he was fighting his heart. I knew he was trying not to feel. It was going to be better for him if he didn't. His life would have to move on from this point. He had to keep it together for his girls, to go on building a family and making memories. The city couldn't all burn down around them, someone had to be left standing to put out the flames and rebuild. I kept my head down as I heard the door open and listened as his slow heavy footsteps from his bowed legs made their way down the hall.

"OK Max, let's take you to get cleaned up," Bud said as he uncuffed me from the table.

Being the wife of a cop in a small town afforded me a few luxuries, dignities if you will. One that I was grateful for was that Bud took me down to an actual shower stall in the back of the place, and with such grace, afforded me a hot shower. It was an older area of the station that the officers now used to shower themselves at the end of a long shift or if they used the decrepit small workout room that sat across the hall. Although he didn't actually stand guard in there with me, I knew he was right out the door. Let's face it, in a town this size, with a family that was once a downright pillar to the community, I wasn't exactly a flight risk. Seriously, where the hell would I go?

I stood under that scalding stream of soul baptizing water and couldn't get Gage out of my head. Not the broken man that walks the earth sullen and scorn, but the one that I married, the one that couldn't wait to be a father and the one that had little girls following him around while working on cars and riding along with him on skid loaders. They were so good for his soul. He just radiated happiness and contentment when they were around. His girls could snowmobile as soon as they were big enough to ride, rode four wheelers before bicycles and could change a tire with the best of them. Even as they got older and their preferences in how they spent their time changed, they always had time for their good old dad. The girls used to laugh and call him a grinch when he would be grouchy, and he wouldn't be able to hold back a grin for long for them.

For them. Jesus. Our whole marriage, except for the first two years before them, had always been for them. Every vacation we took, every experience, everything that we could do to ensure that the girls had a solid upbringing and a great life, we did. We moved to bigger homes, took on extra jobs, bought all the toys. We lived life and we lived it big. They wanted for nothing.

We never thought that they were actually spoiled, just that we wanted the world for them, and we had hoped that the solidity and fierce love and loyalty of the family would serve them well in this world, give them an edge, give them every upper hand that we could. Every move that he and I made in our marriage was calculated towards the end game. Gage was adamant that we paid on huge life insurance policies as soon as we had our girls. For our entire married life, we should have had a brand-new car in the driveway instead of monthly payments that would only be paid out if we died or we cashed part of it in at the age of sixty-five... So that we could then turn around and give it to the girls of course.

I read somewhere that it generally takes four generations for the wealth of a family line to dramatically increase. Looking at the lineage of our family history, we are following that to a T because these girls should be set eventually, at least on paper.

With Gage, nothing is ever left uncalculated. As I am writing this, the girls know about our life insurance policies that they will split and our burial policies. They know that Gage and I each have a certificate paid in full to be used towards our burials to the tune of $19,000 each. Gage has also told them where our plots are that are prepaid, and that the certificate has no monetary value printed on it so go in and pick things out to bury us as cheaply as possible, then hand them the certificate. The life insurance company would then send the girls a rebate for the money not spent. Hell, just burn our bodies, throw the ashes in the lake and get a bigger refund. We live for them. Maybe this is why Gage is so broken now.

As the scalding water hit my scalp and burned slowly down my back, I just stood in the steam thinking about how much we have changed in the course of a year. Change is never easy, but the monster that had been unleashed into our lives had taken the happy little middle-class family, ripped off the shiny exterior and left us bloody, bruised and confused. Gage was a man who lived for his girls and when Maisey pushed away, when she walked out on her life, on our plan for what our future was supposed to be… He broke. And as a result, it fractured our relationship in ways that just couldn't be put back together again. He was always such a strong pillar, the one that we all leaned on. He became lost, needy. He needed more physical and emotional connection and that was never what we were about.

Tears once again rolled down my puffy face as I stood in the shower stall, wishing that I could have been more for him, that I could have been what he had needed to come out swinging on the other side of this. But you have to remember, I too was trying to survive. I too was treading water and gasping for air. I too was dying a little more every time she would lash out at us, every time she would disappear. Every time she pushed us away. I barely had the strength or sanity to be who I needed to be in my day-to-day life, let alone pull my shit together enough to pick up his pieces as well. I know I was pissed at him for it too, and unfairly so. I needed a pillar. I needed strength. When he showed his weakness of stumbling along as well, somewhere I think it pissed me off. Never in our marriage was I coddled, never 'taken care of'.

In fact, at one point in our marriage when we were arguing about something stupid when the girls were little, Gage had had enough, got within inches of my face and hissed at me, "Maxine, I will *never* be your knight in shining armor. There is *no* Prince Charming. Are you hearing me? Never get yourself into something that you can't get yourself out of. Depend on no one."

In the moment that he said those words, I thought they were so vile, I cried about it for days. At that point, we had been married for like ten years and I had felt like I had the carpet ripped out from under my feet, my safety net cut away. I had always thought that he was valiantly standing in the shadows, in my corner, ready to tackle the world together. Through the years, I had come to understand that what he was actually trying to do was make me stronger than his mom and sister had been. Some women need to be rescued. I heard story after story of him and his friends taking care of and rescuing his mom from situations when they were kids, and I see the way that my sweet sister-in-law is doted on hand and foot by her husband. What I hadn't realized was that it really bothered Gage. I think he had a fear that if I was so dependent on him and something happened to him, I wouldn't know how to survive. The irony is that he had spent an entire marriage building me to be strong enough to walk away. I didn't know how to save him; I only knew how to survive and do what I could to save my daughters.

I could see his beautiful face, and kind eyes in the not-so-distant past. He had such a great laugh when he really thought something was funny, and his eyes would light up when he was talking to someone he loved. For Gage, family was his world, and when he lost a grip on those chubby little fingers, the girl with curly hair and a toothy smile, when he lost his grip on her, he just fell to pieces. His soul couldn't recover. He would pull himself together for his Shiloh and we all put on a nice shiny façade for her wedding, but right below the surface we were struggling. I think the kids already knew.

The week after the wedding, we were riding one hell of a low. It was as if all of the stress of the wedding, all of the happiness, all of the closeness of the family being together had worn away, leaving us to once again look at each other and not know what to do any more. How do you love with broken hearts? How can you live in one house when you agree on nothing any more, when you go to sleep angry and wake up even more pissed off? For every time that he would try to back off Maisey, I would push her, cling to her, trying to change her mind, trying to get her to hold on. Then we would reverse and I would have had enough of her pain and he would be trying to fix her broken heart. It was a constant tug of war and in the end, we let go of each other.

There is a haunting sadness about that which just makes me cry every time I think about it, something that our girls will never know until they have children someday. The truth is, you go into marriage because you have found your forever. Your heart pauses every time they are around, you ride out the hurricanes in life together and wait for the calmer tides. You make plans, you grow your family, you plan for the last half of your life.

Somewhere in all of that, through storms and fires and turbulence and just the day-to-days of life, you focus shifts towards putting your children and their needs first. Soon, you are living a life where 'us' is a new metaphor, meaning the whole family unit because the initial 'us' of two has been replaced. Maybe families who don't go through nightmares come out the other side of the storms OK, maybe they do just fine living in the new 'us'. I like to think that we would have. Had we not encountered the nightmare that was Him, the heartache that stabbed Maisey and bled out onto all of us, maybe we would have been OK. But we weren't OK, we could never be OK after we had to let go of each other to survive and save the girls.

I came out of my warm haze in that lonely shower stall as I heard Bud knocking on the door. He knew as well as I, that there was no reason to be worried about me being in there alone, there was literally only a bar of soap and a towel, not even a shower rod to tie a towel to. I was zero risk in here. I knew he was only letting me escape myself, ride out my thoughts in this stream of scalding water out of his own sad heart. We were like family, and I was grateful for the escape.

"Getting out now Bud," I shouted into the emptiness. My voice no longer sounded like my own as it echoed around me. I grabbed my towel and wrapped it around my tired body. As good as standing in that constant stream of warmth felt, I knew my time had come to an end and I needed to get back. There was no saving us now, Gage and I. He was my forever, forever ago. It's time to do what I can to save the girls.

Chapter 13

Where We Began

Staring out the window that was high on the wall of my cold cage, I could watch the sun dance around in the bright blue sky, tempting and teasing me that I was not, nor would I ever be free again to enjoy her warmth and run barefoot through the damp blades of grass on a dewy summer morning. I would never again feel the breeze of a hot summer's day whip across my face as we rode out across the water on our weekend adventures, red Solo cup in one hand and a kid on my lap. Freedom is something that will no longer be afforded to me now. I was lost in thought, staring out at nothing, thinking about how much I had changed, how much we had all changed.

When I was sixteen, I had been dating a perfectly nice guy, who was also sixteen. And as any sixteen-year-old kid knows, friends are very important at that time in your life. My boyfriend at the time was more into hanging around the bonfire with his football friends than he was with hanging around with me. I was bored. I didn't have many friends of my own, my life mostly revolved around his friends. I was restless, tired of spending all those Saturday nights alone. One of the friends that I did have, my very best of friends, had an older brother that had been off at college for a while. He too had gotten tired of the whole friends scene and wanted more out of life than just working and going to school. He wanted someone to come home and visit, someone to look forward to seeing. At the time, at sixteen and nineteen, I don't think you are really searching for your forever, more just looking for fun, a purpose to keep getting up in the morning. That is when Gage, the older brother of my best friend came into my world.

I have always said that he was like a bull in a China shop, and by no means do I mean that in a bad way. He has a personality that is just all-in. He commands a presence in a room and holds the interest of anyone around him listening to his booming voice tell a story and watching his face light up with excitement when he gets to the good parts. He's beautiful, standing only at five foot seven, but with bowed muscular legs and broad shoulders, he could have easily been a wrestler. He wasn't though, as he grew up as a hockey player in Minnesota where from the time that he could get out there on skates, he lived by the creed of protecting his teammates and showing no mercy to his opponents. He protected who he loved and be damned to those who were left on the outside. His ocean eyes, Italian olive skin and playful grin had me from the first time we went out dancing.

When we were dating, I felt special. I felt protected. He was proud. This feeling hung around for quite a few years too, but then life set in.

We were young parents working our asses off to provide for our dreams for what our future family was supposed to look like. Dates get replaced with trips to the grocery store and romantic trips away are replaced with family vacations. Like most young couples, we worked two jobs each for a while, just trying to propel ourselves forward in life. This led to being tired, which led to arguing. Money was always an issue, feeling like there was always a medical bill that needed to be paid or the kids needed something for school that we hadn't budgeted for, or a car would break down.

For many years, this is just how we lived, just functioning, sacrificing ourselves for our daughters, hoping that eventually it would all be worth it. They would grow up, we would get them off to college and our lives would return to what they were together before we had kids, a second life would begin. But things don't always follow the well intentioned yet grueling path that you lay out, do they?

After we had been married for the better part of ten years, there was a sudden shift between us. At the time, Gage had taken a job that had required him to travel for training a lot. The girls were still young, and looking back, I know that he has always regretted those years because he missed out on so much time with them. There is nothing more gut-wrenching than the memory of Shiloh at about eight years old, following him down the long driveway at the cabin on her bike, waving and crying her heart out as he drove away, not to be seen again for another week, as five-year-old Maisey stood with her blanket in the driveway waving her little chubby hand in the air, the evening breeze tousling her majestic curls. But the time spent apart had another long-lasting effect that would rear its ugly head later in our marriage. By him being gone all the time, in order to survive, my life had to move on. So, I fell into the role of a single parent.

Everything fell on me at the time, and for many years after. If the toilet broke, I had to learn how to deal with it, figure out who to call. If it snowed six inches overnight, I had to make sure I got up early enough to get us out the next day. I tracked the money, I paid the bills, I made all the appointments and drove to all of the dance lessons. I also began to harbor a resentment towards him, although unknowingly at the time. Having to be a single parent, a fiercely independent woman was not something that I had signed up for.

I remember when we were dating, early on in our relationship, we would talk about our lives, the way that we grew up. He told me stories of how he and his friends would fiercely protect and defend his mom on different occasions and how she depended on his father and him for all of the 'manly' things that needed to be done around the house, while his mom and sister would lounge in the pool or go shopping.

This was a stark difference to my world where I had no brother to look towards for help with the 'manly' things. My dad worked a lot to get ahead and we moved a lot so most of the time we had no family close by to help with anything. My sister and I did the jobs around the house that boys would do and my mom was the one who mowed lawns, shoveled snow, hung shelving units and paid the bills. I remember thinking back then, when we were talking about life and getting to know each other, how amazing it would be to have a feeling of just being protected and taken care of as a woman. And for the longest time, I did. Gage and I were a united front and blazed trails with the best of them.

But life happens. Guilt, panic and anger happen. I really think that at some point, Gage began to worry about me being able to take care of myself, being able to take care of the girls when he was away. This is when the rug was first cruelly ripped out from under my feet. During this time, when he was gone a lot, we had a house that we were renting as we were trying to sell it. We had rented it out to a guy that we knew, a brother of one of Gage's friends. Long story short, he had stopped paying rent, and with Gage being gone, it was left to me to try getting the rent money.

I was stressed, I was tired and I was lonely. I was trying to just hold my shit together, fearing that we wouldn't be able to make the mortgage payments on both homes unless I got that rent money back. The retaliation from our neighbors, who had been what I thought were close friends, was catastrophic. They lashed out at me and called me every name under the sun. I was heartless and a bitch because I didn't acknowledge that our renter was going through a hard time. I reached out to Gage over the phone, expecting him to have my back, as he always did, expecting to shoulder some of the burden. Instead, I got the biggest slap in the face, the biggest, 'Fuck you' that I had never dreamed flying my way.

With a tired and monotone voice, Gage said to me through the phone that night, "I'm not your Prince Charming, Max, not your knight in shining armor. I told you, don't ever get yourself into situations that you can't get back out of. You deal with it."

I know in my heart that he must have been coming from a place of being stranded, a place of exhaustion. I knew that in my mind. My heart didn't know though. In one phone call, everything that I thought I knew about my marriage had shattered. I felt the air being sucked out of the room and felt my soul curl up in the corner of the room in the fading evening sun and lick my wounds in utter defeat. I had been stripped of my armor, left with no protection. I was naked to the elements and terrified. I was all of this, plus had two little girls that depended solely on me. So, I sat in sadness that night, mourning the marriage that I no longer had to my best friend, and arose the next morning a warrior for these girls, determined to be able to survive the world alone.

That's how we lived our lives for a few years, and although I began to thrive as an independent mom, Gage no longer fit in when he did come home. He realized that in order for us to be able to make it when he was away, we had to learn how to live without him, out of survival. So, we did. We had a routine; I had my own rules and my own ways of discipline. Because of this, when he came home, he felt completely out of place. By him forcing me into a position of having to depend on myself with no safety net, he had helped to create a divide in our marriage.

Soon enough, he could see that his being gone was forcing that divide to rip us wide open. That's when we decided to move to the small town we are in now, the place that was home to all of my childhood memories, where my family was from. We sold our home, and lived short-term at the family cabin on the lake until we could move into my grandma's farmhouse. He took the job as a city cop and I found my way into the local DHS chapter. For a while, our life had gotten back on track. We paid off debts, saved money and bought our little crown jewel of a house, paying cash to build Gage the garage of his dreams.

Our girls grew up, and up until this last year, our life plan that we had so meticulously crafted was starting to take shape. We knew when we would retire, what our pensions would look like, the year we would pay our home off and started dreaming about vacations that we would take, once again alone, just us, the way we started out. We had looked forward to finding each other again, living out the second half of our lives.

When He entered our lives, the strain that it put on our marriage was apparent. We didn't agree on how to deal with anything. The timing was also off because during this time, Gage was going through some midlife crisis type of thing that had nothing to do with our girls or our marriage or even Him and the stress He brought. For twenty-eight years with Gage, he had never been overly emotional, never really a romantic kind of guy.

Suddenly, I was walking on eggshells around him. He was emotional and needed me to reassure him all the time. He became clingy and physically needed to be hugged and touched all the time. He smothered me, if I am being bluntly honest about it. I suppose that the timing couldn't have been worse for him to be going through his personal hell, because I was too busy trying to save our daughter and also mourning the loss of two grandparents at the time who had died just ten months apart.

I was angry too, because for an entire marriage, he forced me to be independent, starved me of any type of an actual romance or the safety of being protected and taken care of, yet now he expected me to do an about face and produce these things for him. It wasn't fair. I was pissed and felt like I just didn't have time to deal with him too. It hurt to see him so lost, but it hurt worse knowing he was expecting me to be his savior when I couldn't save myself.

As I sat on my bed in the cage looking out at the bright sky, I felt my heart race as I thought of Gage. I felt my exhausted eyes fill up with tears that once again began to roll down my face.

"This wasn't where we were supposed to end up. I never meant to lose you along the way..." I spoke in a hushed tone to no one. As I sat there, my heart began to flash through all the snapshots that I have saved up from him, all of the good times. I could see him laughing on the boat, kid in his lap, beer in his hand. I saw him leaning over his red 1987 Camaro while Shiloh was standing by his side. We are at my prom dancing away to Bon Jovi's *I'll be There for You* one minute and on the dance floor of our wedding dancing to George Strait's *I Cross my Heart* the next. He is holding his first born by my hospital bed. He's sitting in the NICU with Maisey. I grin at the thought of him doing a father-daughter dance for Shiloh's dance class and can see him teaching the girls how to run their snowmobiles.

He's laughing while walking into the sunset on a nude beach, calling to me over his shoulder, "You coming with or just going to stand there." After he stripped behind a palm tree. We are laughing in Las Vegas after riding a roller coaster on the top of a hotel. He's trying to teach me to ski. He's sitting next to me, holding my hand at the funeral for my grandfather. He's coming home from work after being gone for a week, excited just to hold us close again.

I lay back on my bed in the cage as I let a lifetime of memories flood my heart and take my brain captive for a little while. I had never forgotten all the good, even when things had gone so bad. I knew who the man that I married was and knew what our lives were supposed to be. At some point though, this past year, I let him go.

My memories had now caught up to speed and I was in a dark cell now thinking of the darkest of times.

"God damn it Max, what do you want from me? I can't fix this! She has broken me," he whispered against the backdrop of tears as we sat in the backyard arguing once again. We had been cleaning out the garage, trying to get rid of all the wedding items left over from Shiloh's wedding. I had been drinking, which was already a point of contention those days because in order to save his own health, Gage had already sworn off alcohol. Although he was doing well avoiding it, he still held on to an underlying anger when people around him drank. It wasn't that he couldn't have alcohol, it was that his liver had decided to start shutting down last year due to his diabetes, so alcohol was no longer his friend, unless he wanted to be looking at a transplant eventually.

At this point, we had already been arguing hardcore for weeks, about her, about Him, about where we are in life and how to deal with what we were going through. There just comes a point in life when something has to give. People can only bend so much before they break. And boy, did we shatter.

"Gage, what am I supposed to do here?" I remembered shouting at him in the garage, a glass of wine in one hand and a bouquet of flowers in the other. "It is all I can do daily to get to work without crying and trying to stay focused and then make it back home in one piece. I lay awake most nights terrified of how all of this might end, scared for her and what she is going through, exhausted from arguing. I am terrified because I just don't think that I can be what you need any more. I can't save you when I am drowning too," I cried while the wine warmed my soul.

"I want you to care, Max!" Gage shouted back, slamming his hands down on the truck he had been tinkering with. "I want you to give a damn about me, about us! Whatever happens with Maze, that's her call, her life. We are still here. Shiloh is still here. There is a whole life to live out there and yet we are sitting here just pissing it all away!"

"Pissing it all away? Gage, I am fighting to save our daughter! Our life *never* included a future without her in it! I may not know what's going to happen, but I can tell you that I couldn't live with myself if I didn't at least *try* to save her."

I can still feel the air painfully being sucked out of the garage and my heart came to a faltering pause as he quietly echoed, "And my life never involved losing you, Max, yet here we are."

Chapter 14

And We All Fall Down…

I thought that writing all of this would be a little more cut and dry, a way to just explain myself, but I am seeing now after I have asked for my second legal pad to write on that there needs to be more clarity of our past in order for the courts to truly understand where we were coming from and why I had no choice where my actions were concerned. I don't quite think I have made it clear enough yet where the pain comes in, where the fear resides and why… What we were truly up against as far as protecting her from Him…

I was deep in slumber in the harsh quietness of the night, after fighting the demons in my mind like I do every other night. Gage was next to me, the snoring apparatus strapped to his face.

When my phone rang out of the darkness, it took my heart a quick second to get pumping again. No one calls in the middle of the night. No good news is ever given over the static of darkness in the latest of the witching hours. Life doesn't happen like that.

"Hello," I half shouted into the phone after my fingers frantically managed to find the button to answer the call in the darkness. I was not mentally prepared for the words that would haunt my heart that crept from the dark echoes of the phone next.

"Mom," a tearful and frightened Maisey was whispering into the phone. "Mom, I called 911."

For what felt like an eternity, but really was only a few seconds, it was like the air had been sucked out of the room and my lungs struggled to inflate. With all of the vengeance writhing through my body and the absolutely paralyzing fear and just plain pissed-off-edness coursing through my heart, I sat up, gripping the phone close to my ear so that I could hear this terrified child who was whispering to me in the night, across hundreds of miles.

This was the shit you are never ready for. You fear for calls like these almost as much as you fear for no calls at all. I live in a world where every phone call makes me hold my breath until I hear what is coming at me from the echoes on the other end. I have played scenarios over and over in my tired mind, along with how I would handle it, how I would react. With every middle of the night silence pierced by the ring of the phone, your heart starts to make deals with an unknown God. Is she hurt? Is she broke? Is she in trouble? Pregnant? At the police station?

Kicked out of school? As always, the underlying granddaddy of all fears, did He kill her yet?

I shook off the haze of my evening slumber and frantically called out to her, my body trembling. At least it was her voice on the line this time. At least she was still alive.

"Maisey, what? What's happening? Where are you?" I helplessly asked. It is an absolute gut-wrenching feeling to know that your kid is in trouble in the middle of the night and you are so far away that there isn't a damn thing that you can do to help... all you can do is captively listen to her cries...

"Mom..." she was quietly sobbing in hysterics at that point. "I just crawled into bed after studying and my window alarms went off in the living room! I ran to the bathroom and locked myself in with my stun gun and called the police. I think I hear something moving around out there Mom! Oh my God what do I do?" she quietly wept. It was in this moment that my heart was shattered yet again.

As a parent, your main goal in life is to protect your kids. You make sure their needs are met, always put your own needs last and ensure their safety. Give them an easy road, or at least as best as you can make it for them. When Maisey had made the decision to go to college a little over three hours away, we spent many hours searching through apartment listings and reviews online, made multiple trips out to the college town to look at properties and finally found one close to her school, yet as safe as we could find in a city that size. I remember thinking that I wasn't thrilled that the unit she had chosen was a ground level apartment, but at the time, she had a roommate that she had just met who was going to be going to school with her. She assured me that it was a great location because she could see her parking space from her apartment, it was located in the only family building and the apartment was right across the hall from the garbage shoot.

To ease my mind, we bought her a stun gun and window alarms for the apartment. I needed to know she was as safe as possible. The decision that she had made initially to move there was hard enough because *He* didn't want her to go. As possessive and controlling as He was, I knew it was only a matter of time before He chased her home. It was fine by me that my naive dear daughter believed that we were keeping her safe from strangers and unknown threats, when in reality the biggest threat she had in her life was the one that she shared her heart and bed with.

It wasn't that we were naive, it was just that we had tried to hang on to hope. We foolishly had believed that if we could just get her away from here, that she would survive. She would hopefully somehow find her fire and be able to rise from the ashes of the singed world that His caustic inferno had leveled. We figured that if we could just get her a few hundred miles away, maybe she had a fighting chance, maybe He would move on, and as harsh as it sounds, find a new girl to prey on. (I know, karma's a bitch and she will get me for wishing that upon anyone...)

What we hadn't truly bargained for was just how desperate He had become without her. She was his lifeline. She made Him whole, made Him feel like he mattered. She gave purpose to His bleak future and made Him feel important and needed. She was His crutch in life, the one thing that gave His perilous balance on the tightrope of life some stability. And she left. And He didn't like it.

I think deep in our souls, Gage and I knew that it was only wishful thinking that He would ever let her go willingly. At that point, we had been fighting this monster for almost a year and every time we would push, He would pull her closer. Our last line of defense that we had was just to get her out of town, get her one step closer to a future where she could truly be happy again, without being tied to the gates of His Hell. Without being manipulated, made to feel less than enough, made to feel weak and powerless.

I had broken down more than once in a fit of rage while holding my beautiful daughter's tear-streaked face and pleading with her to never become dependent on any man. She was stronger than that. I had built her better than that. But a narcissistic asshole knows which buttons to push and when to put on the pressure. He knew exactly what to say and when to say it. And in return, she learned to live with a little less oxygen, a little darker soul and a heart that found a slower pace. She had learned to exist in the mundane and survive the everyday.

Her senior year of high school was the year of 'should have beens'. She should have been hanging out with all of her best friends that she grew up with, hitting the keggers in cornfields and taking hits off joints down by the lake. It should have been a time that she focused on making all of the great last memories of high school, just like in all of the cheesy movies she always loved to watch. This was the year before she was going to spread her wings and leave the nest, the year before she became an adult and life kicked her in the ass. That's what senior years are for. The love, the fun, the nostalgia. Although Moby stood by her side that year, albeit on the outskirts, she missed out on it all (except for prom). Hell, I missed out on it all. I was robbed and it hurt.

Before He came into her life, I was preparing for all of the great parts of senior year! We would have a fun year full of lasts… last homecoming, last powderpuff, last year of marching band, last prom, last after prom party, last preparing scholarship applications in the middle of the night with her, the last graduation parties. And then my plan had been to go shopping with her like all good mamas do before their kiddos move off to college and shop for her dorm or apartment, get her fully stocked on supplies and groceries, and drive away fighting back my tears, heading back to our empty nest where Gage and I would then start the second half of our adult lives. Together. In love. Going on adventures. But this is *not* what fucking happened. This is not the way our lives fell.

I first noticed a change in Maisey about two months into their relationship. There were subtle changes of course, like dressing like a bum going to school and not wearing makeup any more. Suddenly she didn't curl her hair to go to work or school, and always began throwing it up in a bun. All too quickly my brilliant, funny and bubbly girl began to slide, then freefall into the dark abyss beneath her.

She dropped out of the marching band, which she had been in since the eighth grade. She quit the robotics club. She shortened her hours at work, which she had worked so hard to get her certified nursing certification in the first place. She stopped going out with her friends. She stopped showing up at family events. She became a ghostly presence in a home that, at one time, was so full of exuberant laughter and a big hug when you came in the door. She either began to give up on herself at that point or was so focused on taking care of and fixing Him, that she blocked out everything and everyone else.

Desperate times called for desperate measures and by the middle of her senior year, we were about as pathetic and desperate as a family could get. Right after Maisey turned eighteen, she began to run from us. She would stay at His Hell hole for days and weeks at a time. They would just hide out in His psychotic mother's basement doing who knows what. Her grades began to slip. She started to let go of her dreams, and began to make his Hell her reality.

It was during these hard months that I grabbed the reins of her future. She may have been temporarily blinded in what she wanted out of life, but I knew her heart and knew what she was capable of. So even with a heart full of pain and more anger coursing through my body than my body knew what to do with, I pressed on. I contacted teachers, watched her grades, and reached out to school counselors. I made sure every milestone was being hit and that at least on paper, it appeared as if she knew where her future was still leading too. I applied to colleges, posing as her.

It was tough to watch a kid have her spirit so broken that she would risk all that she has worked for her whole school career. This girl had worked since she was fourteen, started taking her college level courses her sophomore year of high school and had her mind set on an end goal of a master's in nursing so that she would be able to change the way people are cared for, be able to provide them with better care. The irony is that the very thing that she spent a lifetime building towards was about to fall down around her, all because her caring heart became a victim to Him.

I had hoped that if I could just keep making it look like she was fine on paper, maybe someday she would see what He had done and it wouldn't be too late for her, not too late to live the life she had imagined. This is why I would stay up late into the night finishing her papers that were due, reaching out to online study groups posing as her and filling out her scholarship applications. It wasn't that I was enabling her behavior, as Gage said that I was, it was just that I didn't have it in me to give up on her. There are some mistakes in life that once you make, you just can't recoil back from. I just tried my best to save her from that. I tried to shield her the best that I could, even if it was just on paper.

So there we were, me doing all of the schoolwork in the middle of the night so that she could stay in a deep sleep in the cave that He had entombed them in. You know the really shitty part? It didn't matter that I worked for the department of human services or that Gage was the town cop. When your kid is eighteen and doesn't want to come home, when she is scared and traumatized and being bullied and hiding from you just to keep the Beast happy, there isn't a damn thing that you can do about it. As parents, you have no rights at all any more. It's like eighteen is a magical number and the person that you love most in this life could throw herself off of this fucking planet and your hands are tied. All we could do was have wellness checks done, where a cop (not Gage) would go to the house and demand to see her in person, ask if she was OK and then walk away if she refused help.

Let me put this into a clearer yet gritty perspective for the people who may be reading this who have been blessed or lucky to not have had to dance with a demon like this... On one evening, Maisey called Shiloh crying. Shiloh knew something was wrong. Maisey was incoherent and not making a lot of sense on the phone. While she was talking, He was being belligerent in the background, either having an anxiety attack, mental breakdown or high on something and yelling at her. The last thing that Shiloh heard was her sister crying for help and Him screaming at her to put the fucking phone down.

After once again restraining my own husband so that he didn't go over there and put an end to this monster once and for all, we drove to the cop shop and spoke with the chief. He took two other officers and went to the house. Gage and I sat down the street in my Jeep with the lights off. In the dark, windows down, it was a calm night. We

239

could see that the only light in the house that was on was one in the basement, where they stayed. We watched as the patrol cars pulled up and did a walk around with flashlights around the outside of the house.

My body had gone numb. I just sat there with Gage in the dark thinking this can't be our lives. This can't be our daughter. I was terrified that He would come to the door. I was terrified no one would answer the door. Part of me prayed to the heavens that He would answer the door, weapon in hand so the officers could blow him away and end this tonight. The other part of me was more terrified that there was a real possibility that He may have killed himself this time, taking her with Him and that there would be no answer. I shuddered to think about a scenario where my husband's colleagues would have to tell him the grisly details of what they found in that basement.

After a few minutes of feeling like I was going to pass out because I hadn't been breathing, a shocking thing happened. His batshit crazy mama flew out of the darkness of the front door. It was so surreal because there were no lights to illuminate her from behind within the house, she just ran out of the front door and almost directly into the poor officer that was walking towards the door with his flashlight. All we could hear from a half of a block away was her screaming. I could see by the glow of the streetlight that she was flailing her arms around and could hear her yelling at the officer. After a few minutes of this, she went into the house and slammed the door, hard enough that we could hear it and it spooked the bats out of the tree directly above her decrepit home, them squealing against the calm darkness of night and flying off towards the glow of the moon over the lake.

It felt like we sat there watching that dark doorway for an eternity. Then, the door opened and my poor broken daughter emerged, like a scared puppy who had been beaten. I exhaled with all the air that I had left in my lungs with relief that she was still alive. We made it one more day.

But there would be no happy ending to this night. The night would end with Gage and I going home once again with nothing to say to each other and crawling in bed to face opposite walls. I would once again will myself to sleep by trying to remember who we used to be and try for a few blissful hours to forget what we had become.

We were told, before we headed home that night, that she looked OK, appeared to have no marks on her and didn't want to press any charges. The asshole was in the doorway behind her and confidently told the chief that He was tired of all of the false accusations that we are making towards Him and at this point we were bordering on harassment. He once again told the officers that it was actually Him who feared for His life as we had made life so uncomfortable for Him. He did not, however, intend on filing any charges against us.

In confidence, chief told Gage that Maisey's pupils were huge and he was confident they were both high on something. But living in a small town did have perks, and chief didn't want to derail the future of the little girl that grew up down the street and who used to stop and help him catch lightning bugs when she was little.

To live in a world where you know something is very wrong with your daughter and you know she needs help, but to have your hands tied is a whole new kind of hell. Families can't survive that. Marriages get torn apart. To lay in bed over three hours away as your little girl is locked in her bathroom with God only knows what on the other side of the door takes the darkness and terror of hell into a whole new context.

I sat there with the phone still pressed against my face, my mind drawing a blank on what I should say when she cried into the lonely night, "Mom, I'm so scared! What do I do?"

There is nothing in the world that prepares you for motherhood. There is nothing in this world that prepares you for this kind of heartache. Holding that phone in the middle of the night, knowing there was not a damn thing I could do to save her was the most hauntingly useless feeling a person could ever feel. It wasn't a rapist who had broken in. There would be no burglar to fend off. I knew immediately that night who had crept into the darkness, crippling her sanity and weakening her mind. What I didn't know for sure was what His intent was, whether He was just trying to spook her into moving home or actually hurt her this time.

"Oh my God! Oh my God, Mom! I can hear someone out there! I can hear them moving around in the living room! I don't want to die mom, please don't let me die!"

my girl was whispering into the phone while sobbing. My heart lay shattered into a million pieces as I slapped Gage in the shoulder to wake him up. He shot straight up in bed, grabbing for his 9mm and yanking the scuba gear off his head in one swift move, a force of habit.

"Maisey, when will the police be there?" I asked as calmly as possible. She gave me no answer as I was left listening to this child's breath on the other end of the phone, labored short breaths of terror. I could hear her fumbling with what I assumed to be her stun gun.

My body began to tremble as Gage shouted out, "What the hell is going on?"

My ears were ringing, head was pounding and I was trying to will her voice back onto the line while whispering to Gage, "I think He broke into her apartment! She's OK, locked herself in the bathroom with her stun gun and called the police."

Gage jumped out of bed, flipped on the light and began fumbling for his clothes. As I strained to listen for her voice on the line, I shouted at him, half-bewildered and half pissed off, "Where are you going?"

"Bringing her home!" was the last thing he said. It would be the last thing he would say to me for quite a while after this too.

I didn't go with. I have no reason as to why I didn't ride along with him that night, why I just let him go into the darkness to rescue her. I just did. Instead, I stayed on the line with her until the police got there. I listened across a very staticky line as she held her breath and ran to the

243

front door of her apartment that was down the hall from her bathroom, stun gun in one hand, phone in the other when the police arrived. I listened as she began to hyperventilate telling the police what had happened. I stayed on the line as the police walked through her apartment, noted broken glass, nothing was taken, and asked her if there was anyone that she would suspect of trying to break in, anyone that may be trying to scare her. I held my breath as she mentioned His name and then listed every reason she could think of to defend him. Then she hung up on me.

Gage had made it to her in record time, shaving almost forty-five minutes off the usual time in the middle of the night. He took her to a hotel and went back the next day with a U Haul. Her time at school was over. He brought his princess back home. This time, however, she was a very different girl who had a very different battle raging in her heart.

I sometimes imagine how that car ride home went. I have since heard bits and pieces from both of them, so I have a pretty good idea. She had lost her will. Maisey had given up. For as stubborn as she was, and as sure of herself she had always been, this had rocked her confidence. She was terrified and didn't want to be so far from home. In a way, He was getting what He had set out to do, get her back home. If He had just scared her enough, if He needed her enough, if He begged her enough... it was always fucking something. She was tired. We were tired. He was like the old irritating piece of gum on the bottom of your shoe that you just couldn't scrape off no matter how hard you tried.

I know that Gage tried to gently talk to her. I know that he told her how she shouldn't give up on being a nurse, or give up on herself because she was scared. He tried to assure her that there was always a way and that she was better than who He had broken her apart into. I know that at some point on their way home, serious talk gave way to what those two always ended up doing... Singing along to 80's rock on the radio. For a big chunk of those miles, there were no more words, no timeline. Just a dad and his daughter driving through the night with a truck loaded full of her life driving towards a new start at another life, singing their hearts out along the way. He rescued her.

Chapter 15

The Knight

As I paced back and forth in my cage, reliving each sorted detail of the past year, suffering through every suffocating memory while trying to decide exactly what needed to be included in this tale of ours, this 'confession' of mine, it was His voice that echoed in head, His cruel and compassionless face that kept chasing away all of the good stuff I was trying so desperately to cling to.

Working at the department of human services for years, I had seen my share of mental illness, unstable families and suicidal youth. Let me tell you that in all the years that I have dedicated my life to helping the helpless and orchestrating new starts and new lives for people, I have never once encountered such empty eyes as His. I had never encountered a person who was so skilled at playing the shitty hand of cards that he had been given in life, effortlessly manipulating systems and people in order to get the most he could out of this life without having to do much of the footwork to get it. Honestly though, it was the mask that He held upon his face that made my stomach churn every time I saw Him or even thought of Him.

When you first meet Him, He is nothing remarkable, no threat really. He's tall and slender, built like any other fifteen-year-old kid, with a blonde tuft of bangs that He tended to keep a little longer than the rest of His shaved head. His skin was smooth, no stubble like most twenty-five-year-olds would have. His face was slightly rounded, like a child. His blue eyes were slightly clouded, usually from being in a daze of prescription psychiatric medications or possibly drugs of a more recreational kind. He spoke softly at first, almost sounding somewhere between uneducated or just scared of life. He never made eye contact. He was, in passing, completely unremarkable.

Until... He lowered his eyes, looked up at you through a furled brow and spread that maniacal medicated joker of a smile across His lips, exposing the gap between his teeth that made him sound like He had a slight speech impediment at times.

Upon visualizing that face and the smile that haunts my heart, I had to run to the toilet in the corner of the room and throw up what little I had eaten. He was like a disease that entered your life so slowly, that you barely noticed him, but in time revealed just how devastating His effects could be. I grabbed the sides of the metal toilet bowl and violently heaved into it while wondering how many other asses had sat where my head was now hanging. It was there, with my chin perched on the edge of the dirty toilet bowl, gasping for air while feeling the slow burn of vomit trickle up into my throat that His unstable voice began shouting in my brain.

"I swear to God I will fucking do it!" I could hear Him screaming through the phone as she was sitting on her bed, exhausted and crying. It had been another night of arguing with her after she had returned back home, another night of trying to get her to see Him through eyes that were no longer dependent upon His approval, no longer hinged on whether He lived or died, no longer making decisions out of fear or guilt. But her will to survive always called her back and held her down.

She had tried to walk her own path, had tried so hard to hang on to her own dreams, but what she had wanted out of life had begun to be clouded or overshadowed by the stories that He spun and the future that He wanted. As I peered in on her from the doorway, my spirit was once again shattered and I knew that she would once again give in to her young heart, throwing herself on the sword to shield the beast yet again. He knew how to play her. He knew how to use her. He knew how to win.

"Please, don't hurt her! I'm on my way, just hang on, I'm coming," she pleaded into the phone as she hopped up off of her bed, turning to face me as she once again was going to put more miles between us.

"Damn it Mom... don't look at me like that! He needs help! I can't let Him hurt her!" she muttered through tears that all too frequently fell. Here we go again. The asshole had bought a dog, a little corgi. (This was the same breed that he would later talk her into buying while she was away at school so they could be the 'parents' of two corgis.) He had no home of His own, no full-time job, no sense of

248

responsibility, but He bought a fucking dog. He did it just to keep her closer. He claimed that He was so lonely when she had attempted to move away to school, that His anxiety and depression was so suffocating that He needed a dog.

He called it His 'therapy dog', but He has never been classified as a person who actually needed therapy, nor had this poor animal been through any therapy dog training. But as He was raised, all He knew how to do was try and screw the system. He knew that His mother's landlord wouldn't allow a dog but figured if He slapped the label 'therapy' on it, the landlord couldn't throw them out. (Hell, they were already screwing the landlord over, as His mama stopped paying the rent a while back, but then jumped on the pandemic train as soon as it became available. When *Covid* reared its ugly head, His mama stopped working, stopped paying bills and sat back and sucked the system.)

After Gage brought our girl (and *her* poor dog) back home, she had tried to start living her life again on her own terms. She started working again at the local care center that she was a CNA at before she left for school. She was starting to rebuild the savings account that He had helped her to spend. She had begun hanging out with her friends again, and Moby was coming home as often as he could on the weekends to see her. She had even begun looking into the local community college to transfer her classes and get her goal of nursing degrees back on track.

Things had begun to turn around for our feisty girl, we had almost begun to let our guard down. Almost.

That night, Maisey stormed out of the house, once again screaming at me in misplaced anger. She didn't want to be His savior any more; she didn't want to be His keeper. But He knew how to load on the guilt, make her feel responsible and bait her to come running back.

"Maisey please!" I screamed out at her in the driveway, once again giving the neighbors one hell of a show. "Just stay! Don't do this! Don't run to Him, He's not your problem any more!"

As she ran for her car, tears running down her face, blonde curls pulled up on the top of her head, she shouted over her shoulder, "He won't let me go, Mom, and I can't let Him hurt himself or anyone else, He's sick!" And she crawled into her car and took off. I stood in the driveway watching her pull away, my heart sick with the familiar feeling of fear and anger. She had taken nothing with her, only her phone. This meant nothing though, I knew that she could disappear for days with nothing but the clothes on her back, like she had done in the past.

With Gage gone, all I could do was go inside, curl up with the animals and wait for her to return. I sat there in disbelief of how far she had come, how hard we had all fought back to get to where we were again. To think that we were once again teetering so delicately on the edge of demise, that we were so close to losing her again, just made me cry. There was nothing I could do at that point besides let all the pain wash over me and let the tears fall. I had been in this state of disbelief and self-pity for a good hour when the phone rang. Once again, fear suffocated my heart as I terrifyingly looked at the number calling in on my cell phone. It wasn't the police. It wasn't Gage or Shiloh. It wasn't her... It was Moby.

I didn't even get words to form when I answered the call and the boy was already talking, rattling on about her and the asshole.

"So anyways, Max," he carried on. "After she called me..."

"Wait... wait... hon... slow down... Maze called you?" I blurted out confused. I had been so engulfed in a depressed state that I was having a tough time shaking off the brain fog that had set in.

"Max, listen, don't worry. I'm on my way home now," Moby said as I could hear him throwing things haphazardly into his car, rushing to get on the road. "Yeah, she called. She called me first when she was on her way over there. Do you know what that sick fuck said to her Max? Do you?" Moby was yelling over the traffic that must have been right outside of his dorm, a good almost five hours away. "He was threatening to kill the dog, Max! Can you believe that? Told her that if she didn't come see Him, He was going to kill his puppy!"

"My God..." was all I could push out of my lungs. The desperation. The fear of a life without her. He was finally at the end of what little rope He had left to cling too. This fear was too real, too close to home. We had always assumed that He was capable of awful things, even joked about how we were a made for TV movie, but this? This cut too close. His desperation was inching closer to some kind of an ending. I knew that he had kicked the puppy in the past, knocking a couple of her teeth out and we were almost certain that he had even poisoned the puppy before too, so that she would get sick and need Maisey to come take care of her. But this? To know that he was fully capable of making good on his threats, it made my stomach violently contract.

"Moby, I can call the police. Let me call the chief…" I began before being cut off by the young guy who was being forced to grow up way too soon, having to play a game that he never wanted to play in order to hang on to her.

"And say what, Max? That you heard He was threatening to hurt His dog? It's just going to piss Him off more. Listen, I am on my way home. Maze is going to keep sneaking away to call or text me, OK? No worries. She called me when she was on her way over and called me again after she got there. He took something and passed out in bed after screaming at her when she got there, then having an anxiety attack. She won't come home until she can get Him to the hospital. You know her, Max. She won't give up on a wounded animal. His mom's home too, so it's not like they are there alone," Moby finished as I could hear the sound of his windshield wipers going in the car.

"Moby, you don't have to come home, I can go over there, I can figure something out. Let me call Gage and see if…" I began again, but was once more cut off.

"I love her Max. She needs me, and I'm coming home. I'll call ya soon," he said before the line went dead. I didn't even get a chance to tell him to drive safe, to be careful or that we loved him. I knew that he would fly as fast as he could safely drive and would slay whatever dragons that got in his way to save the princess that claimed she didn't need saving.

I didn't know what to do. I couldn't go over there because His bat shit crazy mama would have me arrested for stalking. I couldn't call Maisey because she would know that Moby had called me and I would never rat him out. I couldn't call Gage because he would kill the kid and end up in jail himself. So, I dutifully sat in the living room on my favorite two-dollar rocking chair and waited for the phone to ring. It was excruciating. I passed the time by looking through photos and flipping through my social media apps. I wanted to just drink the night away, but then I would be of no help if someone did call. So I sat in a perpetual state of fear and anxiety, much like I had been living my life.

Another hour went by before my boy called me back. "So, He's still sleeping and she is just watching a movie in the basement with the dog," he began. "She's so tired of it all, Max. To listen to her talk just tears at my heart. Do you have any idea how hard it is to keep biting my tongue? I listen to her complain about Him, listen to all the awful things that He calls her and accuses her of... But I can't voice too much of an opinion because then I won't have

her either, and I need her, Max. I need her in my life."
Moby teared up and got quiet.

That sweet boy has been her punching bag for so long,
it wasn't fair. He had done more than his share of
consoling her in the middle of nights when he should have
been studying, gave up his own time of hanging out with
his friends just to be there to listen to her, and gave her
more attention than she has ever given him back. Still, he
hung on. She disapproved of every girl he tried to date,
very rarely took the time to compliment him and yet ran to
him every time she needed a confidence boost. Still, he
hung on.

"Oh Mobes… you are too good to her, but I am so
thankful. What are you planning on doing when you get
here? What is she planning on doing?" I asked, listening
to his windshield wipers swipe back and forth and silently
praying that he doesn't get in an accident on the way or get
a speeding ticket.

"Um… I'm not sure. I know she thinks He needs to
go to inpatient therapy again, so I guess maybe try to get
Him to go? I don't know. I mean, I don't give a fuck about
His ass, but she does. She's the priority here, I just want to
get her out of there safely and I suppose if that means that
I have to help the bastard get to the hospital, I will…"

"Be careful, kiddo. Don't get in over your head. If you
get there and it's too dangerous of a situation, call the cops.
Drive safe. Love ya kid," I said to the teenage knight in
shining armor that was riding in to slay the dragon that I
had been unsuccessful at demolishing. But it was what he

had said in his next breath that warmed me to my soul. I could hear the windshield wipers squeaking away on his windshield and his radio playing a little 80's rock when I heard the quiet voice call out to me over the line from about 200 miles away yet.

"You know what makes it so different this time, Max? This time, she's asking me for help, not pushing me away. Talk to ya later Mama Max, much love!" And his sweet voice was once again gone.

I wish I could tell you that he made it to her in time. I wish I could tell you that he rode in on his horse and drove the little asshole to the hospital and all was well. But life is never a fairytale and there is actually a shitshow around every corner.

What actually happened is that she did call Moby while he was on the road a couple of more times, the final time being when he was about a half hour out yet. The joker had woken up and was screaming at her for talking to Moby on the phone. He called her a whore, a cunt, a bitch. At one point, he actually threw the puppy at her and as she was catching the dog, he nailed her in the ribs with his bony fist. He was threatening to kill them all.

When Moby heard her yelp, he immediately dialed 911. Then he called me. I cannot imagine the pain and the fury that must have coursed through his body on that final half hour drive to make it home to her. By the time he got there, Gage and myself were already with her on the asshole's front lawn while law enforcement was speaking with His mama and loading Him up to take to the hospital.

Maisey had told us on the lawn that night, beneath a clear dark sky, with an eye that was starting to swell and dried blood around her nostrils, that she meant it when she said she was trying to move on with her life and that she didn't want Him back in her world again. However, she also wanted to see Him save Himself and get better.

"I don't want to be the reason, Mom. I will *not* be the reason He gives up on life," she told me while clinging to his malnourished puppy who was shivering with fear, wrapped in a blanket in her arms. I did have a moment of delicious retribution, however, that I relish for all it's worth.

The moment that Moby pulled up to the house, He started yelling at Maze from the ambulance stretcher as the paramedics were loading him in, "Run to him you whore, like you always do!"

At which point this triggered His also psychotic mama and she began yelling at us to 'get off her fucking property or she was going tồ file harassment charges against us and take that damn dog with you'! But our sweet boy just ran to Maze, silently wrapping his arms around her. You could see her body instantly relax into him as she clung to him with one arm, balancing the puppy in the other. When they were together, they were home.

As Moby stood there in the moonlight, holding her safely as the world was a chaotic fire around them, he kissed the top of her head, her messy bun of curls tickling his nose. He breathed in the glorious scent of her, smiled to himself and without even looking up, raised a defiant hand in the air to throw a big, 'Fuck You' sign to the asshole.

The kids headed back to the house a few minutes later after Gage determined that Maisey was going to be OK and didn't need any medical attention. Before Gage got into his car, I stopped him.

"Can't you just come home tonight? It's already so late and this was such a terrifying night?" I pleaded as I grabbed him by the arm, looking into his eyes. But it wasn't his eyes that I was looking into any more. He had become someone else who had also lost their way, unsure if I fit into his world any more.

"Not tonight, Max. Just go home with the kids, OK?" he said as he hugged me goodbye.

So, this was who we were now. When I pulled up into my driveway, I saw the house a little differently. It was my house with my things and my animals. I had always been an avid collector of things, bobbles, mementos and memories. This was something that always had driven Gage crazy, but now with the kids gone and Gage gone, the bobbles and photos and mementos were all that remained, almost like they were snippets of a life well-lived that now sat on shelves or were displayed in photo albums as reminders of my past. I am alone now in my little crown jewel of a home, a far cry from the way our lives were just a little over a year ago. And these little collections that I have hoarded are now what keep me company when the loneliness gets a little too hard to bear.

That night, however, I had a couple of the kids home, which I loved. I fell asleep in my room in the basement, hearing the voices of Maisey and Moby upstairs, as they talked well into the night. For one more night, my little house was alive again. I slept that night the best I had in a long time. I fell asleep thinking that just maybe we were getting back on track, just maybe we would make it after all, and not once did I worry about where my gun was when I was trying to fall asleep.

When I woke up the next morning, the house was still quiet, so I let the dog out and showered and got dressed. When I walked through the living room, Moby wasn't on the couch where he usually crashed when he stayed over. I headed towards Maisey's room and saw them through the door as I turned the hallway corner.

There on Maisey's bed, she was curled up into a tight ball, hair a mess, eye swollen. Moby was draped around her, one arm over her with the comforter, cocooning them from the world. The puppy was at their feet and began to whine when she saw me. I grabbed the dog and quietly slipped back out of the room to let the dog out. As I was standing outside in the coolness of the morning, the concrete driveway cold on my bare feet, I heard the sliding glass door creep open slowly behind me.

"Max, I am so sorry!" I heard a panicked Moby starting to say before I could even turn around.

"For?" I began to ask, but I already knew where this was heading. He was a good kid and never wanted to cause any disrespect.

"Max, you know that I *always* crash on the couch when I am hanging out over here. Like *always*. I never meant to..." the humble knight began before I cut him off.

"Seriously Mobes? Listen sweet boy... we have walked through literal hell this year. You just drove five hours home to rescue your best friend. So you crashed in her room. That seems pretty small in the grand scheme of shit that I have to worry about, don't you think?" I half laughed and looked at him.

"Do you have to use the term pretty small? I mean I like to think that..." he smirked and stopped talking.

"How is she Mobes... Like how is she really?" I asked, not entirely sure that I wanted to know the answer.

As we walked around the back yard waiting for the dogs to run around and finish their business, he told me that they talked a lot that night. She felt depressed, full of anxiety and just plain scared. After everything that she has gone through, she felt like she was just exhausted and mentally not right.

"So what does she want then, Mobes? What's going to pull her through this?" I asked before we headed back inside.

"I think that I have her talked into going over to Five East again. She thinks some therapy will do her good. She just needs a break from her life and needs to learn how to cope, I think. She's going to be OK, Max. She's going to be just fine. Our girl is a fighter. And she's kind of bossy, but I love her." He grinned.

That afternoon, she was packing up some things to take with her before heading over to be checked in at the therapy unit. Sitting in the living room, I could hear her chattering away to Moby in her room while trying to put on a brave face. Her soul had been through so much in such a short amount of time, that I was happy to hear that she could giggle at all any more.

"But what if I don't want to stay there, Mobes? You think I can just leave?" she asked while cramming her favorite hoodie in a bag on top of her nail polish and a few pairs of underwear.

"Yeah goofball," he answered. "You are voluntarily going in for treatment, they aren't forcing you to stay there," he said as I saw a stuffed giraffe go flying across the room towards her. "Do me a favor though, don't fall for any hot guys while you are relaxing in there, OK?"

She laughed and walked over towards him. I could hear her crying and glanced that way. They were standing in the center of the room now, his taller thin body with long arms, just holding her as they swayed back and forth.

"Don't be scared, Maze. This will be good for you," Moby said in a hushed tone, never letting go of her.

They stood there like that in the silence of the house for a few minutes until a very small voice whispered from deep within his arms, "I love you, Mobes."

There was a stunned silence for a few seconds and I am sure that he was grinning as he replied, "I have always loved you too, Maze, and I always will."

She was still clinging to him when she asked, "What if I hate it in there and I want to run?"

And without missing a beat, that charming boy just kept holding her in his arms, making the world seem safe as he whispered back, "You can always run home to me, kid."

Chapter 16

Solace

I am not well. My body has withstood crippling bouts of anxiety and mental anguish, the unbearable effects of utter heartbreak and physically I now resemble either a homeless older woman or a person that should be kissing the walls of a delicately padded room. My breaths don't even come easy any more, for I struggle to just focus on forcing my lungs to take shallow weak breaths. I feel a stifling achy pain in every joint and my scalp even hurts when I run my fingers through my thinning hair. The skin on my body has formed angry red patches that feel as dry as sandpaper, and I cannot scratch them enough with my brittle peeling nails.

To think that I used to be a proud woman who would never leave the house without a full face of makeup and would die if anyone ever caught me cleaning house without a bra on. It's hard to fathom, if you are an outsider looking in, how a series of unfortunate choices can burn your life to the ground and attack your body with utter disregard to any form of defense that you had been trying to conjure up.

As I sit in this cell for this last evening, struggling to get my final thoughts down on paper, it isn't lost on me the shock that my body and soul have had to endure over the course of the previous year. And really, I only have myself to blame for all of it. I was too invested. The day that I gave birth to that precious girl, my destiny had already been set into place. There is no fighting destiny. Even now I can close my eyes and be back in that hospital room in the early morning hours. I am holding her, my Magoo, my little Maisey Alexis in the deep blue sea… Her warm tiny little body is pressed against my heart as I fed her a bottle while watching the early morning news.

"There will be many nights like this little one. Many nights that I will hold you in the middle of the night, rock you while you cry, feed you when you are hungry and stare at you in awe, just like I have done with your sister. The middle of the night will always be our time, when the world is quiet and it's just you and me. We will see many early morning news shows and trashy middle of the night movies. But it's OK my Magoo. It's OK because if I do my job right, someday you will grow up and leave me, but I will always have these moments, feeling your heartbeat with mine in the middle of the night, when all was right with the world," I can remember saying to her, exhausted at five a.m. laying in the hospital, just her and I against the world. It's a fiercely intoxicating feeling to be a mother. And I can tell you now that it is even more satisfying to come full circle and to have battled the beast and won, saving her from a lifetime of hell.

Looking back now, seeing where I ended up, one would have to ask if I had any regrets, would I do anything differently? The only regret that I have in my life was ignoring my beautiful yet stern husband in the first place when he tried to stop her from dating the joker. After all, the demise of my marriage, the breakdown of my family and the mental anguish that turned into a painful descent into hell for Maisey all began with that one wrong decision to allow her to date a man six years older than her when she was seventeen. That is my regret. That is what eats at my heart every day, makes me want to puke when I try to eat and now haunts me at night while I sleep.

There are no other regrets. Let me make this crystal clear, I am only here because of what I had chosen to do. My daughter was too young to fully understand what a narcissist was, to fully be able to comprehend the danger that she was in, or how to get out of it. She was scared, she was trapped, she was depressed and she had been taken advantage of. On the day in question, I saw all the pain that he had caused and realized she had no other way out. I had made the decision in a fraction of a second to protect my family, and I regret nothing.

So here it is, the part where I confess and leave no questions unanswered. It is my hope that the judge, jury and my community will read all of what I have written and at least have compassion as to what we had been put through and how we had fallen apart, to bear witness as to how a family who had been a pillar of the community could fall so fast and be forced to fight in order to survive.

I do not ask for forgiveness, because in my heart I have done nothing that I need to repent for. As I have stated previously, I do offer condolences to His mama, only on the grounds that she is a mother who has lost her child, and I can relate to that, since her child almost made me lose mine. But do I apologize for the act itself, for taking a life to save my daughter's? Ask any mother to choose between any other life and their child's, and they will come out swinging for their child like a deranged uncaged animal every time they feel that they have been threatened. When it comes to protecting your family, there is no room for apologies.

On the day in question, November 14, 2021, I had just gotten off work at the DHS department and had planned on stopping to get groceries. On my way to the store, my phone rang and I noticed that it was Maisey on the caller ID. When I answered, there were sounds that didn't connect from my ears to my mind immediately. There was no 'Hi Madre', from my beautiful girl's voice. There wasn't even a, 'Hello'. The call had been made in panic, maybe in secret? I am guessing the phone was then dropped or tossed to the side.

As I pulled the car over to the side of the road, more than a few miles from home, the muffled sounds were lining up and coming into focus in my scattered brain. I could hear my little dog, Bug, barking in a panicked frenzy. I could hear Him screaming at her, not fully making sense. I could hear her struggling, there were splashing sounds. Her voice only made a few small words that echoed through the panic and the muffled tirades being thrown out around her. The only words that I focused on, the only words that stuck into my brain and woke me up, becoming the force that would push me to the edge of all sanity were, "Mom... Mom..." And that was all.

There was a little more noise of scurrying around and some more splashing sounds when I heard Him scream, "Fuck!" as He started whole heartedly sobbing. Then the phone went dead.

From that second that I heard my sweet, beautiful daughter's voice call out my name, it was as if I went on autopilot. There was a very warm calmness that ran over my body, maybe it was shock? It was as if all the years of watching late night crime shows with my daughters triggered something in my brain and fiction just crashed into my reality. I don't even remember pulling back onto the road, but I do remember dialing Moby's number, who had been home on mid-winter break.

When the poor kid answered, all I could scream out was, "She's in trouble at home, I'm coming, go to her now!"

I can't tell you how long it took me to drive those few miles home, what I was wearing that day or if I ran a red light along the way. I do remember that the car was silent as I drove, and I could hear my heart pumping, echoing in my ears. I can tell you that it almost felt surreal, like I was in the middle of living someone else's life. I had almost the same feeling as when I was doing a late-night lake lap, contemplating if I should just let go of the steering wheel. There are moments in life that are so painful that they just make you want to close your eyes in the hopes that it will all just go away. This was one of those moments. But there was no looking away.

No mother should walk into the scene that I had to bear witness too. When I pulled the Jeep up into the driveway of my little cozy crown jewel of a house, I could hear the screaming coming from inside as soon as I opened the car door. I could hear the dog barking as I leapt from the car, leaving the driver's side door wide open. I noticed right away that the screaming voices were those of His and Moby's. And the thuds that were hitting my living room walls were their bodies being thrown about. One voice was definitely missing.

As I swallowed the hard lump that had manifested itself into my parched throat, I could no longer stifle back the tears as I ran through the side door. The scent of blood, strong with iron hit me immediately, before my eyes could focus in on the carnage.

There was so much blood. I could hear Moby screaming at Him, yelling, "What the fuck did you do? What did you do?" He kept saying over and over.

For His part, His only response was to throw punches back at Moby and scream in his face, "It wasn't me! She did it! She did it! I even called the cops, they are coming!"

I can't really tell you what else they were saying to each other, I don't even know how badly they had each been hurt. Hell, I don't even know if any of my living room was left standing at that point. I do vaguely remember the cat running past me and that only registers because my brain managed to take a snapshot of her running by, leaving bloody pawprints on my ivory living room rug. As I headed towards the direction that she just ran from, I also noticed my beloved tiny dog, perched on the couch, barking ferociously at Him, shaking in anger, protecting us with all her little eleven-year-old six-pound body could muster.

And then my world collapsed. All the oxygen in my lungs was sucked out. I saw her. To see your daughter, one of the greatest lights of your life, laying in a crumpled heap in the hallway outside of the bathroom like a pile of wet bloody clothes, actually stops your heart. You cannot breathe. You cannot scream. I do believe that for a very short space in time, your soul actually leaves your body to float above and assess the situation. Then, in a rush of fury and panic, you are thrust into the nightmare once again.

As I grabbed her to roll her over, a few things immediately stood out to me. There was blood all over. And she was soaking wet. When I rolled her body towards its side, I could see that her beautiful face had been beaten, right cheek bone had swollen into a violent and angry purple hue and her lip was split in half. It was then that I realized that she hadn't been wearing her red plaid shirt, but it was actually her beige plaid shirt that had been covered in water and her own blood.

I looked up, glancing into the bloody bathroom and could hear the tub faucet still running as the red stained water began to lap over the edge of the white porcelain tub and flow down onto the gray tiled floor, soaking the sage green bathmat. I can't recall a moment of the drive home, but the details of that scene are etched in my mind no matter how hard I try to forget them.

I frantically felt for a pulse, which was weak, but there. I could feel her shallow breaths on my cheek as I put my face next to hers. As I was leaning into her, I noticed her arms. I pushed the unbuttoned blood and water-soaked sleeve up over her forearm. She had an angry four-inch slice running vertically from her wrist towards her inner elbow on her left arm, while the right arm wasn't as methodical and not as clean of a cut.

"Suicide? Hell no!" I said to no one as the fighting ensued a few feet from me in the living room.

"You son of a bitch!" I heard Moby cry out as he landed a right hook to the left side of His head. My old wooden planked floors trembled as He hit the floor. I don't remember calling for an ambulance, but I remember having the phone in my hand and hearing the voice of a dispatcher on the other end as He rose and began pummeling into poor Moby's sides, screaming at him,

"She's fucking nuts! She tried to kill herself, you asshole! I found her like that! I pulled her out of the tub and was trying to save her dumb ass," he shouted as Moby tried to fight back.

"Kill herself? Did you see her face? You beat the shit out of her! What did you do to her, you freak? You psychotic sick fuck! Why couldn't you leave her alone?"

Moby shouted out before He threw him back to the ground. The vibrations of the floorboards had vibrated the walls, knocking down my prized antique clock that had been in the family for generations, shattering the bubbled glass and splintering the walnut case into shards of nothing onto the floor. He was straddling Moby now, His hands locked around his throat.

Moby was thrashing about underneath Him as He spoke in an eerily calm and quiet tone, "She wouldn't listen. We aren't over. We will *never* be over. I don't care if I have to fight my way through every last one of you, I will be with her." He hissed, inches from Moby's face as He continued to block his airway. I could see Moby's feet violently kicking about, body writhing on the floor, desperately trying to cling to life. Maybe it was the juxtaposition of Him calmly perched above Moby, trying to squeeze the life out of him that hurled me forward, launching me into the fight. We were all clinging to life at this point, and like hell was I going to let Him destroy us all.

I don't remember going into Shiloh's old room. I don't remember moving the box of leftover tablecloths from the wedding to take out the secure box that held one of my loaded nine-millimeter handguns. I do remember having to step over my daughter's lifeless, wet bloody body. I do remember cocking the gun. I do remember worrying about taking the shot because I didn't want to accidentally hit the dog, cat or wound Moby. I do remember seeing Him jump off of Moby when I screamed at Him to get off. I remember the deranged look in his eyes as He looked at me in horror as I stood in the center of my living room, gun cocked and aimed at His chest.

But what I remember most in that moment is recognizing the life that He had already taken from us. This was the evil that had splintered our family. He is the monster who stalks us while we sleep. He is the fear that hangs in every empty dark room, the stranger in the parking lot, the ghost in your home. We fear being alone, we fear things that go bump in the night, window alarms that go off and who has my stolen house keys. We fear living apart and losing each other. Our lives have spiraled out of control at the hands of this monster. And yet look at Him.

Before me had stood an almost twenty-five-year-old trembling bean pole of a 'man', which I use the term loosely because this is no man at all. He is, and has been, broken. Mentally unstable, abusive homelife growing up. He lives in His mama's basement, collecting disability for His mental issues. He works when He feels like it with no real goals in life, spending any money that He makes on eating out and expanding His high-tech gaming system. He scams every system that He can to get what He wants. He uses people, controls them, destroys their families and their self-worth, drains their bank accounts, then trolls the high schools looking for His next victim. A narcissist. An abuser. A loser. A drug addict. A manipulative asshole who has no soul, no conscience. He nearly killed my sweet girl, and He will not stop.

I could hear Maisey gasp for air as the sirens came rolling down our street. I could see the fear in His eyes before He turned to run. And I can recall the crimson stream that burst out of His back, exploding into a beautiful fireworks pattern across His already wet and bloodied t-shirt as my bullet hit its target. No regrets.

So there you have it. I confess to killing the man I shall not speak of, the boy that ruined our lives. It was me. And I hope that people will understand why it had to be done. I was protecting us. I was protecting her. I have done my job.

Bud just walked by my cell, letting me know that it's time to turn in for the night. Bud is one person that I do feel sorry for. He is such a good man, and it doesn't seem fair that he will be the one to find this, to find me when the sun comes up. I hope he can survive all of this. I hope they all can. Because what is the point of me doing what I did if nothing good comes from it?

As I have alluded to, I have lost my faith along the way, so I am no longer big on the whole prayer thing. I am big on wishes and manifesting what you want into the world, in the hopes that somewhere your wishes will be heard. So on this night, my last night, there are things that I want to put forth into the world.

First, my sweet Gage, husband of almost twenty-five years. I wish for him to be able to find his forever again, she has to be out there. Let her be someone good and kind and beautiful. Let him look at her the way he used to look at me. Let him feel needed and valued again. I want him to feel loved. I want him to have his family back and to be able to experience the joys of being a grandpa that the kids will call Grumps. And let him continue being a good cop, because the world needs more men like he has always been. He will move on, first for his girls, then for himself. I will be just a whisper in the echoes of his life, but hopefully he will smile someday when he thinks of me. Let him find joy in life again, because he always likes an adventure and winging it in the world was what we were always good at.

To my Shiloh, I wish for her to have the world. Let her be one hell of a teacher, let her have fun. Let her and Brody have a healthy family and build memories together. I want her to never be scared to venture out into the world and always try new things because the world is beautiful and scary and worth venturing out into. Her life will be the stuff of storybooks and family will be her priority. She will do great things, and do them with courage, dignity and grace.

And to my Maisey, the most important thing I can hope for her is that she finds herself again. Along the way, she has begun to doubt herself and forget how talented she is. She stumbled a little and forgot who she is and where she comes from. She will be one hell of a nurse, and I hope the area that she specializes in just comes naturally to her. I want her to find the path that makes her heart the happiest, and figure out where Moby fits in to that. Most of all, I hope she holds no guilt. We all face difficult paths in life and sometimes don't make the best choices. It's how you recover and move on from that, how you mend broken bridges and go on laughing and loving and living after it all that matters. May she always know her value, hold her family close and keep loving the people in this world with her gracious heart.

They were always my favorite hello and will be my hardest goodbye.

Chapter 17

A Heart Full of Snapshots

I was satisfied with what I had written. At least the world would know the why behind what I had done. I was lucky that I was a cop's wife, considered to not be much of a risk, as I said previously, it affords you some luxuries. Such as the department honoring my request to allow me to put my confession in writing, to get all my thoughts down on paper with a ballpoint pen on a couple of wide ruled, dogged eared old legal pads that had been scavenged out of the back of a desk somewhere within the department.

Although I had felt accomplished, like my mission had been completed and fruitful, I still didn't feel like it was complete. I sat there at the cold metal desk on the equally cold metal stool that was attached to the floor, staring down at the cracked and speckled gray concrete beneath my feet. The loneliness crawled up through the floor and wrapped itself around my shoulders, cradling my back and sending goosebumps down my arms. My heart felt hollow. My mind was finally empty, aside from the nagging feeling that there was something that I had forgotten, something that I hadn't checked off my wild to-do list that would lead me to my peace.

As I was giving in to the loneliness and getting myself mentally prepared to end this hellish nightmare, something hit my soul with a pissed off fury and I grabbed the pen. I flipped to the last page in the legal pad and ripped it out, placing it neatly on the top of the confession that I had so intricately crafted. With a blinding and painful anger coursing through my soul and all the hate in my heart desperately trying to escape my soul through the tip of a pen, I frantically scribbled the following dedication to Him on the front of my statement in garishly large letters.

The writing no longer resembled that of mine, or any sane person. These reflected the last written words of a woman brought to the edge of sanity, crippled by pain, fear and loathing, desperate to get the last word. One final call out to him, wherever his heartless soul may be. This was what I had left out. I needed closure with Him.

And so I scribbled the following dedication…

To Him, He knows who He is. I will never breathe life into His name or bring Him any form of notoriety by letting His vile name be spat from my pursed lips or escape into the world with a flick of a pen or a few clicks of a keyboard. Without Him, our story would have been much different, it would have lasted longer. I have told Him a thousand times that I would never give up on my daughter, I would save her at all costs, and that He had poked the wrong Mama Bear. Now I look forward to dancing with Him in hell.

As I scribbled those last few words, there was a relief that had calmed my soul. I had righted the wrongs. I had saved them all. I was done. I had the last word. Exhausted, I laid the pen down and rose from that cold hard stool in the cold lonely cell that had held me captive for only a few days, yet would become my final resting place. My soul was so tired. My bones ached. I padded softly across that gray, speckled cement floor and took one last glimpse out of the window.

In the darkness, I could once again see stars poking out of the night sky. In my mind, I thought about what those stars look like over our little lake, as people went on their evening lake laps. What heartache would those stars see tonight around the lake, what problems would they lead the way in sorting out. Were there kids out at Farmers Beach secretly making out and having their first glorious taste of beer or their dad's stolen whiskey? Was there a young couple driving around dreaming about what their lives will look like in a few years after they just bought that sweet little cottage by the lake? Was there a mama out there driving around after another blow up with her daughter, driving the night away just to cry alone in silence and sort out her pain until she had the strength to drive back home and deal with what her life had become?

While fantasizing about the lake laps that I would never again have the glory of taking, I caught a glimpse of my reflection in the windowpane. I exhaled a heavy sigh that I could feel all the way down into my belly. What had I become? How is this pale bony reflection looking back at me through the glass with thinning hair and hollow eyes the same woman who just over a year ago was long distance running, planning a wedding, making future plans with her family and loving her life? How has one year done so much damage?

I raised my pale, boney aged hand to touch my cold pale cheek that had lost all fat beneath it, allowing my skin on my cheeks to sag almost like jowls. I ran my fingers under my bloodshot eyes to feel the hollowness that had sunk beneath my eyes, leaving an already deathly appearance to my expression. I ran my fingers through my once thick and glorious mane of blonde hair, only to feel the thinner graying hair that has been left to tangle in the wake of my downfall. I had been neglectful towards my body while trying to avenge my heart.

I walked over to my bedsheets and grasped one of the cold sheets in my clenched bony fist and gave a tug, as I thought to myself. I knew when I had made the decisions that I had, there would be no walking out of here free. I understood that when I confessed to what I had done, that I would be moved upstate to a larger, more secure facility while awaiting a trial that would have no good outcome. I knew that once I saved my family, once I danced in the darkness and took our future into my hands, that I would end up here. I had no plans to make my family suffer watching me caged for the rest of my life. They have lived through enough hell for all of eternity and I refused to put them through the pain of watching me linger in a cage and waste away.

They wouldn't be able to find their way forward to the light if I was holding them prisoners along with me in all this darkness.

With sure yet trembling fingers, I first folded the twin sized sheet lengthwise in half, just once, then tied one end around the leg of my bed, which had been bolted to the floor. This old building was plenty tall... but nowhere to hang anything from the ceiling. But with enough will power, I think that in the dark corners of my mind when I wasn't able to sleep in here at night, I formulated a crude plan that I believed would work, as long as I had the strength and courage to follow through.

I figured that if I tied one end of the sheet to the foot of the bed and tied the other end in a crude noose around my own neck, I would then be able to just roll over and over in bed, tightening the sheet until I passed out. If I covered myself in bed with the itchy blue wool blanket, it would appear that I was only sleeping, and dear Bud wouldn't find me until the next morning. I would help myself along, I had played out in my mind, by rolling over and over as many times as I could force myself to, then lying face down in my pillow, hoping to move the asphyxiation process along.

I kneeled there, next to my bed, tears escaping down my sullen cheeks. In the moments before I tied the sheet around my neck, there was a calming sadness that overtook my soul, one of loneliness and regret. If only I had never let her date Him. If only I had stayed as strong in my convictions as Gage had. But I wanted her to be happy. I wanted to believe that she could be strong, that we had raised her to know her worth in this world and to fight for what she deserved. Nowhere in my heart was there an inkling that she would have been overtaken and brought down by a cunning, demeaning narcissist. Never in my soul did I think I would have to do what I did in order to save them all.

I actually gagged as I tied the free end of the stained white sheet around my neck and crawled into bed. It felt like I was crawling into my coffin, like this was officially the end. I began to panic, thinking that I would never again see those sweet faces that I had grown in my belly for nine months and brought into this world. Never again would I feel her sand papered hands or kiss those squishy cheeks. I would never catch their scent as they walked away or stand in the doorway waving goodbye as they drove off into their next great adventure. I would never again see Shiloh's long blonde hair blowing in the wind as she effortlessly steered the boat to shore or hear them giggle over something insignificant that only mattered in sister code.

Now crying and heaving while trying to temper my breaths, I crawled under the covers. I hung on to the front of the crudely tied noose with my right hand and made two full rotations, rolling over in bed, causing me to be facing the ceiling once again with a tightened noose. It wasn't constricting yet though, I knew I had to roll at least once more for that, then be strong enough to roll one last time, so that I would be laying on my belly, face into the pillow.

I laid there in silence for a few minutes, searching and begging the darkness for the physical determination to finish this.

As I lay there, moments away from ending it all, alone and broken in the darkness of my cell, I closed my eyes and allowed myself a small reprieve. I let my heart bathe in the glory of their greatness one last time. As I curled my fingers around the noose that bit at my neck, memories began to drift across my heart, once again warming my soul and awakening all the parts of my heart and mind that I had forced to close down in order to be able to carry on after what I had done. My senses were awakened, and I smiled one last glorious smile though dry cracked lips as my girls danced through my mind like little lightening bugs in the night sky above our little lake...

I could see them, running through our big yard in the fall, dressed as a princess and her puppy, rolling in the leaves, our old big lab chasing them until they collapsed and giggled. I can see them in the sun, sprawled out laying on the boat with half-melted crayons and color books munching on grapes and bologna sandwiches. I can hear Maisey, all about three years old, asking me to rub her feet as we lay together on the couch watching TV. I see Shiloh's serious little face as a toddler singing her version of *This Little Light of Mine* in her sweet *Kermit the Frog* voice. I can feel the terror as Shiloh clung to me as doctors pierced her back full of needles for allergy testing and hear Maisey cry out for me when she was having her nose cauterized for those awful nose bleeds that she would get.

I lie there in the darkness, letting the tears freely flow down my cheeks as I allow myself to remember. I needed to feel them, to remember why I am here, what I have slayed the dragon for. The memories kept swirling in my mind and they were getting older now, flashes of Maisey in dance costumes twirling wildly on stage and Shiloh in her soccer uniform running down the field with her ponytail bouncing. The closeness and fun of feeling their bodies lie next to mine as we squeezed into too small of beds at their grandparents' cabins, talking about our plans for the next day at the cabin where, as Shiloh always said, there were no rules.

I relived every memory of every formal dance they had gone to, every dress, every corsage, every date. I saw the warmth in Brody's eyes staring at Shiloh on their wedding day and the way her whole body ignited when he was near her. I watched my kids, Maisey, Shiloh, Brody and Moby, just hanging out, content in my little living room, in our little home, giggling while watching an old movie and listening to Moby doing impressions of the old eighties characters. Their laughter seared my soul. Their faces were burned into my eyes. My heart burst. I savored these snapshots of our lives, grateful to have gotten the time that we had.

I kept my fingers locked at my throat, gripping the noose as I brought my feet up and positioned my body to get ready to turn. It was then that I saw my sweet Gage, the beautiful soul that he had been when we met when I was seventeen and he was nineteen. Those damn eyes and grin that Maisey inherited.

I could hear him call out to me, "Max, we are just so damn good at winging it." I could see the three of them now, Gage and his girls, laughing as they sat on cement donkeys holding fake guns while wearing Mexican sombreros in Mexico, a sign that read, 'Three Amigos' above their heads, giggling while patiently waiting in line to see the *Little Mermaid* at Walt Disney World and watching them run like three little buddies down the beach straight towards the ocean looking for seashells when we went to Florida. We were always good together. Life was always an adventure and we clung to each other. Until we had to let go.

I felt warm all over as I remembered Shiloh's wedding, the dancing, the love, the family. Her radiant smile when she looked at Brody, the way she giggled and spun her sister around on the dancefloor. Gage and I had done something right in life. These were wonderful little humans that we had created. The way that it all had to end shouldn't reflect on who they were, who we had been together, and who they still could be.

I think the loneliest place to be is without them. I hope they know how much they were loved. I hope they know that they were my greatest accomplishment and that if all I was given in this lifetime was twenty-eight years with Gage, twenty-two years with Shiloh and nineteen with Maisey, it was still a lifetime well-lived. We packed everything that we could into the time that we had together, and for that my soul is full. I wish we could have had more time. I wish our lives would have played out the way that Gage and I had dreamt of for those twenty-eight years. We almost made it… Just almost.

It was their sweet faces that I focused on. Those smiles, those eyes. It was their arms that I felt wrap around me when I realized it was time to go. They wrapped me in a warm embrace, and my heart could feel their hearts beating in tune with mine, just like Maisey's koala bears. As I found the strength to save them, the strength to end this and give them their lives back, it was only their voices in my head that kept me company as I shoved my body over once more, twisting the sheet tightly around my neck. I could feel the tight sheet cutting into my neck and could muster only small gasping breaths now. Every ounce of terror in my body wanted me to undo this, wanted me to take it no further. My legs began to flail about in confusion as my fingers clung tightly in a spasmodic grip to the noose. I could feel myself drooling and snot dripping out of my nose. My face was hot and I could feel the pulsing of my heart in my head.

Suddenly, the ringing in my ears and pulsing of blood trying to force its way towards my brain was interrupted by voices.

"Love you Mom," I heard in Shiloh's voice as she wavered, trying not to cry.

"Thanks Madre, love ya," Maisey was saying through tears she had been trying to choke back.

"Max, I love ya. Remember, gratitude turns what we had into enough," Gage was whispering into my ear.

"You are my forevers," I tried to call out, but there was no more air in the room. I tell myself it's OK, their hearts had heard me anyway, and let go of the noose and throw myself violently over one more half roll so that my face is in the pillow.

It takes a lot of will power to force your body to die. Every sense in your body is trying to fight against you. It's not pretty, not for the weak. As a mama, I couldn't bear the thought of my children spending their lives worrying about me in here, how that would change the direction that their lives were going in. They needed a clean break, needed to be able to heal and move on. They needed to be able to live out the adventures that were out there waiting for them.

They couldn't do that with Him in our lives. They couldn't do that with me in here. Yes, they will hurt. Yes, they will cry. But they are my strong, brave, beautiful girls who have their dad to lead them. They will be OK.

I lay under the itchy wool blanket gasping for any oxygen left in the room at all, but it is a futile attempt. My brain can't control the urge to kick my feet about and my hands now have a mind of their own, battling and pulling at the noose around my neck. I force my face into the pillow, feeling my body betray me and pee myself in shock as my system begins to shut itself down.

Suddenly, all is silent and still. My face is hot in the pillow and there is no more pain in my neck. I feel nothing.

The ringing in my ears is once again replaced, this time a song so clear that I would swear the girls are standing in the cell next to me singing, in their sweet little three and six-year-old voices.

The sound of my heart struggling to forge on within my chest was dulling to a muted hum and my ears were reprieved with a blissful silence. My body suddenly relaxed and stopped fighting to hang on to this life. My teeth stopped chattering and all the pressure that had built up in my head just faded away, some sort of a sweet release along with my final exhale.

Maybe it was my consciousness hanging on for just a few more seconds. Maybe their souls really did return to me as they slept that night. Or maybe it was just the final memory that I wanted to take with me, wherever it may be that I was headed. All I can tell you is that somewhere between my body shutting down and my soul leaving the carcass of this world behind, I found peace.

As I lay there, all warm in my bed, completely relaxed as the tears stopped falling, I could hear our voices, their voices on that warm day in my old Blazer. All at once, I am there again, a younger, happier version of myself who was blissfully unaware of the heartache and pain that would be waiting for me in just a few years' time. The sun is shining in on them as they munched on their fries in the back seat. Their little naked toes were wiggling as they lazily swung their feet back and forth in their car seats. I could smell the fries, feel the warmth of the sun and hear the glorious sound of our old dog whining in the back, begging for a fry. All was still right in our world. Dreams were still possible.

Together we slowly sang in sleepy voices, "Maisey Alexis in the deep blue sea, swam so high and she swam so free. With the heavens above… and the valley below and her little fishy tail on the go…" Maybe now she can truly be free.

Chapter 18

The Wedding

I love how their lives moved forward. From where I sit, I still get to see them, see how they are, see that they are safe. Heartache dies when your soul leaves your body. All I know now is love. There is no regret, no pain. I am just filled with an all-knowing sense that they will all be fine for their time left on Earth and that it won't be too long until I hold them all again. For now, all I can do is watch and wait.

I will admit, I have had to pay closer attention to what Maisey needs from me now. She doesn't talk to anyone about me and holds all those emotions inside, only having conversations with me in her head. My Maisey. She knows we are connected.

Always have been. She has always been a believer in the things that she couldn't see, much like myself. She's curious about all aspects of spirituality, yet declines to be aligned with or place all of her faith in any one religion.

So, I started doing the dragonfly thing for her. Once, when her heart was hurting and she was lonely and struggling, about two or three weeks after I left the earth, she was crying in her car and asking me to show her I was around, that she couldn't do this alone and wanted proof. (Just like our kiddo to be so demanding, she always did what she wanted to do how she wanted to do it.)

She mentioned the story of when our sweet old dog, Timber, had died and we were so sad and heartbroken and as we were talking about how great of a life she had with us and how wonderful of a dog she was, hundreds of dragonflies had rose up off of the ground out of nowhere, hovering around us at eye level for only a few moments before fluttering off into the sky. I can't even explain to you how I did it, just know that there is a natural connection between this world that I exist in now and the living things on Earth. It's a vibration that I put out I suppose you could say.

For Maisey, it's my dragonflies. For Shiloh, she needs me more in my natural form, so I come to her looking like myself in her dreams. For my dearest Gage, I am the voice in his head when he needs a pep talk or just needs the reassurance that he will be OK.

Today is a great day! It has been two years since I made my big exit, and there's a wedding going on. I loved Shiloh's wedding so much, all the planning and closeness of family and just the fun that we had. It's fall now, a brilliant October day. The leaves have begun to fall and the docks have all been pulled from the lake. I watched last week as the old paddle boat, Lady of the Lake, chugged off to her winter home on the other side of the lake to hibernate on a beach for the sleepy winter ahead. The cabins have all been closed and the town is quiet, as it is every year after the vacationers and city dwellers leave and the town is left to breathe again and her year-round residents just relax. The ice cream place is closed for the season, and there are flocks of geese flying out of here daily. The townspeople have all returned to their slower pace, once again focusing on their families and neighbors.

They decided to get married out at Shiloh and Brody's farm, just as Shiloh and Brody did. But that is the only similarity. Although a much smaller affair, this one is much more formal. Instead of the bohemian vibe of sunflowers and burlap and paper lanterns hanging from trees along with mason jars and candles next to the hay bales, this time there are rented old, worn walnut church pews that are aligned on the hill with massive bouquets of dark red roses filling vases up by the alter. Although they are using the same arch to stand beneath that my dear Brody had built for their wedding, this time it is draped in a rich red velvet instead of the light country white linen. The groomsmen are dressed in black tuxes with a dark red tie and vest beneath, while the bridesmaids are wearing beautiful red satin gowns, adorned with sequins on the bodice. It is cooler out now, which they had prepared for by also wearing a black faux fur shrug about their shoulders.

Where pumpkins and hay bales sat decorated for Shiloh's wedding, there are now black candle lit lanterns resting atop of antique brass framed mirrors on various white linen draped tables and stands. The guests have begun to arrive, all dressed in formal attire instead of casual flare. The crowd was intimate, as they arrived and moved their way into the church pews on the hill.

I felt the love radiating from the crowd of family, and seeing my sister and brother-in-law and Gage's sister and brother-in-law and all the nephews and our parents made me want to just hold them all and tell them it would all be OK. The sun hung low in the sky, giving off a brilliant glow as it began its descent below the hill.

As slow, quiet instrumental music began to play, a familiar face appeared, walking his way down the crushed red velvet aisle runner. It was our beloved Bud. He limped his way to the arch, where he took his position beneath it as the officiant. (I *love* that he was chosen for this as he was, is, and always will be an integral part of our family.)

The setting sun lent way to a candlelit glow, bringing a certain warmth to a cooler October evening. As the crowd huddled together, I stared at the faces that I loved the most, the ones that always are etched on the forefront of my soul. There truly is nothing that compares to a mother's love for her kids, it transcends all time and space. My soul is so warm when I come this close to them. I feel like I could almost reach out and hold them, but then I remember where I am... what I am no longer, and am content to just watch from afar.

The processional begins and a hush lulls the small gathering of friends. It was to be a small wedding party, that I was sure of. The first ones to walk through the antique walnut wooden doors that were set up on the edge of the hill leading to the isle runner, were Shiloh and Brody.

There was my girl, dressed in red satin, golden curls falling loosely down upon her shoulders. She locked arms with our handsome son-in-law, Brody, who was dressed in his sharp formal tux, but paired with his cowboy boots, because... well... what can you say, that was who he was and we loved him for it. They slowly made their way to the makeshift altar, grinning at everyone they passed. No doubt, it had to have brought back memories of their wedding in the same spot just a couple of years ago. No doubt, it isn't lost on them how drastically their lives had changed within that time.

Next to come bursting through those doors was the other part of my soul, my Maisey, arm and arm with her forever, Moby. She looked so happy, so full of life again! She once again had color in her cheeks and there was a softness to her eyes that had been lost. Of course, those two being who they are decided that they needed to have a magnificent and social media worthy entrance, so they actually choreographed a little dance all the way down the aisle. Once they made their way to the front, they paused for a dip and a kiss while their friends clapped from the pews. They then parted ways to stand on their respective sides of the altar.

As they stood there in their formal best, staring towards the worn walnut doors, anticipating them to open, the music changed. What had begun as an instrumental Canon in D Major, transitioned over to an instrumental version of Metallica's *Nothing Else Matters*. It caught me off guard a little and made me laugh. She really knows him. She really knows what will make him happy.

As the heavy walnut doors were pushed open by my darling nephews, I first locked eyes on him, and he took my breath away. When we were married, all those years ago, he wore a white tux jacket, trimmed in black with black pants. Somehow, he looked even younger now, dapper in his solid black attire with red vest beneath. His skin still held the olive tones of summer and his salt and pepper hair had been sun-kissed, no doubt from the hours they spent out on our boat this year. I smiled as I watched his bowed legs take a few steps forward, seemingly hesitating as he looked around. Tears were rolling down my face and I ached to wrap my arms around this man, my Gage. My forever. But forever wasn't in the cards for us this time around. Instead, I spoke out into the air, allowing the cool autumn breeze to carry my soul to his ears.

"You deserve this my love. You can do hard things. You can be this man again. Move forward for them, make a life with her. Love you always and forever." I watched him close his eyes briefly and gasp as my words made it to his heart, let a lonely tear escape his left eye, then smile and open his eyes again, looking around the hill. He had felt me. He was going to be just fine, he always was.

I eagerly watched as he turned back and held out his hand. She stepped forward, beaming against the darkness in the glow of the setting sun and candlelight. Her simple gown hugged her every curve and her chestnut-colored hair was pulled loosely onto the top of her head, leaving stray ringlets of curls to playfully dance onto her neck and frame her sweet face. She was carrying a small bouquet of dark red roses, and as she looked up at him, her emerald-green eyes pierced through any doubts that his icy heart had been harboring. He surrendered to her. With a big grin, he stepped forward with her, making his way to the altar, where his whole life stood waiting for him.

If I was originally supposed to be Gage's forever, then Maddox must have fallen from the heavens to replace me. He looked so happy. I was actually what brought them together. In Gage's heart, he never wanted to remarry. Of course, he had thought about the possibility of dating and having someone to go do things with and of course, sex, but as far as an actual relationship, a commitment just wasn't something that he had wanted to get his heart entangled in again. In his mind, the first time he married, it was going to be forever, and he had been so sure of that, that when we fell apart, when our world collided with massive casualties, he became broken. He didn't trust the world any more. Many nights he would cry and scream and curse the earth. Our girls never saw his pain. But they did see his happiness when he met Maddox. (They call her Maddy now.)

Maddy is a little younger than Gage. Seven years younger if you are counting, but it works. They met at a grief group not long after I had gone. Our family had reached celebrity status in our small town, so there was nowhere that he could go that people didn't look at him funny or cast their eyes down in pity. At the time, he was really fighting his own demons, and Bud had talked him into a grief group just a town over, in Garner. That's where he found her.

Maddy's story is a little different, as she didn't lose a spouse, but a child. Her son had taken his own life when he was fifteen after battling with depression and confusion about his own sexuality for many years. The poor woman woke one day to find that he had never come home the night before. For two days she lived in a panic induced state, not knowing where else to search or what to do. The morning that the officers showed up at her door letting her know that they found him hanging in a wooded area about two miles from home was the day that her marriage of sixteen years began to crumble, and within six months she was divorced.

When they first met, they would just casually talk, not getting overly emotional. But there was something about her that just drew Gage in. She was loud. She was funny. She was messy and unorganized. He found it refreshing that she was unapologetic about who she was or where she had come from or where she was at this point in her life. She had no other children and didn't push too hard with our girls. But she loved them fast and hard. It was in her nature to be a fierce protector, and like a mother cat who lost her kittens, she took them in as her own quickly.

The whole relationship kind of snuck up on Gage. He was out there having fun, learning how to live again. Doing things we hadn't done since the early years of our marriage. There is something to be said about finding a great love later in your life. Since the kids are grown and gone, you actually have time for each other, you aren't running around exhausted chasing after the kids, running them to practices, doing late night homework, planning vacations around school breaks. Instead, you are back to midweek date nights to nice restaurants and taking last-minute weekend trips to have wild adventures, slowly checking off the bucket list that has built up throughout your adult married life, but had been on the back burner while raising a family.

There were late afternoon boat cruises to be had, barbeques with friends, and days they would call in sick to work just to sneak away together. She would tag along to his car shows and he would go to her pottery and yoga classes. It wasn't long before she had moved in with him, bringing with her a whole new modern style of decor. At first, the kids had a bit of a hard time with that, but after a while, the girls took what they had wanted to keep of mine, Gage tucked a few sentimental things away, and her modern art pieces and faux fur rugs replaced my antique clocks and mid-century modern furniture. She did, however, cherish all my religious collectibles, so they still adorned the little crown jewel of the house.

So it was no surprise then that one evening, after the two of them had gotten back into town from visiting the kids for dinner out at Shiloh and Brody's house, he talked her into a lake lap before heading home. It was hot out that night and he had the windows rolled down, music playing on the radio, just rolling along. They were talking about anything and everything while riding along in my grandpa's old square body pick up that Gage had finally finished restoring after all these years. He drove out to Farmers Beach and jumped out to throw a blanket in the truck bed, helping Maddy out of the truck. As they walked back to climb in the truck bed to look at the stars, he spun around and dropped to his knee.

He took her hand and looked up at her under the glow of the moon, as the water rippled in the wind.

"Maddy," he began. "I thought my world was broken. I thought I was broken and didn't know how to care for anyone or anything any more. But God sent me you. He sent my family you, and you are now the glue that has repaired our cracks. You make life fun again. I want to be with you Maddy. I want to spend the rest of my days with you, laughing, going on adventures, lying in bed on Sunday mornings looking at the paper. I want to go where you go and see what you see. There is a magic about you that just sucks me in and I can't imagine letting that magic ever go. Maddox, will you marry me?" he asked as he raised his other hand to show her the one carrot pear cut diamond that sat on a titanium band.

She was breathless. She was shocked. She was so happy and felt so complete that tears rolled down her cheeks before he could even finish getting his words out.

"Oh Gage! It was you that saved me! I had been so alone in the world, so sure that there was nothing left for me, no further purpose. You woke me up and brought me home. I love your family. I love our family. Honey, I can't wait to marry you!" She sobbed as he placed the ring on her finger and he held her in a long embrace. And then, after crawling into the back of the truck to look at the stars, and spending another hour just talking about life and what she wanted the wedding to be like, they had sex.

Crazy, wild, scared of getting caught, adventurous sex out in the open, in the back of my grandpa's old truck, and Gage realized in that moment that he hadn't felt this alive in years. (I didn't stay around to watch much of the sex part, but I was happy to know that he had found himself again and that he had found someone to make his life worth venturing out and really enjoying life again with. He needed to be more than just a great father and a great cop. He needed to be someone's great love as well.)

As I watched their wedding ceremony, I couldn't help but wonder what the girls were thinking. Did they think of me at all, or was I just a ghost of their past now? I watched as Shiloh listened intently as to what Bud was saying, while Maisey was playfully looking at Moby. Gage and Maddy stood facing each other, hand in hand, saying their vows as the sun went down.

Brody seemed unmoved, preoccupied while digging the toe of his boot into the ground. I noticed that his jaw was flexing, like there was something on his mind. I also noticed that Shiloh wasn't making eye contact with him, which was odd. Maybe I was overthinking it, but there seemed to be something going on between those two. Maybe there would be big news from them soon, oh how

I longed to have been a grandma! But this little family unit that I was watching from afar was going to be just fine. They were going to make it. Somehow, they have all found each other, like a mess of a patchwork quilt that took all the odd pieces that were left over tattered scraps and stitched themselves together a family.

After the ceremony, everyone got ready to drive over to the casino where the reception was going to be held. The kids climbed into Brody's truck and headed off, while Maddy ran back into the house to gather some things and check her hair and makeup. The other guests had already driven off into the darkness when Gage emerged out on the hill, alone. He was putting out the candles in the lanterns and picking up the tables.

Maddy called from the window of the kitchen, "I'll be out in a sec babe!"

Gage walked to the edge of the hill, looking out over the food plot that the kids had been growing for the deer. He inhaled a deep breath and I could hear the shakiness on his exhale.

He brought his hand up to his face to rub his eyes and then dropped one hand to smooth out his salt and peppered beard.

"I miss ya Max," he spoke to the darkness on the hill. "I miss ya every damn day. Even though things weren't the best between us towards the end, I still lost my best friend that day. When we got married all those years ago, we had so many plans, so many dreams. We could never have known... I wouldn't have wanted to know where we would end up. I think a lot about what you said to me once, that you felt like while we were trying to save Maze, just struggling to keep her head above water, we kind of let go of each other. I'm sorry Max. I'm sorry we let go. You are the mother of my children, my best friend for twenty-eight years. We grew up together. I've got you in my heart, Max, always will," he half whispered into the darkness.

Gage didn't realize that he had been crying as Maddy walked up behind him and wrapped her arms around him from behind. She nuzzled her face into his neck, which made him giggle. (He has always been ticklish there...) She clung to him, lifting her face to look out into the darkness.

Like a kindred soul this beauty whispered to him on her wedding day, "You will always love her babe, and that's OK. She lives on in your girls..." And that is when I knew without a doubt that this woman was a soul sister, one who would love my girls like her own and take my place in my future grandchildren's lives. He loved her. Hell, I loved her for the way she loved them all.

As they stood there, locked in an embrace looking out over the hill in the darkness, I put out into the universe my final goodbye to this man that I had spent well over half of my life with, the man who was supposed to be my forever, the man that I would follow to the end of the earth.

I spoke into the wind a final, 'Love you always', that carried into his ear. He gasped and flashed that infamous toothy boyish grin and I saw the glimmer in his eye before

I turned to leave, just as hundreds of fireflies lifted out of the field and hovered around their heads.

Epilogue

Moby

Leave it to Max to want to have a granite bench in place of her headstone. That's just who she was. If you stopped by her house, she would expect you to sit for a few minutes and tell her all about your day before she started grabbing things out of the fridge and cupboard that you just had to take because she 'didn't need it any more'. The woman took care of people. It's just who she had always been. Her love for her family was so strong, so deep, that she would never have batted an eye when it came to saving them. Even if that meant living in a depressed silence, letting go of her husband and losing all concept of a future in this world, if that future didn't include both of her daughters.

What a beautiful day it is! I just can't believe she's been gone for five years already. I used to hate these places, cemeteries, but Max taught me to see them as nothing more than parks, a place to rest your heart and unburden your soul, because the audience in a cemetery is so captive, they aren't going anywhere, won't laugh at the words that you speak or ideas that you may have. And it's where I come to talk to her when we are back home. She would laugh at that, I think, because I know she's all around us all of the time anyways. But I do like stopping here when we come back to town. Today, we are in town because Shiloh is throwing a birthday party for Brody out at their place. It will be good for the sisters to be together again, since it's been a few months, but we try to get together as often as life allows us to.

"She's really doing good, Mama Max, she is," I begin to say as I take a seat on Max's bench, staring up at the tree branches that are swaying in the breeze overhead. The sun is blazing overhead, and the sky is clear. It's going to be a beautiful day. These days, most of our days are beautiful days.

"She is absolutely loving her job Max!" I begin again, speaking as though she is right in front of me because, let's face it, Max is everywhere. "She decided that her calling in this world wasn't with hospice care or even pediatrics like she originally had set out to do. Maisey is now working in a lead nursing position at an in-patient mental health center in North Dakota.

"After you were gone, Max, she knew that is what her heart needed to do to heal. She wanted to help kids, teenagers who are so lost and broken that they had fallen into the lonely abyss. She's helping them, Max. She's even working on her masters now! Can you believe it?" I swallowed the lump in my throat and realized there were tears pooling in my eyes.

"Man, we miss ya Max. It has been so hard without you. Shiloh's good too, of course Shiloh always lands on her feet. She took that teaching job with St. Mary's over in

Garner as the lead on their special education program. Her life has really…" My thoughts were interrupted as I saw her running towards me. There she was, the fierce force of life at only two years old. Her blonde baby hair was a complete mess, wild curls all over. Her chubby little legs were moving as fast as they would carry her and as soon as she got to where I was, her face beamed, and I was blinded by that gorgeous toothy smile (of only a few front teeth) and her ocean blue eyes reaching into my soul. She had my heart and she knew it.

"Up, up!" she shouted and giggled as she raised her chubby little arms towards me. I smiled back and lifted this little goober up into my lap. She smelled like lavender and vanilla. Barefoot, as she liked to be most of the time on nice days, she sat swinging her little feet back and forth, content to just be there, staring at the trees, looking at the flowers that adorned Max's grave. "Fishy song!" she shouted and clapped her hands.

"Fishy song? Should we sing it, Paige Magoo? Do you want to sing your song?"

"Yup, yup!" she shouted, clapping those little hands with pure excitement.

So there we sat, her and I on Max's bench, singing our hearts out to a song that she never knew her Nonna made up. She was too young to know that years ago, this song was sung in the back of an old Blazer, while two little girls ate their fries, exhausted from a day at the lake. It was sung as they lay in their tiny beds in the top of the A frame cabin before they went to sleep for the night. It was sung on the way back to the car after Maisey graduated from high school, and that the girls sang it, as well as Shiloh's song while walking away from Max's grave the day they buried her. This song brought Max peace and gave her something to hold on to when she thought all was lost. This was their song. And now it's hers.

"Paigey Alexis in the deep blue sea, swam so high and she swam so free. With the heavens above, and the valley below, and her little fishy tail on the go..." We sang and clapped over and over while Paige sat there giggling every time we said her name. It was while enjoying this moment of love, this moment of peace and reflection that I saw her walking towards me out of the corner of her eye, a diaper bag thrown over one shoulder and a bouquet of red roses in the other.

"Man, she took off as soon as I put her down!" Maisey laughed as she made her way across the graves to get to us.

"Babe, what can I say, when she's excited about something, she just goes after it, she gets it from you," I tell her as Paige is reaching towards the flowers that Maisey had tucked under her arm.

"For me! Mine!" Paige shouted in excitement.

"Here babes, you can have one," Maisey grabbed one rose out of the bunch and held it out to the tiny chubby hand that was all too willing to grab onto the delicate rose. She held the entire flower over her nose as she inhaled deeply. Her face was in heaven. She was our heaven.

Maisey knelt down in front of the bench, gently cleaning grass clippings from Max's nameplate. She said nothing as she lay the flowers down, stared at the bronze name plaque for just a few seconds and stood back up. She said nothing as she sat down next to me on the bench and stared up at the sky. Her relationship with Max was different. She kept their conversations private. Once when I asked her about it, she told me that when two souls were so alike, they could just feel each other, know what the other was thinking. She felt that there was no need to put her words out into the world that she held for only her mom, that Max will always hear her. She says her mom comes to her in the form of dragonflies, so she is comforted knowing she's around. It's how she has gotten through it all, how she has coped.

"Well, Paigey Baby, I think we better get going," Maisey said to no one after we had been sitting there for a few minutes. "Your mama is going to be pissed if we don't get that cake to her on time."

"Pissed!" Paige shouted out, once again with the hands clapping.

The look of shock on my Maisey's face was priceless. "Baby girl, you can't say that! What kind of an aunt am I? Shiloh is going to love me!" Maisey laughed as she stood and picked this cherub of a child up from my lap. Paige held tight to the poor delicate rose in her chubby little fist, laying her sun-kissed face on Maisey's shoulder as they turned to walk away. That was my whole heart walking away from me at that moment. To be an uncle is only a close second to being a husband.

"You coming, Mobes?" she hollered over her shoulder. "Or do you need a minute?"

"I'll be there in just a few girl," I shouted over the breeze that had picked up.

"You always were mom's favorite," Maisey said as she spun around to throw me one of her infectious toothy smiles. Her golden curls were dancing wildly in the wind.

"You right, girl, you right!" I laughed. "I'll be there in sec," I said, watching the love of my life, my forever, as Max would say, walking to the car.

I sat on Max's bench thinking about all the things that I wanted to say, all of the things that were riding in my heart. I know Maisey doesn't believe that you need to put things out into the world, but I have one thing that I need closure on, one thing that eats at me day and night. I looked over towards the car to see Maisey putting Paige into the car, digging to get her cheesy poofs and sippy cup out of the diaper bag. For a brief moment, I thought about the orange dust that was about to be fingerprinted all over the backseat of my car, but then I saw that magic two-year-old grin and let it all go.

I stood, turning to face Max's grave and began unloading my heart, saying the words that needed to find their way to her to unburden my soul and allow me to move on.

"Max, thank you," I began as the breeze whipped around under the trees. I stared hard at that cold bronze nameplate that held the name of the woman that I didn't get the pleasure of knowing nearly long enough, but whom I owed my life to. "Actually, those words aren't enough. Nothing will ever be enough. I was so enraged with fury that day, when I saw our girl like that. I couldn't see beyond my anger, Max. I was tired. Tired of chasing her, tired of fighting for her, tired of it all. I was just done. Just like you, I tried to protect her, was there for her, chased her down every rabbit hole, just to come out the other end in worse shape than the time before. When you called me and told me she was in trouble, my only thought, the only thing in my head was to run to her and save her. I didn't know how... I didn't know what I would walk in on..." I had gotten lost in the awful memories of it all, the ones that I had tried to block for so long, the ones that haunt me while I slept at night.

"Hey, babe, you coming soon? That cake has to get there on time or she's going to have my head!" I heard Maisey call out through the trees.

"In just a sec, Maze," I hollered back with a wave. The impatience of that girl is one thing that still hasn't changed. When she has her mind set on something, there is no detouring her. Much like how my mind was locked on her that day when you saved us all.

"Max," I began in a more hushed tone as a tear began to slowly roll down my cheek, making its way towards where she was lying beneath my feet. "When I got to that house and saw her there, laying in the hallway covered with blood, face all bruised, body wet and limp, I snapped.

My soul felt as broken as she looked. I held her lifeless body, hearing her wheeze and wasn't sure how much longer she had left on this earth. And the reason for her pain, her torment, her attempt to end it all, was standing right in front of me, He made it so easy to hate Him. So easy to eliminate the problem that had run our lives for the past year. I could hear His words, hear Him telling me that she tried to end her own life. I clearly remember screaming at Him, asking Him to explain her face, why and when He had hit her. I didn't wait for an answer. He fell to the ground crying, holding her."

I paused to look up at the tree limbs swaying above my head and noticed the eerie silence that surrounded me now, as if all of time was standing still, holding its breath, waiting for my admission. I looked back towards the car where Maisey was laughing, picking cheesy poofs out of the car seat now and flinging them on the floor.

"I ran for your gun, Max. The one that we had practiced shooting out at the farm, the one that you kept by your bedside since Gage had been gone out of fear, the one that you had planned to use on Him if you had to. If He broke into your house, if He stalked you, or worse, you had planned on using that gun, Max. We had gotten to the worse. Worse had come for us. I don't remember shooting Him. I remember Him jumping up to run when He saw me, remember you coming in the door as He began to run. I remember the sound of the firing pin and the ringing in my ears as He dropped to the floor, His blood spreading thick like a star across the back of his t-shirt. And I remember you kicking into high gear, grabbing the gun from my hand, holding it in your own, chattering like a crazy person, telling me what to say, telling me what our story would be. You gave me no time to deny you, Max, no time to take the fall. It was as if you had known what would happen, what you would have to do." My voice began to trail off again as my heart began to finally feel at peace, finally being able to unpack all that I had hidden in my soul.

I wiped the tears from my cheeks and glanced up at my whole heart, who was standing over by the car now waving at me and smiling that big toothy grin from ear to ear. She has me. She is my whole world.

"I love her, Max. She's, my forever. You have always known that though, right? I will take care of them Max, I will protect those girls for the rest of my life. So thank you. Thank you for taking the fall to save us, thank you for being the fierce mama bear that you are. Thank you for them." I patted the bench one last time to feel the smooth hard granite before I turned to walk away, to walk towards my forever.

"Oh Max," I spoke over my shoulder as I began to walk away. "Something's up with Brody lately... I can't put my finger on it, but something feels off between him and Shiloh. But don't worry, Mama Max, I got this. Love ya woman!" I spoke and walked away with a full, yet quieted heart. Max had saved us all, and I fully intend on honoring her life and what she has done for us, for me, by protecting them always. It's what family does.

"Geez kid... finally!" Maze was saying as I crawled back into the car. Little peanut had passed out in the backseat, cheesy poof dust all over her sweaty, chubby little paws. She slumped sideways in her car seat, so content with the world and where she fit into it. Her beloved blanket was wadded up under her chin, bare toes dangling from the chubby little legs. She was so innocent, hadn't had her heart broken yet or learned to fear anything. She had the whole fantastic and miserable world waiting for her out there, and I intended to be there for all of it.

"Stay two, kiddo. Stay two for as long as you can," I said through a grin and clenched jaw as I looked at her through the rearview mirror.

I put the keys in the ignition and looked over towards where Max lay once more.

"You good babe?" Maisey asked.

"Never better kid. Let's get that cake to your sister's before she has my balls," I laughed as we pulled away.

On that summer day, in the sun, with those two in the car, all was all right in the world. I didn't know what lay ahead. I didn't know what we were in for. All I knew as I pulled down the cemetery drive was that I was right where I was supposed to be, and she is supposed to be at my side. As I pulled out onto the desolate two-lane highway, I glanced back one last time in remembrance for one more fleeting moment, one last acknowledgement to the woman who left me in charge of them, the woman I owe my future to. It was no coincidence that right as I looked, hundreds of dragonflies lifted delicately off of the ground by where she lay in her eternal slumber, and hovered in the air for just a moment. It caught my breath for a second and I felt her suddenly. I said nothing to Maisey, who was digging through her bag, searching for her phone.

These dragonflies were mine. Maybe Maze was right... when people are so close, when they truly are bonded by their souls, there are no words needed. I grinned and thought to myself, *Love you too Max, see you again soon.*

"Hey Mobes, I got you! I know what you need," Maisey said, noticing my goofy smile.

"We can't... Shiloh is waiting for us. Can we?" I asked, smiling right back at her as her ocean blues danced in the sunlight. Her hair was a mess of golden ringlets all about her shoulders and she just looked happy. Content. She was back to her old self, like the previous years hadn't happened.

"Come on, one lap won't hurt anything," she said as she pulled her sunglasses down over those ocean blues and put her hand on my thigh, giving it a little squeeze. With the peanut sound asleep in the back seat, I rolled the windows down, cranked the radio up, and headed towards the lake.

END... (maybe...)